Look what people are saying about Leslie Kelly!

"Spend an evening of pleasure and fun, and treat yourself to an intensely emotional, funny, spine-tingling, and well-written book. A Perfect 10!"
—*Romance Reviews Today* on *She Drives Me Crazy*

"Leslie Kelly continues to show why she is becoming one of Harlequin's most popular authors."
—*The Best Reviews*

"Leslie Kelly writes with a matchless combination of sexiness and sassiness that makes every story a keeper."
—*Fallen Angel Reviews*

"*Don't Open Till Christmas* by Leslie Kelly is a present in itself where the humor and the sizzling sex never stop. Top Pick!"
—*Romantic Times BOOKclub*

"Leslie Kelly has penned a story chock full of humor sure to bring a smile even across the Grinch's face and lots of steamy sex scenes so hot you will need to turn on the air conditioner to cool off."
—*The Romance Reader's Connection*

Blaze™

Dear Reader,

As a teenager, I completely devoured gothic novels by authors such as Victoria Holt and Phyllis Whitney. But when I started my writing career, I never imagined I'd have the chance to revisit those much-loved classics. Then I heard that the Harlequin Blaze line was launching a gothic miniseries, and I knew I had to give it a shot. I just needed to find the right characters and the right situation.

I had been planning to write the rest of the Santori family stories, and Lottie has always been the one who fascinated me. Since she'd been raised with five older brothers, what kind of man would she be looking for?

The answer was actually easy. Sexy, mysterious and brooding Simon Lebeaux—whom I'd introduced in my August HQN release *Here Comes Trouble*—seemed like *exactly* the kind of man this brash, tough young woman would need. And his home, Seaton House, was the perfect gothic setting.

In writing *Asking for Trouble,* I was thrilled to discover that my love of the gothic format was as strong as ever... and was made stronger with the addition of the steamy sexiness that Harlequin Blaze is known for.

I hope you enjoy the combination, too.

Leslie Kelly

LESLIE KELLY
Asking for Trouble

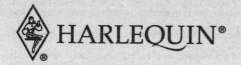

HARLEQUIN®

TORONTO • NEW YORK • LONDON
AMSTERDAM • PARIS • SYDNEY • HAMBURG
STOCKHOLM • ATHENS • TOKYO • MILAN • MADRID
PRAGUE • WARSAW • BUDAPEST • AUCKLAND

ISBN-13: 978-0-373-79284-9
ISBN-10:   0-373-79284-0

ASKING FOR TROUBLE

Copyright © 2006 by Leslie Kelly.

This edition published by arrangement with Harlequin Books S.A.

www.eHarlequin.com

Printed in U.S.A.

ABOUT THE AUTHOR

Since releasing her first book with the Harlequin Temptation line in 1999, Leslie Kelly has become known for her sassy, sexy novels with strong heroines and to-die-for heroes.

As well as writing for the Harlequin Blaze line, Leslie also writes quirky contemporary single-title novels for HQN Books. A two-time RITA® Award nominee, six-time *Romantic Times BOOKclub* Award nominee and 2006 *Romantic Times BOOKclub* Award winner, she has also received numerous other writing honors, including the National Reader's Choice Award. For excerpts, contests and more, visit Leslie at www.lesliekelly.com, or pop in to www.plotmonkeys.com to check out her latest blog.

Books by Leslie Kelly

Don't miss any of our special offers. Write to us at the following address for information on our newest releases.

Harlequin Reader Service
U.S.: 3010 Walden Ave., P.O. Box 1325, Buffalo, NY 14269
Canadian: P.O. Box 609, Fort Erie, Ont. L2A 5X3

To my aunt, Harriet Day, who instilled in me a love of reading and an appreciation for great literature. Thanks for hiding my Nancy Drew books and making me read *The Scarlet Letter* and *Brave New World* in fifth grade. You are an utter inspiration.

Prologue

Simon

ON NIGHTS LIKE THIS, Simon Lebeaux wondered if Seaton House truly _was_ haunted.

The power had gone out again and the cold October wind roared through the cracks in the window moldings to extinguish any unattended candles. At least, he presumed it was the wind.

Though cracking with rage in the stormy sky overhead, the thunder couldn't quite drown out the creaks of the old floor boards just above his head...as if someone were walking back and forth, up and down the second-floor corridor. Slowly, deliberately, with weary, fatalistic repetition.

Yet he was the only one in the place. And had been for months.

An hour ago, hearing loud banging coming from even farther above, he'd gone to the third floor to investigate. He'd found the previously locked doors to several of the former guest rooms mysteriously standing open. Inside them, each long unslept-in bed suddenly bore the rumpled indentation of a human form, as if several of the hotel's long departed guests had just awakened from their deep, restless sleep.

The keys to those rooms remained undisturbed, locked away. Both before he'd gone upstairs, and after he'd come back.

"And the air," he murmured. It tasted so strange—of cloves and citrus. Of secrets and age.

He was not a superstitious man. Yet in the three months he'd lived here—since inheriting the place from his uncle Roger and deciding it would provide the perfect location to recover from his injuries—he'd experienced things that made him wonder. Things that even made him doubt his own senses.

Objects moving from one spot to another. Scratches and whispery noises in the walls. Frigid air trickling in from no-where as he prowled the house, unable to sleep, trying to walk off the pain. And those smells…

"It's the headaches," he muttered as he sat in his office that evening, working on his laptop for as long as its battery charge lasted. He'd become accustomed to the unreliable electrical service here on his stark, private mountain above the town of Trouble, Pennsylvania, and therefore had backups for his back-ups. Not only had he made sure he had extra battery packs, he'd even purchased a second computer. He always kept one fully charged in case he ran out of power during the small number of productive hours he managed to find each day. And so he would never run the risk of an unexpected power outage frying his hard drive—causing him to lose the few precious pages he'd been able to eke out since returning to work.

He could have used the generator out back, but on the two occasions he'd tried it, the thing had caused the lights in the old hotel to surge and ebb. On the first occasion, he'd been struck by the strange rhythm of it—a steady pulse—as though the building itself had a giant beating heart hidden some-where in its depths.

Fanciful…ridiculous. In actuality, he was quite sure the wiring in the hundred-year-old mansion simply disliked such a modern intervention and chose to thwart it.

His own thoughts startled him. *When*, he wondered, had he begun to think of Seaton House as a living entity, capable of choice…of vengeance?

Lifting his fingers from his keys, he brought his hands to his face and rubbed wearily at his temples. Because his *own* pulse had suddenly begun to beat harder. A subtle increase in pressure instantly had him on alert. "No. Not tonight," he said with a groan as he lifted the computer from his lap and set it on the coffee table.

Shifting around on the tired leather couch, Simon lay back, leaning his head against the arm and closing his eyes. He needed to relax. To let go of his anger and his concern that it was starting all over again.

Hopefully the subtle throbbing meant nothing. It would pass. It *had* to pass.

The doctors had said the migraines would eventually go away, as, hopefully, would the memories of what had happened that June night in Charleston. Since the pain was often severe, he sincerely hoped the experts were right.

But in his darkest nighttime hours, when the cloying weight of the hotel and the vivid images in his brain pressed down on him with unbearable pressure, he knew he'd rather live with the headaches than with the memories. If he could banish one or the other forever, he would choose to endure the physical agony and end the still-frame snapshots of memory that tormented him.

The images replayed night after night in his head like a never-ending horror movie. The fear. The pain. The screams. The blood.

The crushed and broken body.

He tried deep-breathing and focused relaxation techniques. Clench, then release, he reminded himself. The fingers— tight, then limp. The wrists—flaccid. Every muscle in the arm going slack, then the shoulders, the neck.

Calm. Breathe. *Float* over *the waves of memory crashing in your skull rather than letting* them *wash over you.*

Amazingly it began to work. The pulse slowed. The throbbing dulled. Eventually, after a few long moments, he felt confident of his success in battling off one of the headaches that, at times, left him nearly incapacitated. *So* confident, he opened his eyes and slowly sat up, almost smiling at that small victory. One he hadn't even been able to imagine when last in the grip of the demonizing pain.

His triumph didn't last for long, because when he caught sight of his computer screen, he knew he had not won the battle at all. He'd merely fallen asleep again. Fallen into that strange place where his dreams and his memories met up and tortured him.

Shaking his head, Simon silently yelled at himself to wake up and end this nightmare. Yes, it was *only* a nightmare. It couldn't be real—he could *not* be seeing what he thought he was seeing.

On the laptop screen where only letters, words and paragraphs had existed a few minutes before, there was now one large, horrifying, bloody image. An image he saw in his mind every single day…but one he'd certainly never expected to see on his computer screen.

He reached toward the horrible picture, covering it with his palm, spreading his fingers apart in an effort to block it out of sight—out of existence. But despite the size of his hand, it could not hide everything. Especially not when each brutal detail was so very, *very* familiar.

"Wake up, man," he told himself. In his dream, he leaned back on the couch and closed his eyes as he felt that throbbing begin again.

Remembering his therapy, he counted backwards from ten, willing himself to rise toward consciousness as if ascending a long flight of stairs. Going from darkness into light. From nightmare into reality.

When he reached one, he slowly opened his eyes and looked around.

"Thank God," he murmured. Because on the screen in front of him he saw letters. And words. And paragraphs. "A dream. Just a dream," he whispered.

Then he saw something else and his heart clenched tight in his chest. Slowly fading from sight on the screen of his laptop was a shape…the shape of a hand.

His hand.

It hadn't been a dream. A hallucination? Christ, was he doomed to be reminded of his past by everything—even his computer, his only connection with the outside world?

He wouldn't be able to stand it. He couldn't live like this, with the pain and the solitude and the grief coming at him from every angle. He'd lose his mind, if he hadn't already.

Because, Simon knew he would go insane if everywhere he looked he saw the image of *her*.

The woman he'd killed.

1

Lottie

THE NEXT PERSON who tells me how great it must be to have five older brothers is going to feel my fist in his or her face. Because, believe me, being the youngest child—and the only one without a penis—in a big Italian Catholic family from Chicago, I can personally attest to the fact that it bites.

I would have been better off being left as a baby on the doorstep of some nunnery in the mountains of Austria. At least I might have had a little action from a cute shepherd passing by with his herd once I grew up.

I'm definitely hotter than a sheep.

Lottie Santori, that's me, the hotter-than-a-sheep girl. Yes, before you ask, I'm one of *those* Santoris—the big family who owns that great pizza joint on Taylor Avenue. If you haven't heard of it, I'm sure you've at least heard of my brothers. Either because of the way they plowed across the football field at St. Raphael's or the way they plowed through every *girl* at St. Raphael's. Most of my friends included.

And yes, before you ask the *next* question, I have a dirty mind and a big mouth and I don't take much crap off anybody.

My brothers, however, still haven't gotten that through their thick skulls. They've been ordering me around, trying to control who I talk to, where I go, what I do and *who* I do, for my entire life. *Tried* being the key word there.

Wish I could say they'd failed completely. Unfortunately for me—and my sex life—they succeeded in keeping me about as celibate as a twenty-five-year-old grad student can be.

Oh, sure, I've snuck in a few affairs, but there aren't many men I meet who don't know—or know *of*—my family. And I swear, the big jerks are like bloodhounds. Because the minute I *do* find some guy who is mercifully ignorant about the thousand pounds of male aggression acting as the defensive line on my virtue, one of them finds out and scares the crap out of him.

I kid you not, when I started ninth grade, they put out the word that if their sister didn't graduate a virgin, they would ban every person from my high school from ever having another slice of my pop's famous deep dish pizza. Anyone from Chicago knows that's about as dire a threat as you can make.

Can you believe it worked? They had all *my* friends making sure my legs stayed shut, and their friends, too. Which really sucked since a lot of those guys were really hot. I ask you, what is the point of having older brothers if you don't even have the benefit of having a built-in supply of potential boyfriends?

Thank God I'd spent a college semester in an exchange program at New York University, where I'd met Chuck. And Dave. Then…umm…Will. Man, had *that* guy had staying power, especially in comparison to the other twenty- and twenty-one-year-olds I dated.

I'd probably been thought of as the easiest exchange student NYU had ever known, but I knew I was potentially cramming a lifetime full of sex into those three months. Damned if I wasn't going to make the most of them.

Of course, from what I've learned about sex since that time, I know I didn't scratch the surface of what *can* be done. Big sigh, there.

No, I didn't learn about it firsthand. But having come

home a sex maniac, then being forced to peek longingly over my big brothers' shoulders at any nice piece of male ass— never *getting* any of it—had left me a little frustrated. Frustrated enough to take things into my own hands. Literally. And since my imagination only went so far—pretty much meat and potatoes on the sex scale, me being the potatoes—I'd had to do some research.

I like research. I'm good at it. Good enough that I'm doing it to pay the bills while I finish my masters degree in journalism.

Solving puzzles and sticking my nose into other people's stories was something I'd excelled at since I was little and used to spy on my brothers and their girlfriends. What can I say? I love to know things. Not to exploit secrets—and I never resorted to blackmail. Well, okay, once in a while when Mark or Nick decapitated one of my stuffed toys or tied my Barbies to the tracks of their Lionel train set, I might have used my knowledge to my own advantage. Like, you know, to get them thunked in the head with a soup ladle by our mother. But not often.

Most of the time, I didn't even do anything with the things I figured out. I just like the process of following steps through to reach a conclusion. Seeing if the things I *thought* had happened really *had* happened.

For someone like me—who's been told I have a wild imagination—getting to that conclusion could be one heck of a ride. My oldest brother, Tony, once commented that if I found a dollar on the pavement, I'd concoct an entire bank robbery scenario about the thieves who'd dropped it, rather than picking the damn thing up and buying a bunch of tooth-rotting candy like any normal kid would.

I guess he was right. Instead of the big picture, I sometimes tend to see the gargantuan one.

So having a little glimpse of sex, you can bet I'd built up

in my mind just how good it could be. Hence my research into the subject. I was very thorough. Lord help me if Mama goes over to my apartment to "help" me while I'm out of town and decides to clean out my closet. If she sees my stash of sex toys and erotica, she's going to have a heart attack and think I'm a sex fiend.

I'm not. I'm just frustrated. If you hadn't been touched intimately by anyone other than the dressmaker who fitted you for your latest bridesmaid gown for the past few years, wouldn't you be?

Bridesmaid gowns. Getting quite a collection of those, I tell you. While I'm on the subject, does anyone in the world know *why* those things always look like fifties prom dresses worn by somebody named Peggy Sue or Bobbie Jean? Is there a law or something that says they have to be butt ugly?

Okay, back to the intimate touching. You should know, the dress-fitting thing wasn't as naughty as it sounds. The dressmaker was one of my sisters-in-law. And the only private part of my body she touched was my bra strap as she measured my chest size.

What was it? Mind your own business. That's a sore subject.

So anyway, yeah, take it from me, it's not easy bobbing around in a sea of testosterone just trying to keep your head above water. I've somehow managed it for twenty-five years now, but I realized a couple of months ago that if I didn't get away for a little while, I'd drown.

I probably could have gotten a job at the bottom rung of a paper after I graduated from college two years ago. But something held me back. Maybe the realization that I wasn't through learning. So after saving up money by working in the family pizzeria for a year, I went back to school and fell right back into the routine of losing myself in intricate stories that I—and only I—could decipher.

The family doesn't get me. Pop thought that when I worked at the restaurant, it meant I'd stay there full-time, which would have suited him fine. And Mama just wants me married and pregnant.

Uh…no. Not happening. Not anytime soon, at least.

That's why I decided long ago to get the hell out of Chicago for some much needed mental relaxation and, hopefully, physical stimulation. So I accepted my psychology professor's offer to become his research assistant for an out-of-town assignment. Which is why I'm in my little car— purchased with my own money, thank you very much; otherwise, I'd be driving a yacht-sized Cadillac bought by my father—chugging up a Pennsylvania mountain toward some place called Seaton House.

And that is why I'm about ready to pee my pants.

Because, to be perfectly honest, the first time I saw the pictures of that place, I was scared to death. I felt this weird chill run down my spine. I even caught myself turning into my Grandma Rosalita, instinctively making the sign of the cross just like she did whenever one of her grandchildren made the mistake of cussing in front of her. Or criticizing Tony Bennett.

I never knew a building could look so menacing. Sounds melodramatic, I know, but it's true.

When I went on to read exactly what had happened in the mansion, which had been transformed into a hotel sometime in the 1930's, the chill had spread from my spine to every inch of my body. With its murderous history, Seaton House would have been terrifying, even if it had looked like Granny's frigging cottage in the woods. No vivid imagination required when it came to this place—its real history was quite dramatic enough.

"It's just a building," I whispered, needing to hear something over and above the wicked crash of thunder and the hammering of rain on the roof of the car.

I didn't grab the radio dial, however, and not only because the reception had fizzled out when I'd started slowly climbing up this mountain. I also didn't need the distraction.

For some reason that made me think of how I used to laugh at the way my dad would automatically reach out to turn the radio down when driving in a thunderstorm. Like he was saying, "Shh, I can't *see* with all that noise." Never got that.

Now I do. I needed every ounce of concentration to focus on the unexpected curves and the washed-out shoulders—guess they never heard of yellow hazard signs around here. If a deer decided to do a rain dance on the road in front of me, I'd be toast. I could easily picture my pretty little car and my pretty little self flying off the edge of a cliff and landing in the river about a thousand miles below.

"It's okay," I whispered again, "almost there, almost there."

After nine hours in the car, I damn well should be almost there. That useless Internet map I'd dug up had predicted six or seven hours on the road. Of course, it couldn't have predicted the wicked storm that had been dumping water by the trailer load on my windshield since I hit the Pennsylvania line. Or the mountain that seemed to go straight up at a ninety-degree angle.

Or the vision of hell waiting for me at the top of that mountain, which was probably why my foot had been much more on the feather side of the scale than the lead one with every additional foot of altitude.

"Don't be a chicken," I told myself, thinking of how utterly humiliating it would be if Mark or Nick—the twins, who were the next up from me in family hierarchy—found out I was scared of some old house. Just because it looked like something out of a Wes Craven movie. Well, that and because a convicted serial killer—Josef Zangara—had lived there in the 1930s. Turning his mansion into an exclusive hotel, he and his business partner had been very successful. But it hadn't been enough for Zangara, who'd gotten his *real* kicks out of kidnapping and murdering unsuspecting victims from the town below.

It was a wonder the hotel run by the infamous murderer hadn't been torched by an angry mob when its owner's crimes had been discovered. From what I'd learned, his partner—who'd bought out the killer's widow and taken over Seaton House after Zangara had been tried and executed—had hired armed guards to watch the place for the first few years after the crimes.

Good thing, because if it had been destroyed, I wouldn't have this job. My professor was paying me to get information for his book on lesser-known serial killers, ones who'd somehow flown under the radar of most of the history texts. And Zangara was included.

The money had sounded great. The idea of getting out of Chicago until the end of the month was even better. Though, honestly, I was glad I'd be going home on Halloween day. I sure couldn't see spending *that* night in Seaton House.

Actually, I couldn't see spending *any* night there. I'd never pictured myself chugging up this mountain scared out of my mind well after dark on a stormy night. I'd hoped to arrive here on a nice, sunny fall afternoon so I could pretend everything was okeydokey. Why had I thought this research assistant thing was a good idea again?

I didn't have time to wonder because suddenly, as if my car had driven into another dimension, I rounded a curve and saw the huge, hulking shape of the hotel directly in front of me.

"Holy shit," I muttered, immediately reaching for my chest, where my heart was pounding like crazy.

Braking hard and throwing the car into Park, I sat there at

the edge of the driveway. I peered through the rain-splashed windshield at the dark, enormous building crouched against the stormy night sky. And gulped.

Seaton House was three stories tall, a fifteen-thousand square-foot stone mansion constructed in the gothic style. I'd easily been able to track the place back to the Seaton in question, a robber baron who'd built it in 1902 after a visit to Europe. The man had apparently had a thing for the great cathedrals there because when he'd built his American palace, he'd demanded flying buttresses reminiscent of the basilicas of Italy and gargoyles that looked like they'd crawled off the corners of Notre Dame.

Those spiky spires had looked threatening in pictures taken during the day. By night, awash with lightning, they looked capable of supporting the heads of Henry VIII's murdered wives.

"Enough," I snapped out loud, trying to stop myself from going down that imaginative path. "Just look."

So I did. I sat there and I looked, letting my visual impressions mesh with what I already knew about Seaton House.

First impressions are usually the best ones, and, after a few moments, I realized what I *really* thought about the hotel. It was mysterious.

Not terrifying.

My heart stopped thudding and my hands stopped shaking. Now, confronted with the actual place, my irrational fears began to quiet and this became just another building. A business establishment with fading white lines striping its parking lot, with a sign pointing to a delivery entrance, and another toward the scenic overlook.

Just an old house turned hotel.

I wanted to sigh in relief. I settled for easing the car back into Drive and creeping closer, studying the place all the while.

Obviously, the millionaire who'd built it had had delusions

of grandeur. The presentation of the house—its location near the edge of a cliff, as if taunting everyone below to look up and not tremble—said as much about its builder as its dramatic design. From his broad, two-hundred-foot verandah, he could have looked out over everything he surveyed and felt like a king.

His delusions hadn't been enough to save him a few decades later. He'd supposedly taken a swan dive off his own cliff in 1929 after losing all his money in the stock market crash.

That's when Zangara had stepped in. He'd been an Italian immigrant—supposedly a minor prince. And right away he'd become known for the interest he showed in the pretty young women living in the town at the foot of his mountain. A number of whom had disappeared during his time in residence.

"Zangara," I murmured, instantly picturing the one grainy black-and-white photograph I'd seen of the man. Dark and handsome with a boyish face, thick black hair and deep-set, soulful brown eyes. He'd looked anything but ruthless. In fact, if I disregarded his long, handlebar mustache, I'd have to describe him as a total Hottie McHotHot. How any young girl from Trouble would have been able to resist him if he'd quirked a finger in her direction, I had no idea.

That was probably why he'd been able to get away with it for so long. The man had been charming and handsome, a prince. He'd been sought after by every single woman in town even though he was married. And when he'd brought in a partner and transformed his palace into a public hotel—providing jobs for a lot of the destitute people in the town below—he'd become a savior.

Who'd have suspected he was behind the disappearance of a slew of chambermaids and shop girls during the depression?

Zangara was, obviously, the one I'd come here to learn more about, at Professor Tyler's request. Having been accused and convicted of killing fifteen women—and suspected of more—the man was surprisingly unknown. Never mentioned in the annals of the most horrible murderers of the nineteenth and twentieth centuries.

Tyler wanted to know why. And it wasn't just my ambitions in research journalism that made me want to know why, too. I was, to put it bluntly, fascinated and wanted to learn more.

Curiosity. It killed the cat. But hopefully not the girl.

Okay. Cool. I was ready for this. I felt calm and collected. Zangara was long gone—electrocuted and buried. Everything would be *fine*.

Even as I told myself I was ready for my stay in hotel hell, I couldn't help noticing—and worrying about—how empty the place looked. It was dark but for a few downstairs windows. There were no lights at all on the upper floors, except for a faint flicker in the very highest window on the north side.

Hey, maybe the guests were just the early-to-bed types. Which might be good…after nine hours in the car, my hair had to be a straggly mess. My makeup had washed off my face in warm beige streaks during my last gas-up because the old station hadn't had an awning. So privacy was a good thing. Hopefully I could just check in, escape to my room, get a good night's sleep, then tomorrow morning meet up with Roger Denton, the current owner of Seaton House.

That was the plan, anyway.

So, taking a deep breath and reaching for my small overnight bag—which I'd thought to leave on the passenger seat rather than in the trunk with my bigger suitcase—I opened the door.

And immediately got drenched. The rain washed down and flooded me as soon as I stuck my head outside. "To hell with it," I muttered as I hopped out, my black leather boots immediately sucking up a few gallons of water from a puddle like a baby diaper sucks up…well, you know.

Not pausing to lock the car, I dashed toward the front of the hotel. Skidding and sliding on the watery gravel, I kept my head down to protect my face from the stinging pellets of freezing cold rain, and literally took the porch steps two at a time. I leapt up onto the verandah, immediately grateful for the shelter of its roof. Shaking out my wet hair, I groaned, imagining how I must look now, with thick, dark curls plastered to my cheeks and sticking to my eyelashes.

Even Zangara himself wouldn't want me now.

While standing up on the verandah, I glanced out toward my car in the parking lot, reaching for my keychain so I could remotely lock it. My brothers were such worrywarts that they'd installed this superfancy antitheft system on it, with all the bells and whistles. Sometimes I considered trying to make the thing stand on its back tires and dance like Herbie the Love Bug.

But as I clicked the lock button and saw the headlights flash in response, I suddenly made a really strange realization. One I should have made as soon as I arrived.

My pretty yellow PT Cruiser was sitting completely alone out there in the parking lot. There wasn't another other car in sight. Not *anywhere*.

Perfect. I was the only guest. Just call me Janet Leigh and yell for Norman Bates because this was exactly how her night started out, wasn't it?

"You're being an idiot," I mumbled as I swept my wet hair back, straightened my shoulders and strode across the veranda to the front door. The striding wasn't terribly effective since a cup of water squirted out of my boots with every step, but I did the best I could, just in case anyone was watching from the closest window.

Grasping the knob, I twisted it…and realized it was locked. Strange. I'd never heard of a public hotel that locked its doors when guests were expected. Especially since it was only 9:00 p.m.

Sighing, I lifted my hand and grabbed the ornate brass door-knocker. I somehow couldn't muster up any surprise that the thing had a weird-looking gargoyle head. Cracking it hard against the door, I waited. And waited. And waited some more.

"Come on, it's fricking cold out here," I muttered as I knocked again.

More waiting.

Really getting annoyed, I lifted that sucker with both hands and slammed it hard against the brass plate, whacking it a few times just like I used to whack my brothers in the head with a Ping-Pong paddle when they were picking on me.

This time, somebody answered. I'd been lining up to take another swing, and the door opened so fast—thrown back almost violently—that I fell forward into the place. Stumbling over my own wet, slippery boots, I skidded, dropping my overnight bag on the slick tiles inside in the process.

I didn't hit the floor. But I still landed against something hard. Something *really* hard. And big. And warm.

Something that smelled downright sinful—musky, spicy and male.

My fingers clenched reflexively as I realized I'd fallen right into the arms of a strange man, whose big, delicious-smelling form was the only thing keeping me upright.

A normal person would pull away and start stammering apologies, right?

I closed my eyes and remained where I was.

How could I not? He was warmth personified and I was freezing. And he smelled…oh, God, *amazing*. That hot scent filled my head until I felt as though I were drawing in his essence with every breath I inhaled.

"Mmm," I groaned, opening my eyes again. Though the light was dim and shadowy, I could easily make out the powerful ropy muscles of his neck. I could even see the pulse in his throat, which was an inch from my mouth.

My fingers were clenched in the soft white fabric of his loosely buttoned shirt, which didn't do much to cover his firm chest.

Put your hands in the air and step away from the hot dude.

But I couldn't make myself do it. I couldn't move backward. I couldn't even look up. Because as soon as I did—as soon as I saw confusion or amusement on this stranger's face—this surreal, intoxicating moment would end. Mystery solved, secrets revealed.

He'd be just another guy with a laugh and a leer. Or bad teeth and a hooked nose. So with one quick, appreciative glance at his strong, square jaw, outlined by a layer of dark stubble, I looked down instead.

The stranger's button-up shirt was open almost to his middle, revealing a swirl of dark, wiry hair and ripples of flexing muscle. Just below his collarbone, I saw the puckered edge of a raw, fresh-looking scar that disappeared beneath his shirt. For some crazy reason, I wanted to lift my hand and scrape my fingers across it. To soothe away the redness. To shiver as I wondered how he'd gotten it.

Lottie, wake up!

No. Not yet. I didn't *want* to.

My wet, jean-covered legs were almost entwined with his and even through the soaked fabric, and his own dark pants, I could feel the powerful warmth of his thighs. Our position was almost sexual, with one of his limbs caught between mine, so I couldn't muster up any surprise when my body reacted in a typical way.

The shakiness in my thighs now had nothing to do with my stumble or my wet boots. A warm current of want drifted through me, making my nipples pucker hard against my thin sweater. And lower I felt a flow of moisture between my legs as my sex swelled against the seam of my jeans.

"Are you all right?" he asked, his voice low and thick. He almost combined the words you and all, his soft drawl giving a tiny hint that he was from the South.

I thought about his question. Was I all right? No. Not at all. I was ravenous and hot, even while wet and freezing. I was aroused over a complete stranger whose face I hadn't yet seen and was wrapped around him in the shadows while the rain still pounded outside and a strong October wind blew through the open front door.

"Still with me here?" the voice said, sounding a tiny bit amused.

That hint of amusement finally pierced through the hazy cloud of sensual awareness that had been filling my head. Blinking rapidly, I cleared my throat and slowly—carefully—pulled away. I regretted the loss of his warmth the moment an inch of cool evening air separated our bodies.

"I'm okay," I managed to whisper.

Then I looked up and saw his face. And my heart stopped.

In the shadowy light spilling into the foyer from a nearby room, I could just make out the thin scar marring the perfection of his forehead. My breath catching in my lungs, I realized his hair was jet-black. Just like Josef Zangara's. His eyes...also nearly black. Also like Zangara's.

He looked angry. He looked forbidding. And he looked like a fricking serial killer.

I was definitely *not* okay.

"Oh, my God," I whispered, already backing toward the door.

Shaking my head—doubting my senses—I quickly chose the storm over the ghosts in this place. When my heels hit the threshold, they kept right on going. Onto the slick wooden planks of the porch. Farther. Farther.

He followed, those intense dark eyes narrowing as he slowly stepped toward me, like some kind of graceful-but-deadly cat stalking its prey.

Graceful. Deadly.

Yes. That pretty well summed him up. Because though my brain told me it was impossible—that I didn't believe in ghosts—I couldn't stop the fear rushing through every inch of me. Did I say I had an imagination that worked overtime in some situations? Well, right now, it was deserving of triple pay.

"Don't come any closer," I whispered.

"Who are you?" he asked, all traces of amusement gone. "What do you want?"

Just to not be slaughtered by a murderous ghost or a rein-carnated serial killer. That's all I wanted. To make it back to my car and put the pedal to the metal and race down the mountain like the hounds of hell were after me.

Not hounds, I quickly clarified. *Hound*. Just one terrifying, murderous creature.

Named Josef Zangara.

2

Simon

SIMON HAD STILL been shaking off the tension and trauma of what he'd seen on his laptop screen when the banging on the front door had finally burst into his consciousness. He was unaccustomed to receiving visitors. Just a cleaning lady from a local maid service company, a mailman, occasionally a delivery of groceries. Sometimes old Mr. Potts, who had recently purchased most of the town of Trouble, stopped by. Other than that, he lived in complete solitude.

Which was exactly what he wanted.

So who would pound on his door during a stormy, violent night, he had no idea. He just knew he didn't appreciate the intrusion—not now, not when he was still so concerned about what had just happened. Doubting your own sanity was difficult enough to do in private. In front of unexpected—and unwanted—guests, it was beyond bad.

When he'd yanked open the door, ready to tell whomever was on the other side of it to stop that incessant banging before his head blew off his shoulders, he certainly hadn't expected a woman to fall into his arms. Or that she'd stay there.

Or that she'd feel so incredibly good.

For a few long moments, he'd remained still, soaking in the surprising pleasure of physical contact. He hadn't experienced that in a long time, and until the dark-haired stranger had landed in his arms, he really hadn't known how much he missed it.

Her soft, curvy body, her sweet-smelling skin—even her tangled wet hair—reminded him that it had been a very long, celibate four months since he'd touched a woman. Considering how very much he *liked* to touch women, that he hadn't exploded out of sheer sexual frustration before now, was the biggest surprise of all.

As a globe-trotting writer of travel guides and newspaper columns, he made a damn good living. And as someone who'd been born with a lot of confidence and the ability to get around the defenses of just about any aloof, sexy woman, he'd never lacked for female companionship. His little black book could probably double as the yellow pages and every one of his friends had harassed him for years about what a lucky son of a bitch he was when it came to sex.

But he wasn't that man anymore. An inner voice of anger and regret, which might have been his conscience or just his intelligent side, was always present now, reminding him of Charleston. It made him acknowledge just how badly giving in to his liking for women had turned out then. A bar pickup with a stranger had seemed dangerous only in the sexual sense—he'd never, in his wildest dreams, imagined how that night would end up. Bloody.

And deadly.

Any man would steer clear of beautiful, strange females after one he'd picked up in a bar had turned out to be armed and violent. The blonde in Charleston—and her accomplice, who had followed them to Simon's hotel room that night—hadn't just robbed him of his money. They had stolen his faith in the basic decency of strangers. So he should have been much more wary of the brunette who'd landed in his arms tonight.

But for some reason, he wasn't. Something had awakened within him. His long dormant sensual side, he supposed. Whatever it was, he had liked having this stranger curl against him as if they were longtime lovers. She'd liked it, too—he could tell by the little sighs in her throat, the soft surrender of her body against his and her warm, womanly smell.

But something had changed. Because the creamy-skinned, dark-haired woman was now backing away from him with horror in her eyes. Stepping closer to the edge of the porch.

A roaring began to build in Simon's head and his whole body grew tense as another image replaced this one. Another woman, another patio. A scream. A plunge.

"Please, stop," he said, forcing the words out of his thick, tight throat as he thrust off the memories and focused on the here and now.

She slid back a little more, until the high heels of her boots moved perilously close to the edge. Though they were only a few feet off the ground—not eleven stories, like he'd been in June when he'd watched a woman fall away—he simply couldn't let it happen. Not this time. So, without warning, he lunged out and grabbed her arm, clamping his hand around her wrist in an iron grip.

She fought, flailing her arms, trying to twist away. "Let go of me."

Her struggle put her on the precipice of the step and he wrapped an arm around her waist to pull her away from it. "You're about to fall." Dropping a hand to the small of her back, he held her with gentle firmness, waiting for her to calm down. He thrust off the pleasure he felt at having her in his arms again, and fought the wicked impulse to drop his hand and cup her ass to keep her from wiggling. Or to keep her exactly where she was. He honestly wasn't sure which.

"Would you relax and tell me who you are and what it is you want?"

She finally stopped squirming, which was a good thing. Because her curvaceous form—though wet and tense—still felt much too good when pressed against his.

Once he was sure she'd relaxed, Simon released her and stepped back, holding his hands up, palms out, in a non-threatening way. The rain still pounded, and a vicious bolt of lightning exploded across the sky, brightening everything around them for a few seconds before plunging them back into near darkness. But that quick glimpse—along with the view he'd had inside, when she'd been in his arms—convinced him of one thing.

The woman was glorious.

All that thick, dark hair hanging like a wet drape around her face only emphasized the creaminess of her skin, the exotic way her dark eyes tilted up slightly at the corners. She had full lips that were trembling either from nervousness or from the cold. High cheekbones, a slim jaw. And a graceful, delicate throat. Beautiful.

But frightened.

Now, however, she seemed to calm down a little. She'd stared at him just as intently during the lightning strike, and whatever she'd seen had made her stop fidgeting.

"Yeah," she whispered. "I think I've regained my sanity."

"What were you afraid of?" he asked, trying to keep his voice low and soothing. "Is someone chasing you?"

She shook her head.

"The storm?"

Another shake. Then, finally, she whispered, "I'm sorry, I was afraid of *you* for a second."

Stiffening, he realized he should have figured as much. Wasn't the whole damn town afraid of him? At least, afraid of the man they whispered about—the one who didn't bear much resemblance to the real Simon. The gossipers had everything wrong.

Well, *practically* everything. The rumors that he'd killed someone were more accurate than he'd like to admit.

"I didn't get a good look at you until just now when the lightning flashed," she added.

That made two of them. Although, she'd seemed perfectly willing to *feel* her way around getting to know him. Not that he blamed her, since he'd had exactly the same reaction to her surprise stumble into his arms.

"You're not…oh, wow, this is going to sound so stupid but for a second, I thought you were…someone else. The dark hair and eyes were all I saw and I overreacted." She laughed softly and even from a couple of feet away, he reacted to that husky sound. "Of course, you don't have that awful handle-bar mustache."

He barked a laugh. "Uh, no, definitely not."

"And you're much scruffier, a lot tougher looking."

He didn't know whether to be offended or not. But he supposed she was right. He *was* scruffy. He hadn't shaved in a few days and had run his hands through his hair to comb it this morning after his shower. He'd also lost weight during his recovery so his clothes hung on him.

His friends and colleagues in Baton Rouge wouldn't recognize him. Definitely the media wouldn't. With a presence in newspapers across the country and a couple of bestselling books, he wouldn't exactly call himself a celebrity…but people knew his name. The papers back home, at least, had gotten used to labeling him as a smooth, traveling playboy with a woman in every town he visited.

They'd probably gotten a lot of mileage out of Charleston. He'd bet the *Fatal Attraction* comments had been flying.

Since he had avoided any hometown newspapers for the past few months, he could only surmise they'd had a field day with the fact that the reckless playboy had finally tangled with the wrong woman.

Oh, so *very* wrong.

"Thanks," he finally said, forcing the memories away by sheer force of will. "I think."

She laughed again. "Well, I mean, it is a good thing. You don't look like him, and you sure felt hard."

He did a quick mental check of his body's reactions and realized she wasn't far off the mark. Their close encounter had affected him more than he'd realized.

Clearing her throat nervously, she added, "I mean, you didn't feel like a vapor or a cloud or anything. Stupid, I know, but I thought you were a ghost."

A ghost. Hmm. Three months ago, yes, that would have sounded incredibly stupid to him. It didn't so much now, though. Not after the things he'd seen and felt since moving here. Ghosts seemed as likely an explanation as anything else for the crazy things that had happened since he'd relocated to this tiny corner of Pennsylvania in an effort to escape his past.

Whenever he'd come to visit his uncle Roger at Seaton House before the man's tragic, untimely death last June, he'd always loved the mysterious aura of the old hotel. His uncle used to talk about Seaton House's dark, secretive past, and had promised to someday tell him about how it had come into the family a few generations before, through Simon's great-grandfather.

He'd never dreamed that *someday* would never happen. That his uncle would be taken away so shockingly a few short weeks before Simon's own world had gone to hell.

He sometimes wondered now, though, if he'd feel differently about this place if he knew whatever it was Roger had hinted about. Despite what guests would sometimes say, and the comments his uncle occasionally made about the place's history, he'd always scoffed at the idea that anything supernatural was going on. Even having a home near New Orleans hadn't made him a believer in the occult. But living here for three months…well, he wished he and his uncle could have had that conversation.

The brunette was watching, appearing almost tentative after her only half-joking admission that she thought he was a ghost. And he wasn't about to add fuel to the fire of her imagination. He would never open his mouth about something as foolish as his occasional curiosity about whether his was the only spirit residing in Seaton House.

"Well, I'm not a ghost," he said, beginning to stiffen and emotionally pull away in self-defense, as he had for the past several months. Now that she'd calmed down, and removed herself from the edge of the porch—and from *him*—he frowned and got back to the more pressing issue. "So, tell me, what are you doing here?"

Another splash of lightning made him realize she'd moved closer to the door and was, in fact, reaching for the knob. "I don't recall inviting you in." That didn't appear to faze her. She pushed the door open and walked back into his house as if she belonged there.

She didn't. He was meant to be alone. The last thing he needed was to do something stupid like letting his interest in a beautiful woman influence his actions. Wasn't he still recovering from the wounds from the last time he'd let that happen?

Real annoyance began to crawl through him, his shoulders growing tight with tension. "Have you ever heard of respecting private property?" he asked as he followed her inside the dimly lit foyer.

"Isn't there any light in this place?"

"The power's out."

Grabbing her bag from the floor where she'd dropped it, she walked toward the study. Her heels made a funny squishing sound as they tapped against the hard tile. "So where's *that* light coming from?"

"Well, yes, of course, make yourself at home," he muttered, not attempting to hide his sarcasm.

Unable to believe he was trailing after a complete stranger—a drenched, gorgeous one—in his own home, Simon strode past her. He stepped into his office, turning in the doorway to block her way. "I have a few battery-powered lanterns. Now, would you mind answering my questions? Who are you and what do you think you're doing barging into my home?"

"Your *home?*" One of her fine, dark eyebrows lifted in surprise. Here, closer to the lantern, he had a better view of her face, the redness in her cheeks and the tremble of her lips that told him she was cold.

"Yes, my home," he muttered as he grudgingly swung out of her way and gestured her in.

"This is Seaton House, isn't it?"

He nodded. The woman opened her mouth to continue, but before she could do so, she let out a few little sneezes. Unable to keep the gruffness from his voice, he pointed toward the fireplace. "Go over there. You look like you're about to shatter from cold."

She didn't hesitate, rushing toward the crackling fire in the massive fireplace that dominated one wall of his office. She held her hands out—pale, slender hands—and Simon saw they were shaking.

Wonderful. A freezing, wet waif had landed on his doorstep, intruding on his solitude when he could least afford the interruption. He was finally getting back to work—returning to his writing after a long hiatus during his recovery. In fact, before the strange image had appeared on his computer screen tonight—or, the image he *thought* had appeared—he'd actually managed to churn out eight pages of the travel guide he was contracted to write.

He needed to get the book done. It was the first step in reclaiming his life. Returning to his place in the world, changed though it may be.

To do that, he needed to be alone. With no distractions. No reminders of how stupid he'd been to let physical desire take the place of common sense.

He'd nearly paid for it with his life. And in his darkest moments, he suspected he *had* paid for it with his soul.

But he wasn't completely lost to the social niceties. Shoving her back toward her car—which had been his first instinct—didn't seem very gentlemanly.

Not that he'd been accused of being a gentleman. At least not lately. "Foul-tempered beast" was, he believed, the epithet one of his unwanted guests from town had flung over her shoulder after he'd ordered her off his property a week or so ago.

Still, he just couldn't see forcing the stranger to get out on the road again during what sounded like the most violent height of the storm. She'd leave the moment it was over. The very second.

Shivering in front of the fire, the woman wriggled out of her coat, dropped it to the hearth, then stood there and soaked up the heat.

Hmm…maybe not the very *second*.

Because damn, the brunette was built like a centerfold. It was bad enough that she had those big, dark eyes and that beautiful face. Did she have to have such mouthwatering curves, too? Even from several feet away he reacted, a warm flow of familiar desire washing over him and pulsing in his groin.

If she were a few feet closer, she definitely would not mistake him for anything but rock-hard man.

No, not again. You're a different *man.*

And she was a different woman. She wasn't an easy blonde in a skin-tight short skirt giving him a sultry glance across a crowded bar on a hot June night. She was *nothing* like that woman.

Spying his half-empty drink on the coffee table beside his laptop, he went over to it, picked it up and slowly drained the neat Scotch. The alcohol only ratcheted up the heat—it did nothing to calm him.

He couldn't help staring at her. Her black jeans were plastered to a generous pair of hips and an incredibly long pair of legs. They disappeared into her high black boots.

Her V-necked red sweater, also soaked, outlined her slim waist and positively clung to her generous breasts.

Correction. More. Than. Generous.

The woman was *very* well built. His hands clenched reflexively at the thought of cupping her, scraping his fingers across her puckered nipples, so sexy and inviting against the sweater.

She turned around, so her curvy butt faced the flames. Smiling, almost purring in delight, she closed her eyes. Obviously wanting more, she shifted her feet a little apart, silently admitting she wanted the waves of heat to slide between her wet thighs.

He stiffened. But didn't take his eyes off her.

Pure physical contentment made her whole body stretch and sway. It was as if each muscle in her body were crying out to be kneaded and caressed by the heat, every inch of her skin kissed by the glow of the fire.

She soaked it up. Indulged in it. Smiled and sighed at the pleasure of sensation.

As he stood there and watched, lazy desire suddenly turned into raging want. It was sudden. Shocking. Overpowering.

This wasn't about looking at a woman and acknowledging she was lovely. It was about seeing the secret, sensual side of a mysterious female and knowing that she wanted to be touched—was *thinking* of being touched—by a lot more than warm air.

And he *did* know. He'd suspected it when she hadn't pulled away from him after falling into his arms. Now, seeing her take pleasure from the warmth enfolding her body, he had no doubt this stranger was one sensual woman.

Watching long, individual tendrils of her dark hair slowly beginning to dry, he swallowed hard as a few strands thickened in soft curls around her face. He would dearly love to see the woman strip off her wet clothing, piece by piece, and stand there, covered only by the golden glow of the flames and her own thick, brown hair.

Lowering his glass, he stepped closer. There was more he'd like to see. A lot more. Like the way her bottom lip would catch between her teeth as a small moan escaped her mouth when she was being caressed. The way those tiny remaining goose bumps on her neck would disappear under the warmth of his touch.

The way her dark eyes would widen and her body arch as he slid inside her.

No.

He'd let his guard down around a sultry stranger once. He'd never do it again.

Clearing his throat, he asked, "Feeling better?"

She finally opened her eyes and nodded lazily. "Definitely. My brain cells are functioning again."

The rest of her looked in tip-top shape, too.

"I think some of the cold rain slid into my head somehow and made me act like a twit when you opened the door."

"Yes, that would explain it," he replied softly, hiding a smile when he saw her eyebrows shoot up in indignation.

She must have seen some hint of humor sparkling in his eyes. "Smart-ass. I was trying to apologize for being such an idiot."

"An idiot?" He wasn't sure whether she meant the way she'd curled into his arms, or the way she'd suddenly flung herself out of them. A part of him—the sexual, womanizing part he'd thought had been lost along with a lot of his blood and part of his chest back in Charleston—preferred to think it was the latter.

"Thinking you were a ghost or something. You don't really look like…him."

"Him?" Simon stepped closer, then sat on the arm of an overstuffed leather chair beside the fireplace. "Please tell me you're not referring to Casper," he murmured. "If I'm a ghost, I'd at least like to think I'm a frightening one."

She chuckled softly, and Simon relaxed a little at the sound. He wasn't used to making small talk with strangers. To light conversation and lighter flirtation. To letting down his guard and laughing. But he was remembering why he'd once liked it so very much.

God, what had happened to the man he'd once been?

The stranger's pale cheeks were now flushed, though he didn't know if it was because of the fire or embarrassment. "No, of course not. It was silly. It's been a long day of driving." Wriggling, she twisted again to face him—and to warm her left side. She tugged at her clothes, but the wet fabric thwacked right back against her skin, the jeans still clinging tightly to her. And the sweater…heaven help him, the soft, red fabric was almost glued to those high, full breasts and the taut, puckered nipples beneath.

He needed another drink.

"For the past hour I was thinking of nothing but how scary this place was going to be, and wondering how I'd let myself get talked into coming here." She laughed softly, a low, whiskey laugh. "But the worse the weather got, and the heavier my eyelids, the more I just desperately wanted to get here so I could get into bed."

Simon coughed into his fist, glad he hadn't just sipped his scotch. "Into *bed?*"

"Sure. That's the only thing that kept me going, knowing there'd be a nice big, warm bed at the end of my trip." She shrugged. "Speaking of which…maybe I should head there and get out of these clothes."

Simon sat there for a moment, trying to put it all together. Finally he got it. The sexy-as-hell woman who'd landed on his doorstep had been *sent* here. She'd landed in his arms. She'd been wiggling that gorgeous ass and smiling that seductive smile and making him hard from halfway across the room just by the way she savored a little warmth.

She was obviously good at what she did. Very good. And he suddenly began to suspect he knew what that was.

"Who sent you?" he asked, slowly rising to his feet. "Was it Adam? My agent?"

She raised a quizzical brow. "No, I don't know anyone named Adam."

"Look, it doesn't matter," he said, thrusting a hand through his hair as the anger and frustration rose within him. Damn his interfering friends. It didn't really matter who had done it, they were all equally as pushy and intrusive. Any one of them could have done this.

Because he had no doubt he'd finally figured out the secret of this sexy mystery woman. Someone had *hired* her to come here and cheer him up. Get him back in the saddle, in one way or another. And all of those ways involved him getting her naked.

Any normal man would probably be very cheered up at the idea of taking this incredible woman to bed. And if she'd showed up on his doorstep four months ago, he would have done exactly that. He wouldn't have let her up until she couldn't walk. Or even close her thighs.

He wasn't that man anymore, however, and he didn't know if he ever would be. So though part of him—a big part—was tempted to help her strip out of her wet clothes right here and now, and take her on the thick, plush carpet in front of the fireplace, he simply couldn't do it. "I'm afraid there's been a misunderstanding," he muttered. "Your... *services*...aren't required."

She tilted her head in confusion even as she tried awkwardly to squeeze some remaining water out of her hair. "My services?"

Why did she have to look so adorable, as well as so damn hot? He couldn't stand the contrast, since both sides of her appealed to him so strongly.

Simon managed to thrust his deep, primal reaction to her away. Crossing his arms and leveling a steady stare at her, he said, "Yes, your services. I'm sure whoever hired you thought they were doing me a favor. But I'm just not in the market." Though deep inside, a tiny voice protested the lie, he added, "You're not what I need."

"Not..."

"So as soon as you dry off, you might as well go to your car and drive back to wherever you came from. Because you won't be sharing my bed tonight."

Her jaw dropped. "Your bed?"

"Right. You are beautiful, I won't deny it, but I'm just not in the mood for a hooker."

3

Lottie

EXCUSE ME WHILE I fall to the floor in paroxysms of laughter. I, Lottie Santori, so untouched in nearly three years that my hymen had probably grown back, was being called a hooker.

The irony didn't escape me.

Funny, on the rare occasions I'd imagined myself being insulted by a man, I thought I'd go all slap-happy on his ass. I mean, on his face. But my first instinct was not to slap. It was to howl. To grab my stomach and laugh until it hurt and tears pricked the corners of my eyes.

Unable to quit it, I shook my head back and forth, snorting at the very possibility that I could have sex for a living. Hell, I couldn't even have it for recreation!

But looking at the man watching me from a few feet away—the incredibly sexy man who bore no more than a superficial resemblance to a mass murderer—I was beginning to question that. Because oh, wouldn't I like to have it for recreation with the man who'd made me feel so incredibly aroused.

I couldn't recall a single moment in my life when I'd felt so sensual and charged up as I had when I'd fallen into his arms. Those moments had awakened something more. Something that had lain just beneath the surface of my skin, waiting—screaming—to get out. Just the touch of his body against mine had brought every hungry, sexual urge I'd ever experienced raging up until I wasn't sure I was going to be able to remain on my feet.

Too bad my own foolish fears had made me stagger away. Though, I ought to give myself a break. Because in the shadowy light, with my wild imagination, he really had looked a bit like Josef Zangara. But now, having had a better look at him, I knew he didn't bear much of a resemblance to the man I'd come here to investigate. His hair and eyes were dark—more black than brown—but there the resemblance ended. His face wasn't soft and dreamy, it was all hard angles. Jutting and strong, not curved and gentle. His deep-set eyes were made even more dramatic by the thin scar running from his hairline, down his forehead, to the corner of his right eye.

Most people's scars looked old, hinting of past wounds—childhood traumas long forgotten. Reminders of one moment of recklessness from years ago.

This one looked fresh. Though slim, the line of white, puckered skin was made more dramatic by the newly healed pink flesh around it. That scar, and the one on his chest, both hinted at some kind of story about this stranger. One I was dying to find out.

Even if he *did* think I was a hooker.

Guess I'd better take care of that right off the bat. "Sorry to break it to you," I finally said, controlling my laughter with one final chuckle, "I'm not a call girl. But, well, thanks for thinking I could be."

He just stared, revealing nothing with that intense gaze and unsmiling expression.

I was babbling, but I couldn't stop. "I mean, I guess you thinking I was a hooker isn't as bad as me thinking you were a serial killer."

The dark eyebrow came down, emphasizing his scar and

the fathomless depths of his black eyes. God, the man was utterly mesmerizing. And I was jabbering like a teenager after an overdose of Mountain Dew. "Look, Mr. Denton, I'm Lottie Santori. Professor Tyler's assistant?"

His head jerked back. I'd finally gotten some kind of response. "My name isn't Denton," he said, a muscle in his jaw clenching. The words came grudgingly out of his mouth like coins coming from a miser.

Confused, I tilted my head, wriggling my fanny a little more toward the fireplace, since the seat of my jeans finally felt like it was drying out. "I'm sorry, I thought you said you lived here. I assumed you were Roger Denton, the owner of the hotel. Is he here?"

He turned away, crossing his strong arms over his chest. The movement made the white fabric of his shirt hug tight against his broad shoulders and muscular back. "Seaton House is no longer a hotel. It's been out of business since Roger Denton—my uncle—died four months ago."

I couldn't help gasping in surprise. "Died...oh, God, I'm so sorry, I had no idea."

"Thank you," he murmured. "Now, since my uncle is not here, and you're obviously...drying...perhaps you should get on the road again before it gets too late."

Here's your hat, what's your hurry. What a congenial guy he was. "Look, Mr...."

"Lebeaux."

Mmm. Sounded French. Sounded sexy. Which made sense because the man was six feet two inches of walking yumminess.

"Mr. Lebeaux, I don't have anywhere else to go."

He didn't move, just stood there watching, as if silently asking what my point was.

"Arrangements were made for me to stay here." Then,

feeling pretty pathetic and knowing I'd just shoot myself if I had to drive out in this weather, I added, "I'm very, very sorry about your uncle's death. But really, the weather's horrible, I have driven nine hours to get here, it's nearly ten o'clock on a weeknight. Where do you suggest I go?"

He leaned his shoulder against a richly paneled wall, his arms still crossed over his big chest. His eyes glittered and his lips lifted the tiniest bit at the corners as he said, "You could go back to wherever you came from. If you leave now, you'll be home before dawn."

At first I thought he was kidding. I'd noticed a couple of times since I'd arrived that he seemed to have a caustic, quiet sense of humor, though he did a pretty good job of hiding it behind a surly sneer. But this time he looked deadly serious.

My mouth dropped open. I could not believe how rude the guy was being. Despite feeling sorry that his uncle had died, I was really getting mad.

That didn't, of course, mean I no longer wanted to jump on him and lick him like he was a mountain of cotton candy. He might be rude, but he was still just about the sexiest thing I'd ever seen.

A loud crash of thunder sounded overhead and I flinched a little. "You can't expect me to go out in that. This is a hotel...."

"*Was* a hotel. I closed it immediately after inheriting it upon my uncle's death."

"And you live here alone?" I asked, unable to keep the skepticism out of my voice. Because, really, who would want to live in a place this enormous—that had once housed a serial killer and the corpses of his victims—all alone?

"Yes." He tilted his head, as if listening for something, then murmured, "You should probably be going. I think the rain has lightened up."

"You've got to be kidding me. This was a hotel as of a few

months ago," I argued, not about to let him push me out. "There has to be a place for me to sleep. For God's sake you probably have forty guest rooms."

He shrugged. "I like to spread out."

I looked for a twinkle in those black eyes but didn't see one. Damned if I could read him. And that was like waving a red flag in front of my face.

I couldn't figure this man out. I *wanted* to figure this man out. Ergo, I had to stay. "You're being unreasonable. You really can't expect me to go back out in that."

Somehow, I knew I was arguing not only for the sake of my job, the research project, but also because I wasn't ready to walk away from the obsidian-eyed stranger whose muscular arms bulged against the fabric of his shirt and whose striking face was only enhanced by his swarthiness and that scar. The one who had, at least a handful of times, checked me out from half-lowered lashes when he thought I wasn't watching.

Not watching? Hell, I hadn't taken my eyes off the black-haired god since we walked into the room.

I liked that he was looking. Because it told me that despite his brusque attitude and coldness, he wasn't entirely unaffected by me. Even if it was simple attraction, he was feeling *something*. Just like I was.

"A half hour ago you thought I was a serial killer. Now you want to sleep under my roof?"

I waved my hand, unconcerned. "I told you, my imagination was just all worked up." Trying to sound pathetic and tired—which I really was, I supposed—I added, "Probably from exhaustion and fatigue after driving in such horrible conditions for so many hours."

"You *can't* stay here."

Grabbing my purse off the side table where I'd dropped it,

I dug out a folded, damp piece of paper. "I have a reservation. I have a guaranteed room here until October 31." I waved the thing at him like a banner, almost daring him to come close enough to take it.

He did. And suddenly my butt wasn't the only thing getting hot. With every step closer he took, the temperature in the room went up a degree. Or ten. My breath got heavy and I had a hard time forcing it out of my lungs because the air was so thick, and strong with his musky, masculine smell. His presence.

He kept coming closer, until the tips of his feet touched the base of the hearth. I was standing on top of it, which gave me a few inches of height, until we were almost eye-to-eye.

Oh, the face… He should be on the cover of magazines. Or a romance novel. With the scar and the hint of a beard, he would make a perfect pirate. He just needed an earring and a gold tooth. Well, not the gold tooth, I guessed. Pirates in real life might have had them, but pirates in romance novels most certainly did not. I should know. They had become a steady staple in my reading diet over the past few years.

Remember that research thing I mentioned?

"You can't expect me to honor a reservation when this place isn't even in business," he said, yanking the paper out of my hand and giving it a cursory glance. "Besides, this isn't even in your name."

I snatched it back from between his fingers. "It's my professor's name. He made the reservation six months ago when he arranged with your uncle for me to come and do some research on Seaton House."

He cocked a disbelieving eyebrow. "And you got in a car and drove nine hours, without even checking on a reservation made six months ago?"

He had a point. I'd meant to do that, honestly. But with all the stuff I had to do to get ready to leave, including getting my other professors to agree to my time off, arranging for my sister-in-law Rachel to take care of my cat, packing, doing research to prepare for my research…well, I'd just forgotten. "It was all arranged," I mumbled, knowing I didn't sound very persuasive.

"By this professor, and my uncle."

I nodded. Wondering if a little more ammunition would help, I reached for my overnight bag. "I have copies of their correspondence. Professor Tyler and Mr. Denton agreed it would be fine for me to come this semester, after midterms. Your uncle said I could have full access to the house, as well as any records, books and correspondence I could find in the library and storage rooms."

He spared a glance at the letters, flinched, then closed his eyes briefly at the sight of the spidery handwriting on the outside of one of the bulky envelopes I retrieved. It was apparently in his uncle's handwriting, and I suddenly felt very mean. "I'm sorry, I know I'm being incredibly pushy," I said, lowering the letters back into the bag.

"Yes, you are."

Dropping my arms to my sides, I felt my shoulders slump. "I just *really* don't want to get back in that car and drive off into the storm again." Swallowing, I quietly added, "Please."

I didn't continue, didn't beg or harass him. I simply let him see my weariness and genuine concern about trying to navigate back down this mountain on such a wild night.

He said nothing, just stared into my face. I held the stare, suddenly feeling a bit light-headed as I lost myself in his eyes. They were so piercing…so deep and secretive. Angry. Stormy. Intense.

Why, then, wasn't I afraid of him? But I wasn't. In fact, his angry facade attracted more than it than repelled me.

Because he was incredibly sexy, perhaps. Because of the

way his body had felt pressed against mine earlier. Because of the aura of excitement oozing from his every pore. Because of the scars on his body that told a story. Because of the hints of dry wit that had come out of his mouth.

Because he was here in this house alone and quite obviously dealing with something that had left him angry and hurt, and he seemed determined to keep it that way.

Just as determined as I was to stay. At least for tonight.

And after tonight…well, we'd see.

He broke the stare first. "All right," he finally said, his voice low and throaty. "You can stay for *one* night. But you leave first thing tomorrow morning. Understand?"

AN HOUR LATER, tucking my cold body between the cold sheets in a cold room on the third floor, I was beginning to regret my persistence. Did I mention it was cold?

"It's your own fault," I whispered as I tugged the old, faded bedspread and thin, worn blankets tightly under my chin. I curled up in a ball and rolled to my side, trying to provide my own body heat by bringing my knees to my chest.

Yes, it was my own fault. Not only for insisting I stay here, but also because I hadn't taken my less-than-gracious host up on his grudging offer to go try to fire up what he called an "ancient" generator out back in the garage. I was trying to be an *easy* unwanted guest—hoping if I wasn't a problem he might reconsider and let me stay tomorrow. So, thinking that if he was fine in the house with no electricity for the night, I would be, too, I'd said thanks but no thanks.

Big mistake. Stick a giant wooden stick between my legs and you'd have a human Popsicle.

"You asked for this," I muttered, trying to distract myself from the shivery twitches of my legs and arms. Not to mention the sight of my own breaths puffing out into the air.

I'd asked for it, and I'd gotten it. I'd been so happy he'd agreed I could stay that I hadn't voiced a single protest when he'd led me up to the shadowy third floor. I'd barely had time to glance at the old paintings gracing the walls—beautiful but disturbing images of this very house and the ragged cliffs surrounding three sides of it.

He'd lit the way with one of his lanterns. Using an ancient-looking iron key, he'd open the door to a room that smelled of must and old age. Without so much as a good-night, Mr. Lebeaux had set the lantern on the dresser, spun around and stalked out of the room, obviously familiar enough with the house to maneuver his way back in the darkness.

Mr. Lebeaux. God, I didn't even know his first name. But I didn't care. Deep down part of me prayed he'd get lost in the darkness and accidentally wander back in here during the night, mistaking my room for his. That he'd crawl in bed beside me like a fly landing in a web.

That would make me the spider.

But I didn't care. I was feeling predatory, unable to shut down the heated images in my mind. Frankly, three years and no sex would probably have made me react to a balding, middle-aged circus clown. With a hot and dangerous, strikingly handsome man like Lebeaux, it was almost more than I could stand.

Despite the cold, my body wanted to kick off the weight of the covers. To writhe around on the bed, twisting my legs, spreading them—anything to ease the ache of want that had become so familiar it was almost part of me now. Though my hair and body had dried, I was still wet, between my thighs, wanting sex. Wanting it badly. Which was why I'd worn a thoroughly inappropriate-for-the-weather slinky nightgown, just on the off chance the man was coming back.

"He's not coming back," I whispered, tempted to get up and put on my sweats and socks. And my coat.

But even the cold couldn't keep my mind off warm, intimate thoughts for too long. Not now that a gruff-talking, black-eyed stranger had brought every sexual urge I possessed out of hiding and started them all doing a kick line deep inside my body.

Somehow, though, I knew it wasn't just desperate sexual hunger keeping me awake. I couldn't stop thinking of my host's dark haunted eyes. He'd been gruff—abrasive, yes—but he was practically wrapped in an aura of wounded sadness, lashing out at the world but only hurting himself.

I knew, deep inside, that he needed warm, gentle hands to heal him. Just as I knew I needed hot, strong hands to heal *me*.

We were exactly what each other needed. Exactly.

"Oh, God," I whispered, staring up toward the ceiling, lit by a bit of watery moonlight that had finally emerged now that the worst of the storm had passed. "I can't leave here tomorrow."

If I had known where my host's bedroom was, I might have risked pulling some kind of female trick. Racing to him in a sexy nightgown to tell him I saw a mouse or something. Lame, I know. But desperate times called for desperate measures.

Unfortunately, I didn't know where the man was. And in this huge house which, he informed me as he led me upstairs, had forty-two guest rooms, I wasn't likely to stumble over him.

Suddenly hearing a creaking sound in the hallway, I sucked in a breath, convinced he was about to knock on my door and ask me if I wanted him to keep me warm with his big, hot body. I thought the sound—footsteps—paused in front of my doorway, and held my breath for the longest time.

The door never opened. The footsteps never moved away. And I figured my overactive imagination had been running away with me again.

He wasn't coming back. So I had to stay beyond tonight, had to get him to *let* me stay…for both our sakes.

I ran over several different scenarios. Calling my professor and having him appeal to the man was probably not going to help. Lebeaux didn't appear to be the helpful type, like his uncle had been. So he probably wouldn't encourage anyone snooping around in his house, digging up secrets about its past.

Maybe the secrets of the house would be enough, though. Because my host hadn't revealed by so much as the flicker of an eyelid that he had any idea who I was talking about when I'd called him a serial killer. Perhaps he didn't even know about the bloody secrets hidden in these walls.

"So I'll tell him," I muttered. "I'll tell him and he'll be so fascinated he'll let me have the run of the place."

Including his bedroom. Wishful thinking, I know. But I couldn't help it.

Have I mentioned that I'm fricking horny?

It wasn't just how badly I needed to get laid that had me scheming in my bed well into the night. I was sexually attracted to the man like I'd never been to anyone else. And I was fascinated by him. Why was he hiding out here in this drafty old place all alone? Why was he so secretive, so angry?

Then there were the scars.

Oh, you can bet my imagination had been on overdrive about those. Had he been mauled by an animal?

No. Not enough gouges to be claws.

A car accident?

The injuries seemed too precise and limited.

Shot. Or stabbed.

As much as I hated to admit it, I believed that could be the answer. The scar on his face looked thin and wicked, as if a blade had traced a quick route from his hairline to the corner of his eye. And the one on his chest wasn't as long and looked more surgical, as if he'd had to be cut open to have something removed. Like a bullet?

Yeah, yeah, I was going off on tangents. See an appendix scar and imagine a shootout at the OK Corral, that was my m.o.

Only, that wasn't any appendix scar unless the man's appendix had decided to take up residence near his heart. And the darkness in his eyes wasn't from someone who'd had some minor little surgery.

He'd been wounded. Physically and emotionally. I knew it like I knew every word on the menu at my folks' restaurant.

But I didn't know enough, I wanted to know more. *Had* to know more. Like any good researcher, I was filled with curiosity.

Like any hot-blooded woman, I was filled with desire.

I wasn't leaving here until both had been satisfied.

Hoping the man wouldn't toss me on my ear at dawn before I'd had a chance to wear down his defenses with my vivid serial killer storytelling ability—or my cleavage…hey, I was desperate—I suddenly thought of another stalling tactic. He couldn't very well *make* me leave if I was incapable of going anywhere.

Hopping out of the bed, I cringed as my bare toes hit the cold, wood floor. I guess people who'd stayed here wanted the whole authentic shebang. Personally, I'd take a thick plush carpet over icy feet on a splintery floor any day.

Grabbing my purse, I dug around until I found my keys. Trying to tiptoe in case my host's room was directly below mine and he was down there in his bed, all hard, muscular, and naked—*stop it*—I made my way toward the window. It overlooked the front parking lot, where my pretty, perky car sat like a freshly cracked yellow egg sitting in a skillet.

This probably wouldn't work. But it was worth a shot.

The window was the old-fashioned type, thickly paned with warped glass. The paint on the frame was cracking and dingy—fitting in with the aura of abandon that permeated this place. Blowing off some dust, I quickly found the latch and unfastened it. Newer hotels didn't have windows that opened—probably because of the fear of leapers. This one, though, slid up after I applied a good bit of pressure to it.

A strong, frigid gust of moist wind burst into the room, sending the curtains straight back. My hair, too.

Shivering, I leaned out the window, my keychain in my hand, and prayed I wasn't too far away. The nifty little safety system my brothers had installed didn't merely lock and unlock my car remotely. It also had a safety device to prevent theft. The engine could be disabled with the flick of a switch.

So I sent up a silent apology for being so dishonest. I prayed it would work. And I flicked.

Nothing happened. Not a damn thing. I was too far away.

Muttering a couple of really inappropriate words that would make my mother reach for the Ivory soap to wash out my mouth, I fumed a minute, thinking about what to do. This could be a sign from above that I was just not meant to do something so dishonest. Someone up there was telling me so.

Someone down here, however, was saying I just needed to get closer to the car. I guess it was the little fishnet-wearing devil Lottie sitting on my shoulder. She had, throughout my life, been able to tie, blindfold and gag any haloed angel who ever tried to take up residence on the other one.

Not thinking about it for a second longer, in case I lost my nerve, I hurried to the door and opened it, cursing the squeak. The outside hallway was dark, so I turned on the portable lantern Simon had left for me, keeping it on the lowest possible setting.

Fortunately, I was just a few steps away from the stairs, and I quickly made my way down the first flight. Pausing on the landing, I peered over the railing to the foyer below, to ensure the coast was clear.

I saw nothing. Just shadows and shapes in the ink-black night, which was almost enough to send me scurrying back to my room. But I resisted the urge. I simply had to make it down the second flight and out the front door, push a button, then race back up here and leap into my bed before I froze to death.

Speaking of freezing, I really should have put my clothes back on before setting out on this midnight jaunt. I was still wearing just my silky white nightgown with thin spaghetti straps and a plunging neckline.

Hey, I went to bed hoping Simon would suddenly remember he had to tell me something, remember? Had to be prepared. I just hadn't been prepared to have a maniacal impulse to disable my own car so I could get the chance to stay here for a while.

If I went back upstairs, I might lose my nerve. So I proceeded forward, creeping down one silent step at a time. The door to the office was firmly shut. Only the tiniest hint of a glow was visible beneath it, probably from the last burning embers of the fire. It was after 1:00 a.m., he had to be in bed.

Beneath my bare feet, the marble tiles were like blocks of ice and I hissed with every step. Tiptoeing, I finally reached the door and unlocked it. I said a quick prayer that it wouldn't squeak, then slowly tugged it open.

No squeak. Thank heaven.

"And they say Chicago's cold," I whispered as a gust of damp, frigid air blew in and assaulted me. The Windy City had nothing on this mountain. I needed to perform my act of sabotage and hightail it back upstairs quickly.

Shivering, I stepped right outside the door, whimpering at the frigid wood floor of the verandah. When I quickly pressed the button on the keychain device, a single flash of the headlights on my car told me it had worked. I was just thankful the horn hadn't beeped the way it did whenever the car was remotely locked.

Not that it probably would have mattered. The storm had certainly eased, but low rolls of thunder continued to churn in the sky and silent bolts of lightning appeared here and there to brighten up the night. The rain no longer came down in sheets, it merely sluiced a steady drizzle of icy moisture onto the already soaked ground.

I liked storms. Oh, not driving in them, obviously, but I liked looking at them. Smelling that electric scent of power and feeling the moisture in the air before the first drop of rain fell. When safely under shelter, I often liked to watch lightning dance across the sky in the distance, knowing I was safe and it couldn't reach me. Getting a bit of a thrill by pretending maybe it could.

But it was late, I was freezing and I needed sleep. Tomorrow would be a big day, the make-or-break time when I had to put all my skills to work to get my host allow me to stay. The car trick would buy me some time. The rest was up to me.

Turning to head back inside, I bit back a scream when I saw a door opening farther down the verandah, one room past what I knew was the office. The white curtains hanging on the French door blew wildly in the night, dancing in the wind, creating a strange misty fog of fabric. And through that fog of fabric stepped a dark figure.

I couldn't move. Not one inch. I stayed there just outside the front door, watching the figure emerge about twenty feet away. It wasn't until after he'd disentangled himself from the sheers that I knew for sure it was my host.

He was dressed as he'd been earlier, but his white long-sleeved shirt wasn't buttoned at all and it blew out behind him just as the curtains did. He didn't flinch, didn't make any concession whatsoever to the frigid air. He simply walked to the railing and looked up at the sky.

I'd thought at first that he'd heard me, or seen the flash of headlights, but he never even looked my way. I remained frozen still, not moving for fear I'd attract his attention and have to explain what on earth I was doing out here. In my nightgown. My very sexy, filmy nightgown that was pressed against every inch of my body because of the wind.

Hmm.

Not even really deciding to do it, I cleared my throat. He jerked his head, saw me standing there and just stared. Hopefully the wind and my slinky nightgown were doing nice things for my butt and hips.

He was silent for so long, I began to wonder if he'd been sleepwalking. Finally, unable to take the tension, I came up with a quick explanation for my presence.

"I'm sorry," I whispered, my own voice cracking. Clearing my throat I said, "I hope I didn't wake you. I, just…remembered I hadn't locked my car."

"Lottie?" he said, coming closer.

The hesitation in his tone told me he was confused, as if he'd thought I was someone else. Who that someone else could be at this hour in this desolate, abandoned place, I had no idea. "Yes. It's me. I am so sorry if I woke you."

He continued moving toward me, his bare feet making no sound on the wet planked floor. Still he made no concession to the weather, his shirt continuing to blow around him, as did his thick hair.

The man looked dangerous. It's-the-middle-of-the-night-and-he's-a-stranger dangerous. But somehow, I didn't care. I made no effort to leave and had no virginal, self-protective instinct to cross my arms over my chest. How could I when the glorious man was staring at me like a seductive wolf at a plate of lamb chops?

Reaching my side, he finally murmured, "You shouldn't be out here."

"Neither should you."

He raked a slow, thorough glance down my body, obviously able to see my breasts almost to the nipples in the low cut gown. The thing fit well, with a supportive bodice that pushed my already more than generous curves up to Penthouse quality heights and I could probably hold up a flagpole with my tight, overflowing cleavage.

I'd often thought how silly men were about women's breasts. More often than not, I'd considered mine a nuisance whose sole purpose was in getting out of speeding tickets or picking up a fellow college student. Those guys always reminded me of ten-year-olds, as they did their usual rub-squeeze twist see-what-I-get-to-play-with thing that they all considered foreplay.

Now, however, I was feeling different. Lebeaux wouldn't be like that, I knew it. He would know exactly how to touch me to elicit only feelings of blissful pleasure and pure eroticism.

I wanted that. I wanted this dark, sultry stranger to stroke me, to run his fingertips down my cleavage, then catch my nipples between his fingers and lightly squeeze them. I shivered, feeling the tips of my breasts get hard and tight against the silk and could think of nothing else but how amazing it would feel if he were to lick me there, sucking hard while dropping a hand between my legs.

"What are you really doing out here?" he asked, his voice low, almost a growl.

"I told you."

"You came down here, dressed like that, just so you could do something to your car?"

At last, a question I could answer honestly. "Yes, I swear to you, I did. I didn't intend to stay out here and was heading right back to my warm— To my bed. But then you came out."

"And you decided to…stay?" Not waiting for an answer, he lifted his hand and brushed the back of his fingers on my shoulder. "You're freezing."

Freezing? Oh, no. I felt very, *very* hot.

I could have made some lame *well, you could keep me warm* comment, but we were already way beyond that level of silly, light flirtation. Instead, I inched closer to him, using his body to block the wind, smelling the warm, masculine scent arising from his skin. His shirt continued to whip around and now I could see more of the scar just below his collarbone. Not to mention the ripples of muscle and taut, wiry hair.

I couldn't resist. Lifting a hand, I laid it flat on his chest, feeling the beat of his heart. And his heat.

He didn't say anything. He merely acted. Without a word of warning, he slid both his hands into my hair, cupping my head and tugging me forward. Any gasp of surprise I might have made was drowned out by my own heart, which thudded like crazy as he lowered his mouth to mine.

Then our lips met. Opened. Tasted. Thunder pounded…or maybe it was just the low roar of pleasure rolling through me.

The rain picked up again and lightning flashed somewhere nearby. I wasn't aware of any of it. I couldn't focus on anything except the warm lips and smooth tongue giving me such pleasure.

I've been kissed. A lot.

This wasn't kissing. It was sex of the mouth.

Groaning, I rose on tiptoe, loving the strong, steady way

he cupped my head, fingering my hair as his tongue plunged deep. I savored it, licking and sucking, sharing each breath with him, certain I'd never experienced anything more exciting in my entire life.

And then it was over. He ended the kiss, yanked his hands back and put them on my shoulders. Spinning me around, he literally pushed me through the door, into the house. Muttering, "Go to bed before you freeze," he turned and stalked toward the open door, where the white curtains still whipped furiously in the night wind.

With one final, heated glance in my direction, he disappeared inside.

4

Simon

SHE HADN'T BEEN LYING. Her damn car wouldn't start.

When his unwanted houseguest had informed him this morning that there was something wrong with her bright, shiny and new-looking car, Simon had half suspected she was lying. The woman was nothing if not determined to stay here and dig up whatever secrets her professor had sent her to find. She'd started in on him while sipping the coffee he'd grudgingly shared with her before escorting her out the door.

He'd brushed aside her suggestion that she stay and tell him more about this house he'd inherited from his uncle.

He was more tempted than he'd wanted to let on, mainly because of the strange things he'd experienced lately. But a long restless night—during which he'd been tormented by just how amazing she'd tasted when he'd given in to his insane impulse and kissed her—had convinced him it wasn't worth the risk. Having her under his roof would be torture of the worst kind, since he just couldn't trust his own judgment these days.

He wanted her. He'd wanted her from the minute he saw her and now that he'd had her in his arms, he only wanted her more.

Aside from her physical attractions, he wanted some of that brightness—light and life—that seemed to envelop her like an aura.

But he didn't trust her. He trusted no one.

Besides, he wasn't entitled to her. He didn't *deserve* her.

So he'd convinced himself this morning that it was best to let her go. That he didn't need to know anything more about Seaton House than what he already knew. After all, this wasn't his home, it was merely a shelter. A refuge from the storm his life had become since he'd been released from the hospital in July. He didn't give a damn if Jimmy Hoffa were buried in the basement. He simply didn't want to hear about it.

Especially not from *her*. Lottie, she'd insisted he call her. Pretty Lottie—short for Charlotte, she'd told him with a disgusted groan—who cleaned up centerfold-quality stunning.

She'd distracted him much of the previous night already. For that, he supposed he ought to thank the woman. For once he hadn't gone to sleep with the sound of screams echoing in his head or the memory of the slow drip of blood down his face and the taste of it on his lips. The pain of the knife. Or the bullet.

No. He'd lain in his bed long into the night, picturing *her* silhouetted against the fire, her hair glinting gold under the flames. Her lips pursing out as she dropped her long-lashed eyes closed to savor the warmth. The red sweater plunging between those full breasts and the long legs highlighted by the tight jeans. And then later, wearing that windswept nightgown that had molded tightly against every inch of her body, barely concealing that body from his hungry eyes.

Of course, she hadn't been wearing *any* clothes in his dreams. She'd been naked and so had he as they'd explored every inch of one another. His long, deep, erotic dreams had made him wake up in the middle of the night with a hard-on that made it impossible to go back to sleep. So he'd prowled the house a little, as he often did, listening to the creaks and the groans, none of the sounds able to drive out the voice in his head that screamed *murderer*.

He'd finally forced himself to return to bed, managing to find a few restless hours of sleep that had, once again, starred his houseguest and had, once again, been X-rated.

One bad night had convinced him he didn't need her hanging around distracting his waking hours, too. But she hadn't been lying when she'd come back to the front door a few minutes ago—after she was supposed to already have driven away, off his mountain and out of his life.

Not quite believing her claims of car trouble, he'd grabbed the key out of her hand and gone to check for himself.

It was dead. Completely flat. He tried pumping the gas and twisted the key in the ignition again, but got absolutely no response.

"Dammit," he muttered, popping the hood and getting out the driver's side door. Ignoring the light drizzle of cold autumn rain, he went around to the front and lifted the hood. He had no idea what he thought he'd find by checking out the engine. What Simon knew about auto repair could be summed up in three letters—AAA.

Still he gave it a shot, figuring the irritating brunette on the porch would expect him to. He tinkered a little bit, knowing enough to see that the spark plugs were connected and the battery looked shiny and new.

"Are you sure you have gas in it?" he asked, swinging his head around to peer at her over his shoulder.

She nodded, not stepping out from her sheltered spot beneath the awning. Staying nice and dry. "Positive. I gassed up less than a hundred miles from here last night."

Knowing he'd exhausted the last remnants of his automotive knowledge, he slammed the hood down, pocketed the key and strode toward the house.

"No luck?" she asked, her big brown eyes wide and innocent as he joined her on the porch. Her lower lip was jutted out in a tiny pout of frustration.

He wanted to bite it.

He settled for grunting. "No."

"Gee…it was running just fine when I got here."

"Do you have an automotive service?" he asked, forcing himself to focus on the objective—getting her to leave—and not on her soft, delicate face and full red lips.

"I do."

Excellent.

She followed him back into the house. "But I can't call them."

"Why not?" he snapped.

She held up a small cellular phone. "No signal."

Not surprising. One would think that sitting on top of a mountain would give him access to some kind of cellular signal, but his own phone rarely worked. "Use the one in my office."

That pouty lower lip disappeared into her mouth.

"What?"

"I think the storm knocked out your phone service, too. I already tried."

Damn. Double damn.

Not taking her word for it, Simon went into the office and grabbed the receiver from its cradle. Nothing. Not even static.

Slamming it back down, he thrust an angry hand through his hair, flinching as the tip of his index finger scraped across his scar. Not from pain, but from the surprise he always felt whenever he was reminded of his close brush with death. And of the visible disfigurement that would always serve as a reminder of who he was and what he'd done.

The hospital had offered to have a plastic surgeon fix his scars up a little better. Simon had turned the offers down, figuring the world deserved to see the real man.

Lottie obviously noticed his reaction. Immediately coming close to him—close enough for him to feel the heat of her breath on his throat and the suggestive scrape of her body against his—she gently reached up and pushed his hair back off his forehead.

Her touch was incendiary. Simon had been touched by plenty of nurses and doctors while recovering from the attack, but he couldn't recall ever feeling like one of them had started a flaming inferno on his skin.

This woman's touch did that. Her long, delicate fingers were cool and pale, so why they'd bring instant heat, he had no idea.

Or maybe he did.

"How did it happen?" she asked softly. She didn't have to say anything more for him to know she was referring to his scars.

"None of your damn business."

She tsked, not offended by his rudeness. "Are you always so unfriendly? That's not a very good personality trait for a hotel owner. Even Norman Bates was friendly."

"I'm *not* a hotel owner." Frowning, he added, "Besides, the jury's still out on the Norman Bates thing, isn't it?"

"I dunno, I've survived so far."

"The day's still young."

She snickered. The woman had one hell of a thick skin.

"It's a good thing you're not in this for the long haul," she said with a cheery smile. "Because the hospitality industry makes a big deal about having a positive attitude and I don't think you're cut out for it."

As if he'd want to be. "I'm crushed."

She continued as if he hadn't spoken. "I should know. My family's in the restaurant business—Santori's, on Taylor Avenue in Chicago. It's my second home…if I'm not at my apartment, I'm at the restaurant."

He assumed she had a point.

"Anyway, one thing I know, you have to have a certain type of look to succeed in the service industry."

"A look?" he asked, feeling dizzy from her jabbering.

"Yeah, you know, one that says you know how to smile."

His lips twitched. But he quickly pushed them down into a frown. "Do you ever shut up?"

"I'm the sixth child. No. I never shut up. I learned at a young age that if I want to be heard, I just have to keep on talking."

"Well you're certainly adept at it."

Shrugging, she asked, "What's your name?"

The sudden subject change startled him enough that he finally managed to tug himself away from her. Away from her breaths. Her stares. The brush of her lush breasts against his chest. The smile that had made him rock a little on his feet. "What?"

"Your name," she said as she slid down to sit on the arm of the leather couch. "Your first name."

"It's Simon."

"Well, Simon," she said, "it looks like we have a problem."

He quirked a brow. "*We?*"

"*I* have a problem with my car, and *you* have a problem with a houseguest."

"Okay. *We.*" Not seeing any way around it, he mumbled, "Get your stuff. I'll drive you down into town. You can call a repair shop from there."

"And then what, wander around some small Pennsylvania town with the crazy name of Trouble for hours waiting for my car to be towed and fixed?" Before he could answer, she added, "And is it really called that? The map wasn't misprinted or anything?"

"Yes. Yes. And no."

Obviously zoning in on the answer she didn't like in that succinct response, she glared. "There's no reason I can't wait here. I'll stay out of your way. You won't even notice me."

Fat chance of that. She might as well have said he wouldn't notice it if a bird took up residence on his head. "Forget it."

Continuing as if he hadn't spoken, she added, "And by the time you drive me down the mountain, the phone service will probably already be back on, so there's really no need. We'll wait it out for a little while."

The woman just couldn't take no for an answer. "Are you hard of hearing?"

"No." She smiled, a gleam making those brown eyes sparkle. "Just used to having to be stubborn to get what I *want*."

The way she emphasized the word *want* made him curious about just what she did want. When she licked her lips and shifted, his curiosity doubled. Crossing his arms and leaning back against his desk so he half sat on the edge of it, directly above her, he decided to ask her, "So what is it you want, Miss Santori?"

Her lips parted. As she licked at them, Simon could see a slow hint of color rising into her creamy cheeks.

"I *don't* want to be any trouble."

"Too late."

"But if I have to wait around for a couple of hours, I'd much rather do it here—where I can perhaps do some of the work I came all this way to do—rather than at some nasty, greasy garage in town."

It made sense. For *her*. Not for him.

As if seeing he was about to refuse, she hurriedly added, "I've come so far, and if I go back empty-handed, not only am I out the cost of the trip, but I won't get paid."

"What kind of employer is this professor of yours? It was his responsibility to make sure the arrangements were confirmed."

She sighed. "I know. But it's a private project. He's old and doesn't have much money. I certainly can't ask him to pay me for work I didn't do."

She sounded surprisingly sincere. And the hopeful look on her face made him curious enough to ask, "So what, exactly, is it you think you can do here in a few hours?"

That color rose a little higher and her gaze shifted. She stared somewhere in the vicinity of his throat, then looked down. He could almost feel her stare rolling over his body, from his neck, down his chest, across his lap.

If he didn't know better, he'd very much suspect Miss Santori wanted to inspect something other than the history of this house. When she lifted her eyes and boldly stared into his, he suspected that something was *him*.

Ridiculous. He was an embittered, scarred, surly man— as she seemed fond of pointing out. And she was a young, fresh, smart-mouthed student with a smile as bright as the sun and a figure that could make a grown man fall down and beg. She'd kissed him back last night simply because he'd startled her, or else she was grateful he'd let her stay.

He hadn't seen what he thought he'd seen. He was simply transferring his own heated attraction onto the woman, which only proved how jaded his experience—and solitude—had made him.

She finally cleared her throat. "I'm here to learn more about Josef Zangara."

"Who?"

She looked surprised. "He owned this house and, with a partner named Robert Stubbs, turned it into a hotel back in the nineteen-thirties."

At last, a name he recognized. "Stubbs was my mother's grandfather."

Her surprise turned to shock. "Oh, God, I had no idea! The house has been in your family that long?"

"I suppose. I grew up out west and never even visited here until after my mother died. At that point, I decided I wanted to try to get to know her only brother better. My uncle Roger mentioned that the house had been handed down from his grandfather."

She slid from the arm of the couch, landing on the seat of the sofa, appearing deep in thought. "Fascinating. So you have a serious connection to Stubbs. I hadn't gone too far with him since Zangara is the focus of the book." She looked up, beginning to smile, her expression excited. "You might be able to help me more than I thought. Stubbs knew Zangara better than anyone."

Growing interested despite himself, he murmured, "Who was this Zangara character again?"

She didn't even look up. "A serial killer who slaughtered fifteen women and buried them on the grounds of this estate."

Oh. Was that all.

"Are you joking?"

She shook her head. Simon slid down to sit beside her on the couch. "You're serious? This house was owned by a serial killer? Why have I never heard of him?"

She turned to fully face him, lifting one leg and tucking her foot beneath her cute ass, then draping her arm across the back of the couch. "That's what my professor's book is about. Twentieth century serial killers who somehow didn't make it in the history books. There was so much interest in the H. H. Holmes case because of that world's fair book last year, he thought now would be a good time to pursue this project, which he's been thinking of doing for years."

Stories about murderers and their crimes were not high on Simon's reading list, so he had no idea what book she was talking about. Nor could he spend much energy thinking about it, not when she was so animated, leaning forward until he caught the floral scent of her hair and the spicy sweetness of her skin. Her bent leg almost brushed his own, her knee about an inch from his thigh, and Simon had to resist the urge to drop his hand over it. To cup that leg, tug her over onto his lap and settle her astride him

If he ever made love to this woman he wanted to do it just like that. With her naked, riding him, her hair loose and wild around her face and her nipples close enough to feast upon.

He shook his head hard, forcing himself to focus on her job rather than his wild fantasies of something that was *not* going to happen. "What is it you think you can find here at the house?"

She looked around the office, which had once been the mansion's library. The shelves still bulged with dusty hardback books—novels, resource periodicals, ledgers and journals. She didn't have to say a word. He instantly got her point.

"You really think you can find something useful?" he asked, finding himself a little caught up in her excitement, against his own better judgment.

She nodded, leaning closer, her eyes sparkling. "I do. Zangara has been a real mystery. We know he did it—the bodies were found buried on the grounds along the cliffs and he was convicted of the murders. But no one ever knew *why*. And he was executed without ever even admitting his guilt."

Simon remained quiet, not sure how to respond to this truly unexpected revelation. He apparently didn't have to. Lottie wasn't finished.

"Even his partner, your great-grandfather, could never offer any explanation as to why he might have done it. He was one of the star witnesses in the trial because he'd found one of Zangara's kidnapping victims, who'd managed to escape, cowering in his office."

"So, what, you think you're going to find this Zangara's secret journal, in which he revealed all of his dark, twisted thoughts?"

She grinned. "That'd be good." Shrugging, she added, "But no, I don't expect that. Your uncle's letters said there were boxes and boxes of old correspondence, newspapers, guest registries and scrapbooks. I have no idea what I might find in them, but I would like to look."

He didn't say anything for a moment, thinking of her request. He had work to do today—his publisher had been incredibly patient waiting for him to turn in his latest installment in his *Guide to Southern Cities* series. But they wouldn't wait forever. And he needed to get the project done, not only for his career but because he needed to put Charleston behind him in *every* way. He was practically recovered physically. It was time to work on his mental recovery, and getting back to work was a big part of it. Having her here for even an hour more would be a complete distraction.

He prepared to say just that. But somehow, something else came out of his mouth. "All right, Lottie."

Her smile widened. And he immediately regretted not having better control of his vocal cords.

Quickly trying to do some damage control, he continued. "I'll give you a few hours to look through the boxes of papers in the storage room, and you can take what you need with you. But as soon as the phones come on, you call for repairs." Knowing he was about to wipe that smile off her face, he added, "And if we don't get phone service soon, come hell or high water I'm driving you into town this afternoon."

THE PHONES CAME BACK ON at noon. Going to tell her, Simon found Lottie down in the basement storage room, where he'd left her this morning. She'd been sitting on the damp cement floor, surrounded by boxes, with papers strewn on every available surface, including her lap.

She'd looked so disappointed when he told her she could

call for a tow truck that he nearly regretted making her leave. He quickly squelched the regret. Allowing her to stay would be a colossal mistake, not only because he needed to work, but also because she was too much of a damned temptation.

He just couldn't handle someone like her. Not now. Not yet.

He'd learned a life-altering lesson about letting himself be tempted and blinded by his attraction to a beautiful woman. While he didn't envision Lottie pulling a knife or a gun on him like the blonde in Charleston, he wasn't ready to let himself put it to a test. He wouldn't be vulnerable again anytime soon, not to anyone.

Deep within himself he acknowledged the final reason he wouldn't let her stay. Because a part of him *wanted* her to. And he didn't deserve to get something he wanted.

He had blood on his hands. A woman was dead because of him.

No. He didn't deserve the kind of lightness and sunshine Lottie Santori would bring into his world.

After leading Lottie to the phone in the small, private kitchen, he returned to his office. The drizzle from this morning had turned into an afternoon deluge, but thankfully no thunder or lightning threatened to knock the power out again.

Still, the gray sky looked forbidding. The small amount of daylight oozing in through the heavy velvet draperies was weak and watery, bathing the room in shadows that even the strongest lamp could not banish. Since the power had been on this morning when he woke up, Simon hadn't bothered lighting a fire in the hearth, so he didn't even have that golden glow to bring the room to some acceptable level of illumination.

"Doesn't matter," he muttered as he sat at his desk and opened his laptop. Booting it up, he watched closely as the screen came to life. As the familiar blue desktop and icons appeared, he released a breath he didn't even realize he'd been holding.

"Nothing," he whispered, laughing a little at how ridiculous he'd been last night to think he'd really seen the photograph he *thought* he'd seen on his computer.

But as he breathed deeply in relief, he caught a strong whiff of a strange, spicy odor. Recognizing that bitter orange scent he'd smelled before, his pulse began to pound in his temple. The thought of a sudden migraine—which was often signaled by strange smells—made him want to thrust his fist through the computer screen and howl.

He'd never suffered severe headaches in his life until Charleston. Then again, he'd never felt a knife slice his face open and a bullet tear through his chest before then, either.

"Not today," he muttered, remembering how he'd practically willed an attack away the night before.

This time, he was careful to close the laptop, not wanting any surprises when he opened his eyes. Then he lowered his lashes, leaned back in his chair and rubbed at his temples, willing the pounding away.

He waited for several long moments, concentrating on his breathing. Then, slowly raising his head, he opened his eyes.

The pain had eased. The computer was exactly as he'd left it. Everything was normal.

Except… "What the hell?" he mumbled, quickly rising from the chair. Feeling a little dizzy, he dropped a hand to the surface of the desk to steady himself. Then he looked toward the window again, wondering if his mind was playing tricks on him.

Never taking his eyes off the bit of glass revealed between the heavy drapes, he moved toward it. Where he'd just seen… had thought he'd seen… "No. It was just a trick of the light."

There was no one there. He could still hear Lottie on the

phone in the next room. He hadn't seen a woman passing by the window, moving slowly as if drifting across the veranda.

He *hadn't*

"Simon?"

Spinning around quickly, he let go of the desk, almost losing his balance. Before he even straightened up, Lottie had darted across the room and slid an arm around his waist to steady him. "Are you all right?"

"Fine," he said. "Just fighting off a headache. Got up a little fast."

She could have let go. He was steady and perfectly capable of standing on his own. But she didn't. She stayed there, with one hand splayed on his back, the other on his stomach, her fingertips perilously close to the waistband of his pants.

His breathing grew choppy again, though not because of any phantoms in the windows or strange smells. It was entirely due to *her*—the warmth of her body pressed against his, the brush of her hair on his cheek.

Once again, her closeness reminded Simon how very much he missed human contact. Eroticism.

He wanted to drag her sweater off, and his shirt along with it. To lay her down on his desk and explore every inch of her body, feasting on those magnificent breasts, burying his face in her stomach. And lower.

"You're too thin," she murmured, her fingers tracing patterns on his hip. "Hard as a rock, but you look like you've been sick."

He said nothing, trying to work up the strength to tell her he was fine and she could let him go.

Or to just grab her hand and bring it to his mouth to kiss her palm and nibble her fingertips.

"What's wrong? *Are* you sick?"

Knowing she was asking about much more than his unsteadiness, he remained silent. He wasn't about to bring this beautiful woman into the hell of his reality. Better to have her think he'd been in some kind of accident than to know the truth about him. The dark, vicious truth. "I'm fine."

"Okay, keep your secrets," she murmured. Then, with a frown of regret, she stepped away. "But if you're feeling dizzy, maybe it's because of whatever incense you were burning in here."

Though he'd been about to step away from her, Simon suddenly couldn't move. His whole body rigid, he asked, "What did you say?"

"Well, I *guess* it was incense. There's a funny smell in here."

He grabbed her wrist, holding her tight. "You smell it?"

Nodding, she didn't tug away, didn't look at him as if he were crazy or hurting her, which he knew he might be.

He released her wrist. "I'm sorry."

"It's all right." Then she turned and looked around the room, sniffing again. "It's gone. But I would have sworn I smelled this sweet, nasty odor, like overripe fruit when I first came in the room."

"Oranges," he said, keeping his voice low and steady, not revealing just how much her words meant to him.

"Yes, that's it. Like orange blossoms dying on a tree."

Simon didn't know what to say. He couldn't say *anything* for a moment, so he merely stared at her.

For three months now, he'd been associating the strange smells with his migraines—figuring they were figments of his imagination, his brain's way of preparing him for the onslaught to come.

That was the easier explanation. The other was that he was simply losing his mind, going crazy out of guilt and rage. Smelling things that weren't there just as he'd been seeing and hearing things that weren't there.

But now this beautiful dark-haired woman was telling him she smelled it, too. He hadn't imagined it, his brain hadn't invented it. Which made him wonder just what the hell was going on in his house.

"Lottie," he murmured, not even thinking about the words before he said them. "Why don't you stay awhile?"

5

Lottie

I WAS STAYING.

Even though I had no idea why Simon had changed his mind, I wasn't about to argue with his suggestion that I stick around. Especially not after what had happened in his office, when I'd realized just how unsteady on his feet he'd really been.

I had been hot for the man since the minute I landed in his arms when I arrived. Now, though, I was feeling something else for him. Concern, protectiveness, I guess. Funny, since he did his best to project this big, angry, growly guy persona. But I knew, somehow, that he was in trouble.

With five older brothers and loads of male cousins, I knew how men reacted to being sick. They hated being helpless, and usually raged forward through fevers or accidents until they fell over in a heap and were no good to anybody, including themselves.

Something told me that's what Simon Lebeaux had been doing. I hadn't been kidding when I'd said he was too thin. Oh, his build was amazing—I could feel the rippled muscles of his stomach when I'd put my hand there.

Hmm…my, oh my, had it been tempting to slide my hand lower. Maybe pretending it was an accident. Just to see if he was as stunning from the waist down as he was from the waist up.

Aside from his strength, however, I *had* really noticed a hint of gauntness. I didn't doubt that he was recovering from some kind of accident, like the ones I'd been visualizing in my room the previous night. And though I'd asked if he'd been sick I knew, from the scars, that in actuality he'd been injured—*stabbed or shot.*

Why he'd chosen to lock himself away in this creepy old house to recover all alone, I had no idea. But he wasn't going to be alone anymore.

"It worked, I'm staying," I whispered, laughter bubbling up inside me as I made my way to the kitchen.

I probably should have been feeling a lot of Catholic guilt over the whole car thing, but somehow, I couldn't. "It's for his benefit, too," I said, trying to convince myself that my lies were well-justified.

No lies were, I knew that. But my presence was going to help him, not hinder him. Whether he liked it or not, I was going to at least see that the man got a few proper meals and took care of himself for a few days.

Maybe by helping take care of him physically, he'd open up about what was going on in his head. I know, wishful thinking. Men aren't cut out for that. But I could always hope. Because one thing was sure, something was weighing heavily on him and it wasn't just his health. When I'd mentioned smelling the incense, he'd looked ready to drop to his knees and propose to me, as if he thought I shouldn't have noticed the odor but was thrilled that I had.

I wouldn't mind having the man on his knees in front of me. Proposing something sinful. Then *doing* it.

Shutting my eyes, I leaned against the kitchen doorway, which I'd just closed behind me, and let my head fill with possibilities. I was staying in a secluded, private place with a dark and sensual man. A man like no one I'd ever met, who I wanted with every molecule in my body.

I just had to make him want me, too. Last night—when he'd kissed me—he'd wanted me then. Oh, he'd definitely wanted me.

But in the daylight hours, Simon Lebeaux was much more in control of himself. Curse the luck.

"Lottie? Everything all right?"

Jerking upright, I whirled around and saw him standing on the other side of the kitchen. "Where did you come from?" I asked, wondering how on earth he could have gotten past me when I was blocking the damn door. And how pink my face must be considering I'd just been picturing the man naked and tied to my bed. Or tying *me* to my bed. Either way would work.

Like I said, I'd only had meat and potatoes. The closest I'd ever come to kinky sex was when my very first lover got a little overanxious with his repetitive, boring thrusting, missed the mark and almost went in the back door. *Yow*.

Simon cleared his throat. And my face probably went from pink to flaming red as I wondered what on earth the man would say if I admitted what I'd just been thinking about.

He pointed to what I had thought was just a pantry. "Hidden access to the office. My uncle used to use it since this was his private part of the house and he liked to stay away from the public areas when he could."

I'd already figured he was sticking to the private rooms. Much of the hotel was closed and obviously unused—like a larger, professional-size kitchen and an adjoining room that appeared to have once been a small restaurant.

"Secret passages. This place is like a Clue game board."

"There's no conservatory," he murmured, completely straight-faced, though his voice held that same hint of wry humor I'd caught once or twice before.

I couldn't help grinning. "And hopefully no candlesticks."

"Lanterns only," he replied. "Though I am afraid I do carry a rope in my back pocket."

And a lead pipe in his front one? Now I knew he was joking because when I laughed out loud, he joined me. He actually laughed.

Oh, Lord, if the man had been handsome somber, he was absolutely amazing when he laughed. Though he still hadn't shaved and that layer of stubble on his jaw had thickened and filled in a bit, I could still see a pair of dimples in his cheeks.

Dimples. In *this* man's cheeks.

It was like seeing him for the first time, and deep inside, I felt something flutter and uncoil in my stomach. Not lust— not this time, anyway. But a warm appreciation for the man I'd just caught glimpses of beneath the surly facade.

The man I wanted to get to know better.

"Well, I'll be sure to watch out for your…rope, then," I said with a saucy wink.

His eyes glittered and for a second, I thought he was going to reply with a flirtatious comment of his own. But he quickly stiffened, the glint of humor fading away, as if he'd just remembered who and where he was.

I didn't want him to retreat into himself again so soon. "So, any warnings about where I should watch my step so I avoid tripping over the bodies?"

"I'm quite sure you don't have anything to worry about. Seaton House has hardly been a hotbed of crime, not since your Mr. Zangara was in residence, at least."

His voice was so smooth, sometimes holding a tiny hint of an accent but most times just sounding sexy and self-assured. Very educated. Cultured.

"Where are you from, anyway?" I asked.

His eyes shifted and he walked to the fridge, helping himself to a bottle of water. "I grew up in California. Now I live—most *recently* I *lived*—in Baton Rouge."

So why are you here? That was the next question, but I wasn't going to ask it. I'd already sensed he was shutting down, so I quickly backpedaled, wanting him relaxed. Open and happy.

Naked wouldn't be bad, either. But I'd get to that later.

"You said your mother was Robert Stubbs's granddaughter. I knew he and Zangara had children around the same age. I just didn't follow Stubb's family line. Did your mother ever mention remembering him from her childhood?"

"No." He opened his water bottle and lifted it to his mouth. As he sipped, I watched the movement of his throat, saw every swallow, noted the way the cords of muscle flexed beneath his skin. My legs wobbled a little bit even though I was wearing sneakers instead of my high-heeled boots.

When he'd finished, he added, "She hated this house. She told me once that she wished the whole place had gone up in flames when a big section of the third floor was destroyed by fire when she was a teenager. She never came back after marrying my father and moving out west."

"Maybe because she knew its history."

"Probably. It wasn't exactly the kind of thing for a bedtime story. And the few times my uncle talked about their family, it was to say their grandfather was a miserable, mean-spirited, miserly son of a bitch."

Hmm. From what I had found so far, that sounded *exactly* like Zangara's partner, who'd come from my hometown of Chicago.

"So what happened to Zangara's family?" he asked, looking interested in spite of himself.

"After your great-grandfather bought them out, his wife and son moved somewhere down south to start a new life. I tracked the boy up to the nineteen seventies in Atlanta, then lost him."

Crushing his plastic water bottle, he asked, "How do you do that, anyway? Tracking people?"

"It's not that difficult, especially in the Google age. If you have someone's social security number and date of birth or death, it's a breeze tracking their whole work history through the social security administration."

"And if you don't?"

"Makes it a little tougher, but if you know approximately when and where they were born, and you're patient, old newspapers, land transfer paperwork, marriage licenses—they can all come into play. Of course, family bibles and personal correspondence can help, too."

He nodded absently, then rubbed his jaw. "If you don't find what you need in the storage room in the basement, check out the attic. There's an access door at the north end of the third floor corridor."

"A spooky old attic?"

With a wry look, he admitted, "Complete with cobwebs, old dressmaker's dummies and wooden trunks big enough to hold one of those bodies you're so worried about."

I grinned. "Cool."

"You're a morbid little thing, aren't you?"

At five-eight, I wasn't used to anyone calling me little. But since this guy had a few inches on me, not to mention many pounds of solid muscle, I decided it was appropriate. Besides…I sort of liked it. "Not morbid, I just like mysteries. Like to dig into the past and see what I can find out. I loved puzzles as a kid."

"And the game Clue." Opening the refrigerator door again, he poked around a little bit, then closed it without retrieving anything.

Realizing he was hungry but wasn't going to make himself a meal out of the healthy foods in the fridge, I rolled my eyes.

Typical man. If there weren't any cold leftover pizza, he couldn't be bothered to eat anything. Mmm, pizza. I already missed my pop's deep dish. And though I'd been happy as a bunny to get away from them for a while, I already missed my family a little bit. Even my lunkhead brothers.

Deciding to make sure he got at least one decent meal today, I pushed past him. "Go sit down."

His eyebrow shot up.

"I'll make us lunch. It's the least I can do since you're letting me stay."

When he didn't move toward the table, I put my hand on his chest and shoved, just as I would have with one of my brothers. Only, like my brothers, Simon was a big man. And whether he'd lost weight or not, he was a sold hunk of muscle. So he didn't budge.

That didn't mean I took my hand away. No, I sort of left it there, splayed on his broad chest, feeling his heartbeat against the tips of my fingers. Beneath his thin, loose shirt, I could feel the raised skin of his other mysterious scar, and something made me move my index finger up and down it, as if I could ease away any last remnants of pain.

He didn't say a word, didn't move a muscle. He simply stared at me, his breaths slow and steady, making his chest rise and fall beneath my touch. Those dark-to-the-point-of-blackness eyes blazed as he stared at my face. He appeared ready to rip my hand off for daring to put it on him.

Or rip my clothes off and take me up against the refrigerator.

I swallowed, using all my determination to remain completely motionless, knowing the wrong move would break the intense moment. He'd back away, storm out of the room or simply retreat back into casual conversation.

And I didn't want that. I wanted him to go forward, not retreat.

Finally, moving so slowly I almost didn't realize he was doing it, he stepped closer. It wasn't until I felt his shoes touch mine that I understood why my leg was suddenly feeling so warm. It was because his was so close, his body radiating heat. At the brush of his chest across my sweater, my nipples tightened and my breasts felt heavy.

I have often complained over the years about inheriting the more-than-generous Santori women's cup size—and the back problems that go along with it. But right now, I saw the benefits. Because while he hadn't taken me in his arms, our bodies were touching, ever so delicately. That light scrape of his shirt on the very tips of my nipples was more sensual than any heavy petting I'd ever experienced. The almost-there caress heightened the anticipation. And the tension.

He moved his arm up slowly. But he obviously hadn't lost his head over the idea of getting his hands on my breasts the way my former lovers—college guys—always had. Instead, he covered my own hand and pulled it away from his chest.

A sharp stab of disappointment hit me low in the belly. It quickly disappeared when I realized he wasn't letting go. In fact, he'd twined his fingers in mine and pushed my arm behind my back until both of us were touching my backside. Then he took hold of the other and did the same thing until he had me completely immobilized. I couldn't move my arms. Couldn't back away because the counter blocked my path. Couldn't do anything but stand there and breathe him in.

I should have been scared since I barely knew him. And since mystery and danger dripped off the man in buckets.

Instead, I was excited as hell. This could get wild. He could be rough, demanding. Overpowering. I might have gone from meat and potatoes to steak tartar in one touch.

Oh, thank heaven.

"Are you always so bossy?" he growled.

I somehow found the strength to nod once.

"Anybody ever do anything about it?"

Licking my lips, I shook my head and managed to whisper, "Uh-uh."

"Maybe it's time someone did."

I had a really good someone in mind.

Scared—excited—I just stood there, waiting. Finally, after a long, breathless moment, he tugged me closer, until my body was crushed against his. Even though I was half out of my mind with want, there was no missing the ridge of arousal I felt pressed against my crotch. God, he was big. Hard. And I could barely remain on my feet.

Simon dipped his head closer. Dying for his kiss, I tilted mine back, closing my eyes and parting my lips, breathless with anticipation.

When he did kiss me, though, it wasn't the hungry, deep and passionate encounter of the night before. Instead, he did something completely shocking.

He caught my lower lip between his, sucked it into his mouth and bit on it. Lightly. But deliberately.

I almost came right then. Hot waves of pleasure radiated through me, rocketing in a frenzy to pound between my legs, which went weak. As if he knew it, he pulled me closer, his fingers tightening around my bottom as he hoisted me, until I was almost riding that massive erection.

He licked away the spot where he'd bitten, as if easing some nonexistent pain. When what I really wanted was for him to nibble and nip at my entire body.

But oh, I think I could forego his teeth because his tongue was utterly delicious, sliding across my lip. I tried to wriggle closer, to catch his mouth with mine for the kind of slow, drugging kiss I knew he could provide. Simon, unfortunately, seemed to have finished doing whatever it was he wanted to do. Because he suddenly let go of my hands, allowing me to slide down to stand on my own feet, and stepped back.

His eyes were stormy, his frown fierce, as if *I* had been the aggressor and had stolen an unwilling embrace from *him*.

Not that I'd been unwilling. Oh, no.

"You shouldn't be here," he muttered.

"I'm not going anywhere. You said I could stay."

I heard that note of belligerence in my voice that had always served me well when dealing with my brothers. Of course, with my brothers, I always had the threat that I'd tell my parents about *something* they'd done to back it up.

With this man, I had nothing. Nothing but bravado and sheer force of will.

We were at a checkmate moment and I held my breath waiting for his next move. When he made it, I wanted to cry in relief. Because fortunately, force of will seemed to be enough. Though a muscle in his cheek clenched, making that strong jaw of his jut out, he finally nodded. "All right. But only for a day or two. Get what you need and then go back where you came from."

Turning away from me, he strode toward the door. Before exiting, though, he looked back at me. "And just stay out of my way because I'm going to do my best to pretend you're not here."

LATE THAT AFTERNOON, after sneezing about twenty times in a row due to the rank air permeating the basement, I decided to try a change of scenery. I'd gone through a bunch of old mildewy boxes that contained lots of paperwork on the hotel. Guest registries, comment cards, advertisements, bills of sale for supplies and groceries. All appeared to be from the past twenty years or so, when Simon's uncle had been running the place. Right up until this past June. I even found my professor's name on a hotel reservation sheet.

I needed to go back further. So, remembering Simon's words, I made my way to the third floor, started testing doors and found the one to the attic. Climbing up the narrow wooden steps, I made my way carefully, because they were steep and hard.

It was a good thing I was so interested in my topic, because it had been hell doing what Simon Lebeaux had asked of me this afternoon. Stay away from him? How on earth could I do that when all I *wanted* to do was touch the man, soothe his scars, let him know he wasn't alone.

That or throw my arms around his neck and my legs around his waist and beg him to take me.

"Not a good move," I whispered as I waved a hand in front of my face in the dusty, cobweb-ridden attic. If I made a move too quickly, the man was liable to toss me out on my butt. Subtlety was required. Though, to be honest, subtlety wasn't one of my strong points. My brothers and sisters-in-law often accused me of having the tact of a tanker truck.

What can I say? I'm a modern woman. I have opinions. The fact that they're usually correct and other people are so often wrong wasn't *my* fault.

Since the attic revealed itself to be cavernous—covering the entire width and breadth of the house—I decided to explore it in sections. The overhead lights, just bare bulbs hanging from loose wires extended down the center of the room, weren't providing much light. But some late afternoon sunshine had finally peeked out from behind the clouds, and a bit of it was drifting in under the eaves on the west side of the house.

That's where I started. I kept my attention on the old, lidded boxes stacked along one rough, nail-studded wall, not even gazing through the shadows at the rest of the enormous space. And I didn't really want to, either. My first, tentative exploration had been quite enough, thank you.

I had gotten over my initial case of the willies about Seaton House, but there was something a little creepy about being alone in a huge room full of dust, moth-ball scented air and secretive history. Simon had mentioned the dressmaker stands, so those didn't freak me out too much when I first spotted them standing around in silent sentry over the room. But there were other odd things, such as a large, old-fashioned wooden rocking horse with only one eye and a cracked leather saddle. I felt as if I were being winked at by a crusty-skinned wolf fresh from eating Little Red Riding Hood's granny.

Something that looked like it belonged in a torture chamber, but turned out to be one of those old belted fat-busting machines I'd only ever seen in movies, blocked part of the aisleway. So I hadn't gone too far back. But even from twenty feet in the door, I saw endless sheet-draped objects in varying shapes and sizes.

I knew most of the graying sheets were covering nothing but old furniture. Still, the Scooby Doo fan in me couldn't quite get over the idea that somebody was lurking under one of those things, ready to pop out and scare me to death.

"Stop being such a twit," I muttered, since my nervousness was so out of character. I'd always been imaginative, but I'd never been a wimp.

Lottie the hard-ass, that was me. Had been that way since kindergarten when some rotten third grader had told me there was no Santa Claus. I'd been so pissed, I beat the hell out of him on the playground. But when my brothers confirmed it was true—begging me not to tell our parents the Santa secret was out of the bag for fear none of us would get any presents anymore—I'd felt genuinely betrayed. I'd been skeptical of all fantasies and fairy tales ever since. That was, perhaps, why I always tried to find plausible explanations for the things I experienced. Even if those plausible explanations involved bank robbers dropping dollar bills or secretive men hiding out after being brutally attacked.

It could have been an accident, a voice whispered in my head. But I knew it hadn't been.

Anyway, my imagination might have been a little wild, but it was always grounded in reality. No supernatural stuff. Which made last night's lapse into terrified dementia a little surprising. Still, I had to give myself a break. I'd been tired, bleary-eyed, my mind full of images of the awful things that had happened in this house. So I'd mistaken a hot guy for a ghostly serial killer. Sue me.

Wanting to take advantage of the remaining daylight, I got to work. Though I had fully expected to find more of the same boring stuff from the basement, to my surprise, I stumbled upon some older paperwork in the very first box I opened. The schematics and ancient blueprints from the house were neatly folded inside it, along with carpentry notes, bills of sale and neatly written receipts of payment.

"Getting closer," I whispered, even as I marveled over how little the original builder of this place had paid for a thousand square feet of marble tile, which was still in evidence in the foyer downstairs.

I got so wrapped up in the minutiae of life in the early 1900s that I barely noticed the passing of time. It wasn't until I was squinting and holding an old letter up to my nose to make out the elegant, neat script-handwriting that I realized how dark it had become. Whatever outside light had lent it-self to my efforts was now gone and I was left only with the bare, yellowed bulbs overhead.

Okay. That was enough for the day. I'd found some inter-esting information—though not what I'd been looking for—but at least I felt sure I was in the right place now. Plus, I'd stayed out of Simon's sight all afternoon, so he had hopefully decided I would *not* be in his way and could therefore stick around. At least long enough to finish my job, and, hopefully to help him in some way.

And maybe have some fabulous sex, too.

With that pleasant thought in mind, I repacked the box, then tiptoed out of the maze toward the door. I held tightly onto the rail as I made my way down the stairs, realizing that the light from above made absolutely no headway down here. I hadn't noticed it earlier when I'd arrived, but the fixture at the base of the steps was missing a bulb. I could just make out the empty socket the near darkness.

Glad to be getting out of here, I reached for the doorknob and twisted it. But it remained completely immobile.

"Oh, great," I muttered, "the damn door sticks."

I started to wriggle and jiggle it, putting my weight against the door as I did so. It didn't give an inch.

"This can't be happening." I stopped what I was doing and thought about it. When I'd come up here a couple of hours ago, the door had opened smoothly enough, not even creaking on its old hinges. And the knob had twisted easily under my hand.

If the door is stuck...wouldn't the knob still move? a voice in my head asked.

Yeah. I was pretty sure it would. Which meant only one thing.

This door wasn't stuck. Somebody had locked it.

6

Simon

STAYING SHUT AWAY in his office throughout the afternoon, Simon forced himself to focus on his work, on the book he was contracted to write, which was already three months late.

Not on the woman in his basement. The woman whose mouth he'd sampled again earlier this afternoon.

The woman he was dying for.

"Hell," he mumbled that evening, realizing he'd just typed the same sentence twice.

Knowing it was useless—that his brain was tapped out and whatever bit of creative imagination he had left was going to be busy picturing Lottie Santori standing in his kitchen *naked*—he gave up. And gave in, at least a little, to the mental images that had tried to crowd into his head all afternoon.

He couldn't stop picturing the look on her face, the way her pink lip had grown red and swollen when he'd tasted her. The way she'd parted those lips, practically begging him to lick the inside of her beautiful mouth.

With one hard shake of his head, he forced the thoughts away again, knowing he could never face her tonight if he didn't. It was going to be hard enough looking her in the eye, knowing he probably ought to apologize for what he'd done.

It would be worse trying to hide the fact that he wanted to do it again.

Glancing at his watch and realizing it was seven-thirty, he frowned. He'd completely lost track of time while reading over the notes he'd taken during his two weeks in Charleston and putting them into his work in progress. Fortunately, he hadn't been wounded until his very last night, so he had a lot of information to use. More recently, he'd conducted some final interviews and gotten statistics from city officials by e-mail, which should provide him with everything he needed.

Because God knew he'd never go back. At least, not until the trial. And he was still hoping a plea deal would mean that would never happen.

Shutting down his computer, he left the office and wandered into the kitchen, half expecting to see Lottie there, making dinner. He never had gotten that lunch she'd offered earlier. They'd been very *distracted* immediately after she'd suggested it.

But the kitchen was empty. Silent except for the low hum of the refrigerator. The lights were off, here and everywhere else on the first floor—other than the office—which surprised him.

Wondering if she'd gotten caught up in whatever she'd found in the basement, he went down there, but that, too, was dark and deserted. Shadowy. Moist. He certainly didn't blame her for choosing to work elsewhere.

"But where?" he whispered.

A sudden, disturbing thought made him hurry back upstairs. After what had happened this morning, had he scared her off? Had she decided she wasn't safe in the house of the crazy murderer on the hill, packed her bag and left without a word?

Her car was still parked outside. Besides, no one had come to work on it, so his fear had not only been irrational, it had been stupid.

But he was still incredibly relieved she hadn't gone. He didn't pause to analyze why, beyond acknowledging that he shouldn't have felt so glad she had stuck around. He barely knew Lottie, and he'd been wanting her gone since the minute she'd arrived.

Liar.

Maybe at first he'd wanted her gone. But somehow, during the one day she'd been here, he'd remembered that he used to be a social person. He'd liked people. He'd particularly liked women.

The wrong women, in some cases.

Going out to the front porch, he couldn't help glancing toward the edge of the lawn, another fear rising inside him. It had been only four months since his uncle—who'd lived here all his life—had taken one fatal misstep off the edge of those cliffs. And something told him Lottie was in some kind of trouble. Call it intuition strengthened by three months of near solitude, but whatever the case, he wasn't about to wait around for her to wander back.

Because she might not be able to.

Taking the steps three at a time, he ran across the still-wet grass, the starry moonlit sky providing adequate light. As soon as he reached the closest drop-off, though, he realized he should have grabbed a flashlight. "Stupid," he muttered. But unwilling to leave without taking a cursory look, he peered down into the rocky darkness, where the mountain cut away sharply toward the valley—and the town—below.

It was useless without more light. "Lottie!" he called, then repeated the call twice more. If she was hurt or stranded, she could at least yell out and signal her location.

Nothing. The night was silent except for a light breeze rustling through the dried leaves beneath the massive maple and oak trees that marked the boundary of the lawn. Uncle Roger had planted them decades ago, hoping to keep curious hotel visitors away from the dangerous cliffs.

If only they'd kept *him* away.

Simon's concern now gripping him so tightly his chest ached, he strode toward the house, knowing he had to get more light. He hadn't made a full search, so he'd do so now then he was calling the police down in Trouble. But before he got to the porch, he heard something that sounded like a voice.

Stopping abruptly, he yelled, "Lottie?"

"Up here, *I'm up here.*"

He looked up, seeing nothing but the night sky, then noticed a glimmer of light under the eaves at the very top of the house. "The attic," he murmured, immediately realizing where she'd gone.

Okay, so he'd overreacted. He'd been the one who'd suggested she search the attic, and it should have been the first place he'd checked. But somehow after Charleston, he'd found himself immediately fearing the worst rather than thinking logically, as he always had before.

The bullet had taken away a chunk of his optimism along with a chunk of his chest.

"Simon, do you hear me?" came the faint cry.

"Are you in the attic?"

"Yes! I'm locked in, please come let me out."

Locked in. His relief was so great, he almost wanted to laugh that she'd managed to lock herself in on the top floor. Then he wanted to yell at her for scaring him so badly.

"Why the hell would she care?" he muttered as he jogged back into the house. He quickened his pace as he headed up the two long flights of stairs, mentally acknowledging that Lottie owed him nothing. He had no business being so damned worried about her just because he hadn't found her right away.

He needed to get past this. To stop overreacting to this kind of situation. Even if he explained it to her—about his uncle and about what had happened in Charleston, when he'd watched a woman plunge to her death—he didn't think she'd understand.

How could anyone understand? Even Simon, himself, couldn't make sense of the crazy twists and turns his mind took these days. From half believing the house was haunted, to immediately fearing his beautiful young house-guest was in danger, he'd gone from having the creative mentality of an analytical nonfiction writer to a Stephen King wannabe.

When he reached the third floor corridor, he heard her pounding from the far end. He also heard some rather choice language coming out of her beautiful mouth and couldn't prevent a half smile. Damn but the woman was feisty. Dramatic. She brought life and light into this drafty, shadowy old house and he could barely stand the thought of how dark and empty it would be when she left it.

He liked her. He liked having her here. Too much.

If he *didn't* like her, it probably would have made things simpler. Because there was no doubt he was attracted to her. And if attraction had been all he felt, he could have just taken her to bed and been done with it.

Everyone kept telling him he had to get back in the saddle. That he couldn't let what had happened the last time he'd picked up a woman make him swear off sex for life.

He wasn't ready to swear off sex—hell, no. But he would never again do something as stupid as pick up a stranger in a bar and bring her back to his room.

He didn't know if anything he'd ever experienced could have prepared him for that—for an attractive woman practically wrapping herself around him in a public place, begging him to take her upstairs. Then, when he did, letting a male partner in behind them.

When they'd both pulled weapons and demanded his money, he'd given it to them. Simon wasn't stupid.

That should have been the end of it. Why hadn't that been the end of it? Why hadn't they taken his cash and credit cards and gotten the hell out?

Why did things have to get so bloody?

He'd learned a lesson. A valuable one, which made him again question his decision to let Lottie stay here. She wasn't quite a stranger—the paperwork and letters from his uncle proved her identity, and her mission, at least. But she wasn't exactly someone he knew very well, either. "Yet she's still sleeping under my roof," he muttered, knowing he was playing devil's advocate to pump up his own reservations.

There was no more time to consider it, though. Reaching the attic door, he dug the old-fashioned keyring out of his pocket. He had no idea how she'd managed to get in and lock the door behind her without the key. "Hold on, I'm here. You'll be out in a second."

"Thank God," she exclaimed.

He grabbed the knob to hold the door steady while he inserted the key. But strangely, the knob twisted in his hand. The door opened, and Lottie Santori, red-faced and furious-looking, practically fell out.

She landed, as was becoming her habit, right in his arms. "Thank you, thank you, thank you," she muttered, pressing a couple of quick kisses on his cheek, as if she couldn't restrain the impulse. Her body pressed against his from shoulder to thigh and he couldn't resist dropping his hands to her waist, cupping her and holding her still.

The woman definitely knew how to express her appreciation. Her soft curves molded against him and her arms encircled his neck. Her thick, dark hair brushed his face. And his relief that she was okay simply overwhelmed him. Unable to resist, he bent and covered her mouth with his.

She instantly melted into him. Tasting her tongue, Simon heard her tiny groan of pleasure and echoed it. Lottie tasted sweet and spicy, which suited her so well. Lazily exploring her mouth, he met her tongue in thrust after slow thrust.

She tilted her head, lifting her arms to wrap them around his neck, her fingers twining in his hair. There was no frenzy, no insanity as he'd expect to feel after such a long, celibate period without a woman in his life. No. This was smooth and relaxed, not a prelude to anything more but a delight in and of itself.

He liked kissing. He'd forgotten how much.

He especially liked kissing *her*.

Lifting one hand, he cupped her cheek, realizing how cold her skin was. Icy cold. Such a contrast to her warm mouth and her hot, *hot* body.

Lottie shuffled backward, drawing him with her, until she was leaning against the corridor wall. When she bent her leg and lifted it, scraping her thigh along his hip, he groaned at the intimacy of it. She was tugging him hard against her with one leg while she tilted her pelvis into his. He could feel the heat between her legs and smell the hot, unmistakable musk of female arousal.

It would be easy—so very easy—to unfasten her jeans and take her right here, right now. Judging by her whimpers and the nearly frantic way she was rubbing against him—as if getting off on the feel of his erection against her crotch— that was exactly what she wanted. And the way their tongues tangled—mating, thrusting, giving and taking in a long, lethargic dance that imitated the way their bodies would dance when they came together—only emphasized it.

No. That couldn't happen. She'd intended to give him a kiss of gratitude for God's sake, because she *thought* he'd rescued her.

He was no damn hero. And though he was no damn saint, either, he somehow managed to end the kiss and lift his head.

She rose up on tiptoe, whimpering, not even opening her eyes. As if she wanted to start it all over again. But Simon resisted, taking a deep, controlling breath and easing back a few inches.

"Your cheeks are cold," he said with a soft laugh, trying to tease the aura of sex and sensuality out of the air.

She stared at him, her big brown eyes dreamy and out of focus, her lids half-closed in lazy, wanton invitation. But he wasn't accepting that invitation.

He was *not*.

Finally, as if she'd recognized his resolve, she nodded. "Yes, it was pretty cold. At least twenty degrees colder than that icebox I slept in last night."

Chuckling, he said, "I offered to fire up the generator."

"You didn't seem very enthusiastic about it."

Shrugging, he admitted, "It doesn't work very well." Then, knowing their brief talk had succeeded in cooling them both off, he asked, "So, are you okay?"

She nodded. "Just chilled. And a little freaked out. I guess my imagination started to get away from me. I was envisioning people under every one of those stupid sheets up there."

He suddenly remembered what she'd been yelling…that she'd been *locked* in the attic.

"Lottie," he said, taking her hands in his—cold hands, too—and tugging them away so he could step back. "Why did you think you were locked in?"

She gave him a *duh* look. "Because I *was*. At first I wondered if you were trying to scare me into leaving, playing a prank. Believe me, if you'd rescued me an hour ago, I would have come out swinging."

Lucky for him. He much preferred her coming out kissing.

"But I figured you wouldn't do that, especially when I heard you calling for me outside. I'm glad you came back toward the house and heard me shouting back." She lifted her hands, studying the backs of them, which was when he realized they were red and scratched. "I guess I pounded too hard."

Frowning, Simon grabbed her hands and turned them so he could take a better look. "They're raw. You were banging on the door?"

She nodded. "Yelling my guts out, pounding, kicking."

Her throaty voice told him she wasn't exaggerating. She sounded a little hoarse.

"I didn't hear a thing," he said, wondering how he was going to tell her she had not been locked in. He had the feeling she wasn't going to like hearing that bit of news.

"This house is too darn big," she said, not trying to remove her hands. She seemed to like the way he was holding them, carefully stroking his fingers against her abrasions. When the tip of his index finger brushed the tip of hers, she winced. "Ouch."

Seeing small red blisters on the tips of two fingers and her thumb, he asked, "What happened here?"

"I think I burned myself," she admitted. "I didn't realize it until I came down the stairs, but there's no bulb in the light fixture at the bottom of the stairwell. I wasn't about to stay perched on the step pounding on the door with the little tiny bit of light spilling down from above. So I had to go steal one from up in the attic."

Did the woman have no common sense? Unable to resist, he drew her hand to his lips and kissed the tip of each finger, resisting the urge to suck them into his mouth.

Shaking his head, he asked, "Couldn't you have shut the lights off and let them cool off before trying to unscrew one?"

She snatched her hand away and frowned. "In case you haven't realized it, the only switch for your stinking attic is down here by the door. And if you thought I was going to march down in the dark, flip the switch *off* and then climb back up into that black hole of death, trying to *feel* my way to a cool lightbulb, you're nuts."

Well, when she put it that way…

"I wasn't thinking at first," she grudgingly admitted, her temper cooling as quickly as it had heated up. "I just grabbed. Once I realized it was hot, I found a rag and twisted the bulb off, then brought it down and felt around until I could get it into the socket."

The woman was damn lucky she hadn't electrocuted herself. He could just imagine if she'd jammed her finger into the live socket while poking around in the darkness. This story was getting worse and worse. And he still hadn't found a way to tell her the door must have only been stuck, since it certainly had not been locked.

"You really ought to fix that door so it doesn't lock like that. It's dangerous."

Knowing he had to be honest with her, he walked over to the door and pushed it shut. "This is one of the original locks to the house."

"Yeah, well, maybe you should replace it then."

"Yes, I should," he murmured. "But my point is that it's an old type of fixture that can only be locked or unlocked with a key. There are no buttons or switches." Opening and closing it a couple of times, he added, "There's no way it can be accidentally engaged."

Her eyes narrowed as she began to catch his meaning. "You're wrong. It was locked."

"It must have been jammed, Lottie."

The strong jaw jutted out and her dark eyes glittered. "Simon, I tried twisting the knob several times. It wouldn't move at all."

He simply stared at her, certain she must be mistaken. But the woman wouldn't back down, wasn't changing her story at all.

"That door was locked."

VIVID NIGHTMARES interfered with Simon's sleep. Not about Charleston, but about his uncle Roger.

In the months he'd lived in Seaton House, Simon had grown more angry about the way his last remaining relative had died. The unfairness of it, the lousy whim of fate that had sent the sixty-year-old man wandering out on the lawn on a foggy morning, then plunging over the side of a mountain.

His uncle had died an awful death.

And all through the night, Simon kept seeing it over and over in his mind, hearing the plaintive calls for help that had never reached anyone's ears. He saw his uncle's final, lonely hours. When he woke, a slick sheen of sweat covered his skin and hot moisture pricked the corners of his eyes.

"God," he whispered in the semidarkness of early morning. His covers were wrapped around him, as if he'd thrashed in the night.

Knowing he wouldn't be able to get back to sleep, he got up and headed outside, determined to walk off the anger and sadness. As he often did in the early hours, he found himself heading for the cliffs.

The morning had dawned gray but not misty, unlike what it must have been like on his uncle's last day. Standing at the farthest point on the south side of the lawn, Simon was able to see down into the town of Trouble. He could easily make out the main street, the roofs of the grocery store and the diner. And, rising on a hill just past downtown, the house owned by his one and only friend in the area—Mortimer Potts.

He had to laugh. Mortimer was an eighty-year-old millionaire who liked to dress up in sheik robes and camp out in an enormous tent in his backyard. If that wasn't a statement about how radically Simon's life had changed, he didn't know what was.

"What's funny?"

Startled, he swung his head around and saw Lottie standing a few feet away from him. He hadn't even heard her approach in the damp grass.

Apparently an early riser, too, she was dressed in running clothes—sweats and sneakers—with her thick, dark hair swept up in a ponytail on top of her head. Her breaths came in shallow pants, as if she'd been jogging already, though it was only seven-thirty.

"Don't run along the cliffs," he said, barking out the first words that came to his mind.

"Well, good morning to you, too."

He cleared his throat. "Good morning." Then he repeated his warning. "The cliffs are uneven along the edge. You don't want to be running within ten feet of the drop-off, especially not when it's dark out."

She walked over, still panting. She'd apparently been out and about for quite a while. He wondered if her night had been as restless as his. And what the two of them might have done about that restless night, had they happened to be sleeping in the same room.

"Simon?"

Seeing her eyeing him curiously, he cleared his throat. She'd obviously said something to him but his mental imaginings had made him deaf to whatever it was. "Sorry?"

"I asked if you were all right. You don't look well. Have you eaten this morning?"

"Got a second career as a nurse going, have you?"

"Got a second career as a vampire I don't know about? You're pale enough," she said, her tone just as sarcastic.

After a pointed look up at the sun, which cast a few rays of light between the morning clouds, he glanced at her and quirked an eyebrow.

"Okay, you're obviously not a pile of vampire ash in the sunlight," she admitted, sounding grumpy. Cute. "But if you keep starving yourself and hiding away in that office, you're going to look like Dracula."

"I thought you were here to research the history of the house, not harass me into eating."

Her fists hit her hips. "Harass? Please. You haven't seen harassed yet. You want to know what real harassment is, ask my brothers."

There she went being cute again. So tough and bossy. He wanted to know more about her. "Brothers? Big family?"

She nodded. "Five of them. All older."

Ouch. Five older brothers. If he hadn't already known he couldn't get involved with this young woman, that would have driven the point home.

"Fortunately," she added, as if sensing his immediate reaction, "they're all back in Chicago, not here watching my every move. How about you, any siblings to torment you throughout your childhood?"

He shook his head.

"Cousins? Anything?"

"No. No one."

She frowned. "Wow, I've often wished I had about twenty or thirty fewer males bossing me around but I can't imagine not having *any.*"

"Twenty or…"

"With the cousins and second cousins, yeah. My parents each come from huge families and they all took that Catholic 'go forth and breed' thing a little too seriously."

He smiled, liking her frankness. As usual. "My father was an only child, and my mother's brother…" He glanced down the mountain. "Uncle Roger never married. He spent his whole life here." Lowering his voice, speaking almost to himself, he murmured, "And he died here."

Her hand touched his arm—lightly, offering comfort, warmth. "I'm sorry. I still regret barreling in and mistaking you for him the other night." Clearing her throat, she added, "How did he die?"

Simon remained silent for a moment, though the story certainly wasn't any big secret. Still, it wasn't easy to talk about. Even at the funeral, when most of the town had come up to offer him their condolences, he'd barely managed a word to anyone.

Which probably explained why they all thought him an antisocial villain now. Well, that and because he'd thrown so many of them off the grounds after he'd moved here in July. He'd not only pushed the welcome wagon back down the mountain, he'd slit its tires and emptied its gas tank, too.

Lottie, of course, couldn't know, though. Somehow, standing here so close to where it had happened, he felt compelled to tell her. "Uncle Roger apparently came out here for a walk very early one morning in June, as he often did. But this time, he lost his footing." Staring down the hillside past the rocks and mounds of dead plant life and spiny, decrepit tree limbs, he could almost see the elderly man lying there. Waiting for help that never came.

"He wasn't found until a day and a half later, after an all-out search had been called by the Trouble police. By the time they spotted him it was too late."

"Two days…" Lottie's hand clenched reflexively on his arm. The color fell out of her cheeks and her bottom lip trembled. "No one heard him, no one knew?"

"The hotel has never done much business and there were only a handful of people staying here at the time. The staff didn't get worried about his disappearance until that night and didn't call the police until the next morning."

Moisture appeared in Lottie's pretty brown eyes. "Simon, I'm so sorry. I didn't mean to bring up something so painful."

"You didn't. I was standing here thinking about it, anyway." Not sure why he was admitting it, he added, "I dreamed about him last night. I think your stories about this Zangara character have made me start to wonder if this house is… cursed. My mother certainly thought so."

He had been about to say haunted but had quickly changed his mind. Little Miss Tough-talking Santori didn't need to hear about his own crazy imaginings. Even if she had jokingly suggested last night when they'd shared dinner in the kitchen that a ghost must have locked her in the attic.

She'd laughed. He hadn't. Not because he believed any spectral entity was playing pranks on his guest. But because the incident was one more he had to add to the list of strange things taking place in Seaton House.

"So," he said, shaking his head hard in an effort to change the subject, "with five older brothers, I can see where you get your mouth."

Her shocked expression told him he'd succeeded in redirecting the conversation. "I beg your pardon?"

"Tell me," he asked, as if she hadn't spoken, "any of them ever spank you to get you to behave?"

Her eyes widened. "*Spank* me? Are you kidding?"

"I bet you could have used a spanking a few times in your life."

"It'd take a man a whole lot stronger than any of my brothers to give me a spanking."

He should have known better than to taunt her because suddenly Lottie licked her lips. "Unless I *wanted* him to."

Naughty girl. He almost laughed but the heat in her eyes changed his mind.

Knowing he should change the subject, steer back into neutral territory, he instead took the card she'd thrown down and upped the stakes. "Is that what you're into?" Damn, it had been a long time since he'd played these kinds of wicked word games with a beautiful woman. And something wouldn't let him stop. Instead, he inched closer. "Kinky pleasures? Pain? Domination?"

She swayed closer, too. Her deep, even breaths indicated an internal reaction…desire. Arousal. "Were you trying to find out when you bit me?"

He lifted a hand to her neck and brushed back a bit of hair, trailing the tips of his fingers on the vulnerable spot near the base of her throat. "I didn't bite you."

Her head dipped to the side slowly as she arched into his touch, pleading for it though not saying so out loud. "What would you call it then?"

"A taste." Unable to stop himself, he leaned down and pressed his mouth to the warm skin on the side of her neck, just above where it met her shoulder. "Just a small taste." Opening his mouth, he sampled her skin, licking lightly, then nibbling with his teeth until she hissed and started to quiver.

"Taste me again, Simon," she said, her voice throaty and insistent. And before he could reply, she'd taken what she wanted, twining her hands in his hair and tugging his head up so their mouths could meet.

This wasn't lazy and sweet, a kiss of thanks like the previous evening. Lottie thrust her tongue into his mouth, exploring ravenously, all the while pressing her body against him. She was wild, determined, and when she shoved his jacket off his shoulders and slid her hands beneath his shirt, he couldn't manage a protest.

Her fingers were cold, her touch blazing. Never letting the kiss end, she sucked his bottom lip into her mouth, sinking her teeth into it in retaliation for yesterday.

He thought the cliffs had begun shaking beneath his feet, but he couldn't focus enough to be sure. Unable to resist, he dropped his hands to her hips, sliding his fingers beneath the heavy sweatshirt she wore to stroke the fine, smooth skin of her waist. Again, she demanded more. Covering his hand with one of hers, she tugged it up until his thumb was brushing the bottom curve of one lush breast.

She wriggled, reaching up under her own sweatshirt and obviously unfastening her bra, because suddenly the constricting fabric loosened and that big warm mound of flesh dropped into his palm. He groaned, savoring the intimacy.

"Oh, Simon, yes," she whimpered against his mouth, arching harder, as if begging for a firmer touch.

This should stop. He needed to stop it. But he couldn't, not without going just a little bit further.

Finding her puckered nipple, he caught it between his fingers and squeezed lightly until she sobbed in the back of her throat. Every stroke brought a quiver to Lottie's body. Every gentle tug made her moan.

"Taste me *there*," she whispered hoarsely, her mouth lifting just barely from his.

God it was tempting. *She* was tempting. But the sudden shift of a few pebbles tumbling down over the cliff brought him back to reality with a quick snap.

Sometimes he really hated reality. He'd have given anything to continue. Having touched her, he wanted desperately to see her, to cover that hard nipple with his lips and suck it until she begged.

As she was nearly doing now.

But they were outside on a cold autumn morning, standing at the edge of a mountain, not far from one of the most hellish spots he'd ever known.

That, more than anything, enabled him to regain control.

Dropping his hand, he pulled her shirt back into place. "Lottie," he whispered, "enough. That's enough."

"Like hell it is." Her fingers clutched his shoulders, her nails digging into his muscles there.

He caught her hands and forced himself to step back. "This was a very bad idea."

"Nothing that feels this good could be bad."

She was wrong. Because *he* was bad—bad for her, bad for himself. He'd fallen so far he didn't know if he'd ever be able to pull himself out of his emotional pit, and the last thing he needed to do was drag her down into it with him.

So with one final, regretful squeeze of her hand, he turned on his heel and walked toward the house.

7

Lottie

Funny, I've been in this drafty, shadowy old hotel for a couple of days now but my reasons for being here have slowly changed. I thought I was here for work—to find out anything I could about Josef Zangara and his wicked life in order to help the professor with his book. And in that regard, I'd had a little success. Another visit to the attic—with the key tucked safely in my pocket, and a bench propping the door open—had provided some interesting information this morning. Information I wanted to share with Simon.

But if something happened and I had to leave here tonight, it wasn't the *work* that would be so hard to leave behind. It wasn't even the sexual attraction I'd felt for Simon Lebeaux since the moment I'd stumbled into his arms.

It was the man himself. He was the *real* reason things had changed. Oh, sure, I still wanted him as much as ever. When he opened the attic door last night and let me out, a part of me considered doing a whole lot more than giving him a thank-you kiss. A take-me one would have been much better.

And this morning on the cliffs? Whoa, mama, I still shook when I thought about it. I sensed the man could play my body like a virtuoso could a fine instrument, wringing out every last, perfect note I was capable of reaching.

But—and this is the ironic part—something has changed. I am now living under the same roof with a dark, sexy, mysterious stranger. And the me-so-horny-me-love-you-long-time lust I'd been experiencing since, well, forever, has sort of been replaced by something else.

I'm worried about him.

I hadn't liked seeing him standing silhouetted against the early morning sky today at the edge of those cliffs. Now that I know his uncle had died there, I *especially* didn't like it.

He thought I'd been out jogging or something. Ha. Me. Jogging. The only reason I'd jog is if it was five minutes before closing time at the supermarket and I'd run out of Ben & Jerry's.

In actuality, I'd heard him leave. I'd slept like crap so I was wide-awake early this morning when I heard the front door to the building slam shut. Peeking out the window of my third-floor room—the still freezing one, by the way—I saw him striding across the lawn and just had the impulse to follow him. I'd already been dressed, wearing the sweats I'd slept in—cold room, remember? I'd totally given up on the idea that he'd stumble into my room by mistake so I'd ditched the filmy white nightgown my second night in the place. So I'd just yanked on my sneakers, and, of course, a bra, and had taken off after him, practically racing out of the house.

Like something bad would happen to him if I didn't get there fast enough.

How weird was that? To be so protective of a man who, despite his leanness, was muscular enough that he could probably break me in half? Why did I want to wrap my arms around him and tell him he wasn't alone, rather than stripping naked and begging him to *do* me?

Well, okay, I still wanted to do that, too. Fortunately, I guess the two aren't mutually exclusive. Nothing said I couldn't be *naked* when I wrapped my arms around him and told him he wasn't alone, did it?

But right now, I couldn't say what I wanted more. As much as I longed for him—especially after that deep, languorous kiss we'd exchanged outside the attic door yesterday and the more frenzied, passionate one today—I wanted to help him, too.

I wanted him to confide in me. I wanted him to trust me. I wanted him to unburden himself to me.

And I wanted him to make love to me.

"This can't go on," I whispered that afternoon as I finished typing some notes into my laptop. I'd been working all morning in the attic, running to the top of the stairs, to peer down and make sure the door was still open. But, getting hungry, I decided to go downstairs for lunch, detouring to my room to make some notes first.

Fortunately, Simon had a wireless Internet network set up in the house and I was able to hop onto it to send some of my findings to Professor Tyler right away. When I'd realized the network was completely unprotected, with no firewall at all, I'd given Simon a hard time about it. But I hadn't been able to deny the truth he'd pointed out: who around here was going to hack in to it?

He was right. But considering some of the weird stuff that happened in this place, I personally thought he should be a little more careful. No, I hadn't seen any white filmy ghosts floating around, and I hadn't been locked in the attic again. Still, one or two times I'd found myself listening intently, certain I'd heard the sound of a woman's laughter coming from somewhere else on the third floor. And today, when I'd come back to my room to type my notes, I'd found my bed made. Perfectly made. Like quarter-bouncing perfect, as if the room were completely unoccupied.

Now, I'm not a total pig, but I'm not exactly a neatnik, either. I had felt nearly certain that I hadn't made the bed this morning.

Laughing as I told myself the ghost of a former maid must have done it, I still made a point of locking my door when I left. Silly, I know, but I had to do it. This house was huge—somebody could slip in here and pick up anything they liked. My laptop, for instance, and neither Simon nor I would ever notice them.

Shrugging off my worries, I decided to go downstairs, make a good meal and get Simon out of that damn office and away from that damn computer where he was constantly working. Writing, he'd said, though he hadn't elaborated.

It was time to get his attention. Nothing was coming of me being quiet, staying out of his way and trying to remain beneath his radar. I couldn't keep tiptoeing around the house, hoping he wouldn't notice me so that I could stay and worm my way into his life. And I wasn't about to lock myself in the attic again and wait for him to rescue me—even for another one of those crazy, hot, sexy, kisses.

Funny. He'd rescued me. When what I so wanted to do was rescue *him*.

I couldn't do that if he didn't let me get close. "So maybe I need to make him let me get close. In a very dramatic—personal—way," I mumbled.

If I wasn't going to be the pursued, then I needed to be the pursuer. In the past, during my NYU days, I hadn't had to do much more than smile at a guy or wear a tight, low-necked sweater to get what I wanted.

Simon…well, he wasn't some on-the-make college kid. He was a strong, serious man in full control of his desires. Usually. There'd been a few moments—intense, hot ones—where I'd seen a hungry look in his eyes. He sometimes watched me when he thought I wouldn't notice. The way he'd kissed me told me he was not unaffected by me. Not at all.

So maybe it was time for me to pull out all the stops, go into vamp mode and try to seduce him. Seduce my way into his confidence—and his *life*—by way of his bed.

Gee. Tough job.

"I'm up for the challenge," I said, smiling as I shut down the laptop and headed downstairs, going straight to the kitchen. As I dug out some fresh veggies and pasta to make lunch, I thought out my plan for seduction.

It probably wasn't nice, using a man's own innate weakness against him. But considering I was every bit as weak as a man when it came to libido, I didn't consider it beneath me.

My mother would be shocked. She shouldn't be, though. Because while she'd like to think I'm a lady, I think even she knows it's a lost cause.

God knows she and my grandmothers had *tried* to make me a good girl. You know the kid with the funky tartan jumper with the thick, black, patent leather straps that buckled over the shoulders? And the matching black, patent leather shoes? Yeah. That was me. Complete with pigtails.

In eighth grade.

And I'm not talking about the typical school uniform everybody had to wear. Oh, no, they took me out in *public* like that. I hadn't owned a pair of jeans until I was fourteen and I'd had to save up the money I'd earned busing tables in the restaurant to buy them myself. Even then, I had to wear them under my skirts whenever I left the house, then tear the skirt off as soon as I got down to the street.

The older women in my family seemed as if they were from the dark ages. Honestly, though, they were just very old-school, second-generation Americans. My grandparents had all come over before my parents' births, but just because their houses had been on U.S. soil didn't mean those households weren't entirely immersed in Italian culture. None of the older Santori females ever wore pants, much less *dungarees*, as Mama calls them. I don't think I've ever seen my mother in anything other than a dress.

Clothes didn't make the girl, that was for sure. Despite everyone's best efforts, I'd been hell on wheels from childhood on, and my brothers knew it better than anyone. Once when the twins had laughed at me for having to wear a frilly hat on Easter Sunday, I'd pried open the boxes of Raisinettes they'd gotten in their baskets and replaced them with lookalikes from our pet rabbit's cage.

I'm damn good at getting even.

Which, I guess, confirms that I've never been a lady. And I've always been willing to fight dirty to get what I wanted.

I wanted Simon. Now it was time to stop goofing around and get him.

"You're making a real lunch?" a voice said. Simon had entered the kitchen while I was busy planning my seduction campaign and I hadn't even heard him.

Painting a serene look on my face to hide the excitement I knew must have been lurking there, I nodded. "Pasta primavera. Sit down and eat before I shove you down and spoon-feed you."

Part of me was hoping he'd threaten to do something about my bossiness again, just like he had yesterday.

I wasn't that lucky.

"Why are you so determined to make me eat?"

"Why are you so determined to resist? In case you didn't know it, the thin, pale look went out with Byron and Shelley."

"With girlie names like Byron and Shelley, they deserved to be thin and pale."

He didn't smile, but again there was that twinkle in his eye. I liked his quick comebacks. I liked *him*. And he was in no way thin and frail-looking. Just lean. And hard. Like an uncoiled length of steel wire.

But I'm Italian. My family owns a restaurant. If a man's not eating, I take it *very* personally.

"Well, Simon Lebeaux does not. It is much too sexy a name to fit a tragic romantic poet."

"Lottie Santori, on the other hand, suits the bossy, mouthy broad scenario very well."

My jaw fell open. He'd called me a broad. Furthermore, the man was *smiling*.

"With that charm, it's no wonder you have ladies lining up here to keep you company."

"Who needs ladies when I've got you?"

"Whoa, zing," I said, unable to prevent a grin, especially since I'd just been thinking the same thing. I wasn't a lady—and we both knew it. "Who would have guessed there was a smart-ass under that dour, frowning face?"

"I'd say takes one to know one but it sounds so third grade."

I laughed, liking this side of him. He was relaxed, leaning one shoulder against the doorjamb as he watched me finish off the Alfredo sauce and toss it in with the pasta and veggies.

Without being ordered again, Simon sat at the table, watching as I brought two plates over and sat across from him.

"*Mangia, mangia*," I said, as I'd heard my mother say several times a day every day of my life.

Still smiling, he dug in and ate the way a man should eat my fine Italian cooking. I'd learned at the apron strings of the best, and if he hadn't devoured the huge plate of pasta I'd put in front of him, I'd have been highly insulted.

Realizing his approachable mood was providing an opportunity to learn more, I decided to take a chance on getting him to open up. "So what is it you're writing?"

"A book."

"Don't tell me," I said. "A story about a scary hotel?"

He smiled wryly. "No, definitely not." He didn't elaborate until I gave him a pointed stare, then he admitted, "I write destination guides for a publisher that caters to the tourist industry."

"Cool."

"Plus a syndicated column called 'Tales of the Traveler.'"

I sucked in a surprised gasp. "Oh, my gosh, I've read that column! The *Trib* carries it."

He nodded.

"I haven't seen it for a while."

Turning his attention to his plate, he forked a heap of pasta and muttered, "I've been on sabbatical."

Recovering. He didn't have to say the word, I *knew* it.

But I wasn't about to push it, so I instead said, "So you do a lot of research, too. That's something else we have in common."

"Aside from our ebullient personalities?" He didn't even crack a smile, but continued to eat as if he hadn't made such a huge exaggeration.

"Yeah. Sure. Right." Remembering some of the paperwork I'd found in a trunk in the attic this morning, I said, "Speaking of ebullient personalities, your great-grandfather was apparently a real piece of work."

Simon finished his lunch, put the fork on his plate and leaned back in his chair. I resisted the urge to smile when I saw him glance toward the pot on the stove. "Why do you say that?"

Not even hesitating—much less asking—I stood, grabbed his plate, walked over to the pot and refilled it. "I found some paperwork today that showed how he got controlling interest in this hotel. There were some copies of correspondence he exchanged with his partner while he was sitting in a jail cell in Pittsburgh."

"Oh?" He was interested. I could see it in his eyes as he accepted the plate and started eating again.

"Zangara needed money to hire a high-priced attorney. Apparently he wanted to mortgage his share, to just borrow money against his interest in Seaton House, but he couldn't find any takers. So he turned to his partner, Robert Stubbs, asking for a loan. But Stubbs refused. He forced him to sell out altogether at a rock-bottom price."

Simon shrugged. "I told you my mother couldn't stand the man and my uncle Roger never had a good thing to say about him, either."

Reaching for his glass of water, he sipped from it, then murmured, "I guess being able to hire a better lawyer didn't make much difference to Zangara."

"No, it didn't. The newspaper accounts say the jury was out thirty-seven minutes. After he heard the guilty verdict, Zangara had the only emotional outburst anyone ever witnessed. He lashed out at everyone, especially Stubbs, who he blamed for taking advantage of him and leaving his wife and son homeless. He swore revenge, you know—a curse upon your house, I'll haunt you to your dying day, all that stuff." Laughing, I added, "Maybe it was Zangara who locked the door on me yesterday."

Simon's good mood evaporated so quickly, I almost wondered if I'd imagined it. Where an easy, casual, charming man had been sitting across the table a moment ago, there was now a rigid, tight-jawed stranger who'd stopped eating halfway through his second helping.

"That's absolutely ridiculous." He rose from his chair, grabbing his plate off the table and taking it over to the sink.

He dumped out a plateful of food. Grandma Rosalita would be making the sign of the cross and whispering the rosary.

"Superstitious nonsense," he added.

I was about to agree—to tell him I'd been joking, that of

course I didn't believe in ghosts, despite my rather vivid imagination. But before I could do it, Simon had muttered a thank-you for lunch, then stalked out of the kitchen without another word.

Leaving me very curious about what, exactly, had set the man off.

SINCE SIMON AND I had been alone in the house for a few days, walking down the front steps and seeing a woman bent over, washing the tile floor in the foyer came as something of a shock. It was late afternoon and I'd spent the past several hours alone, going through more cartons as well as the drawers of old pieces of furniture in the attic. I'd ventured farther back in the room but still hadn't explored more than a third of it. There was just so much to see, so many fascinating side trips that had nothing to do with Zangara and everything to do with the price of a new-fangled dishwasher in 1952 or the guest comment cards of 1961.

I wondered how on earth I was going to get through everything in the time I had left. As much as I'd like to stay, I really was going to have to get back to Chicago—and school—soon. I was still thinking about that when I came down the stairs and saw the heavyset, middle-aged woman on her hands and knees, scrubbing the floor.

Apparently hearing me, she looked up. The startled, frightened expression on her face was almost comical. She jerked so hard her hand slid out from under her and she nearly went face-first into her bucket.

"Are you all right?" I asked, rushing over to help her, trying to avoid slipping on any wet tile.

The woman nodded, watching me warily as she shimmied backward, then rose to her feet. "Who're you?"

Introducing myself, I watched the expressions of fear ease a little on the woman's face. She looked around, her gaze resting on the closed door to Simon's office, then whispered, "Do you mean to tell me you're staying here? *Sleeping* here at night?"

I nodded. "Yes." Figuring the house's reputation had the woman on edge, I added, "And believe it or not, I haven't seen a single ghost."

"Ghosts," the woman said with a scoffing laugh. "It's not the dead you have to be worrying about." Her milky gray eyes shifted toward the door again. "It's the living."

She meant Simon. I knew it and I immediately stiffened. "If you're referring to my host, he's been perfectly charming and amiable."

A bit of a stretch, but the woman had ticked me off.

"Huh," she grunted, skepticism dripping off her. "You're fooling yourself. You shouldn't be here."

"If you're so concerned, what are *you* doing here?"

Shrugging, the woman bent to her pail again, dumping her rag into it and then straightened, rubbing her back as if it pained her. "Good pay. I come up once a week to tidy up." She jerked her head toward Simon's office door. "He stays in there the whole time, leastwise I think he does. I wouldn't be able to do a lick of work if he was watching me with those cold, sinister eyes of his."

I wanted to slap her. I also wanted to laugh. Because Simon's eyes were heated and intense, nowhere near cold and certainly not sinister. "You obviously don't know him very well."

"I've been cleaning this place and bringing him fresh groceries every week since he showed up. I guess I know him as well as *you* do," the woman replied as she opened the front door and walked out on the porch. I followed.

"The whole town knows all about him," the woman said as she tossed the dirty water from the bucket over the rail onto the lawn.

I wasn't sure the soap suds would do much for the flower

beds but I was fuming too much to pay attention. "I don't think any of you know him at all. Not a single person has called or come up here all week. He could have fallen over dead and no one would even know."

"Which is exactly the way he wants it."

She did have a point there, but I wasn't going to admit it.

"You listen well, miss. If I was you, I'd get out of here right away." The woman looked around, rising on tiptoe to try to peer past me into the shadowy recesses of the house. I knew she was trying to make sure Simon wasn't around to overhear. I also knew I was about to hear something new about my host. "He's a killer."

Uh, yeah, I'd definitely been right. And I damn sure didn't like it. So I, uh, sort of went Lottie on her. Yelled a little, told her to take her mop and ride it back down to wherever she came from. Or shove it somewhere. I don't remember exactly all I said.

I only remember one thing. That when the woman was gone, scurrying away to her station wagon and tearing out of the parking lot with a rattle and a belch of smoke, I realized Simon was standing right inside the doorway.

He'd obviously heard every word.

"I don't need you to defend me," he said, his voice soft, his tone even. Impossible to gauge.

"She's an idiot."

He didn't budge. "I repeat, you don't have to defend me."

"Well, you're sure not doing a very good job of it." Transferring my anger onto him, I strode back into the house. "Sitting up here, all locked away and glaring, you're just feeding the imaginations of narrow-minded people like her."

"You think I care?"

No. I supposed he didn't. But it bothered *me* that people thought so poorly of him.

This man might be moody and temperamental. He might even have an aura of danger and mystery.

But a killer? *Ridiculous.*

One thing was sure. Until Simon joined the land of the living—let himself come to life—he wasn't going to make any effort to change people's minds. He hadn't been lying— he just did not care. He was like a man emotionally dead, completely and utterly alone and adrift from the rest of the world.

I wasn't going to stand for that any longer. Whatever had happened, I would help Simon Lebeaux get past it, open himself up again and let go of the bottled anger and coldness he tried so hard to hide behind.

I was running out of time to let him slowly come to rely on me as a friend while secretly lusting for my hot bod, so it was definitely time to step up the pace. There was only one way to do it. Frankly, I couldn't think of a better way to bring a man's emotions to life than by awakening his libido.

It was for his own good. I intended to seduce the man out of his darkness if it was the last thing I ever did.

8

Simon

SIMON DIDN'T KNOW exactly when he realized Lottie was trying to seduce him, but by the time they finished dinner, he had no doubt that was the case. His first hint had been her feet coming down the stairs for dinner.

She'd been wearing those hot, sexy black boots with high heels and silver chains draped over the foot. They had obviously dried out and now fit snug and tight against her calves. What the hell was it about high-legged boots that instantly made a man think of sweaty sex and sin? But it was true. For a long moment after she'd come down, he'd been unable to picture anything but Lottie Santori, wearing nothing but those boots, lying open and waiting for him on his bed.

Yeah. The fuck-me boots had been clue number one. He'd been imagining all kinds of things as he listened to the sharp heels click on the kitchen tile as she buzzed around playing housekeeper, trying to act like nothing was out of the ordinary as they ate. Somehow, the way she sashayed around in her skin-tight jeans—her sweet, curvy ass swaying with every step—didn't make him feel very much like eating anything except *her*.

He told himself that wasn't what had inspired him to shave this afternoon.

He suspected he was lying.

Because all day long he'd been mentally hearing her begging him, over and over, to *taste* her. A beautiful woman with the most amazing body he'd ever seen had begged him to suck her nipples and he'd walked away. No wonder he hadn't been able to think of anything else all day but how badly he wanted to kiss every inch of her.

Dinner made it a lot more obvious. She was no longer sitting back and letting things happen spontaneously, like grateful kisses, or sultry encounters beneath stormy skies.

No.

The way she leaned over the table to refill his glass or pass the salt, causing her hot pink blouse to gap away from her chest, revealing plumped up, mouthwatering cleavage, cinched the certainty in his mind. He was being seduced. Lottie had stopped playing the earnest student slowly working her way into his life and gone right for his weak spot. His cock.

Not that it was weak. Hell, no. He'd had to keep his chair pulled closely in to the table throughout dinner just so she wouldn't see the bulge in his lap.

Whatever her game, she'd definitely scored the first point. Because he was going to have a hard time getting up after dinner without her noticing her success.

So do it. Take her. Have done with it.

It was tempting. Especially now that, having spent a few days living under the same roof with her, he no longer had any doubts that he could trust the woman. She hadn't tried to murder him in his bed…in fact, her biggest crime was that she was a pain in the ass about trying to take care of him.

Sweet. Nurturing. He wouldn't have expected it of the brash young woman but he knew it was true. She came from a world very different from his own. And from the things she'd said about her family, he knew they had helped create the person she'd become. She was full of life and laughter and happiness.

Everything he was not.

God, he wanted her so much he thought about doing away with the pretenses, grabbing her arm and pulling her across the table onto his lap. Screw the dishes, screw the hour, he'd do her on the kitchen floor, he was that desperate.

Funny, it wasn't his own self-disgust that stopped him from doing it. It was the realization that he owed her more. She deserved to know whom she was having sex with. Especially after she'd so vehemently defended him against the foolish, gossipy old cleaning lady this afternoon.

What, he wondered, would she say if he told her the woman was right? That he *was* a killer?

Not a murderer. No. But a killer nonetheless.

He might have been trying to save his own life by fighting back after he'd been sliced in the face and shot in the chest by a couple of scumbags bent on robbery.

But he'd ended that night alive. And the woman had ended it dead.

He *was* a killer. No matter what Lottie Santori thought.

"I need to get back to work," he said, pushing back from the table before finishing the last of his dinner, which she'd once again skillfully prepared.

"What?" She blinked, eyeing him with disbelief. "Good grief, Simon, it's seven o'clock. You've worked all day. Can't you even enjoy a decent meal?"

"Thank you," he muttered, meaning it. "You didn't have to go to all this trouble. But I appreciate it."

"Don't you walk out on me," she snapped. "Is stalking off your answer for everything?"

"I'm not stalking off." *I'm such a liar.*

She leapt up from her chair and shoved her own plate at him. "You know what? It's my turn to walk out in a huff. Appreciate this, buddy. You can wash the damn dishes, I'm going for a walk."

And out of the room she went, heading out the back door, her righteous indignation wrapped around her like a gauzy scarf.

Huh. This was the sweet, nurturing young woman he'd been imagining? Simon couldn't prevent a smile as he carried the dirty dishes to the sink and began rinsing them. He liked the angry, feisty Lottie. He liked the sexy, sultry Lottie. He liked the nurturing, caring Lottie.

He liked everything about her. And that was just bad news. The last thing he needed was to get himself tied in knots over a woman now, when he was finally starting to come out of his long, dark tunnel.

But he didn't want her to leave. Not only because he'd miss her, but also because with her in the house, it had almost begun to seem *normal*. He'd had no more headaches, noticed no more strange smells. There'd been a few odd moments— her getting locked in the attic, for instance. But for the most part things were going well for the first time in months. All because of her.

He'd grown accustomed to having her here. And he already dreaded the moment when she'd leave.

As Simon finished the dishes, something made him peer harder out the window over the sink. A movement. Something metallic had caught and reflected the light on the back porch. Leaning close and peering out into the darkness, he tried to determine what it had been.

It took a moment but he finally figured it out. "What the hell?" he muttered when he realized the glint he'd seen had been the reflection off the metal struts on an old buggy that Uncle Roger kept on display on the back lawn. The thing had been there for years and tourists who stayed at the hotel often liked to get their picture taken in it. His uncle even said he would occasionally lend it out to the town below when they wanted to hitch a horse to it for a parade or some local carnival.

Practically a fixture at the hotel, there was absolutely no reason to be startled by the buggy…except he *had* been. It took a split second to realize why.

It was moving.

Despite blocks at the base of the four wheels that prevented it from going anywhere, the thing was in motion. If it rolled a few more feet, it would hit the gentle slope in the backyard and cruise right down to the edge of it.

The lawn ended at the cliffs.

A sudden, horrific thought leapt into his mind and Simon's heart thudded in his chest. Dropping the plate he'd been drying, he barely heard it shatter on the floor. He ran for the back door, bursting outside.

The evening was cold and damp. The entire month had been soggy and the ground was mucky and slick. He skidded and slipped as he ran down the steps onto the wet lawn, but he didn't slow down.

"Lottie!" he yelled, as he headed for the buggy, without looking around for her. There wasn't time.

She didn't respond. For all he knew, she was safely around the front of the house, praying to the automotive gods to get her car running so she could get out of here. Away from a moody bastard like him.

But he couldn't be certain of that.

When he reached the carriage, he grabbed a hitching bar across the back, trying to stop it with sheer brute force. His feet could find no stable ground, however, and the thing pulled him to his knees, dragging him behind it as it hit the slope.

"Simon?" He heard the voice from somewhere ahead of him. Ahead of the wagon. Near the cliffs.

"Shit," he muttered, letting go of the buggy, knowing it was pointless. He was on his feet, sprinting around it as the old conveyance picked up speed. With his heart pounding in his chest, he yelled with every step. "Lottie, get out of the way. Get the hell away from the cliffs!"

He finally saw her, standing near a large, man-size boulder that Uncle Roger used to tell guests was the do-not-cross line for the back lawn. Just beyond it, the yard fell away in a jagged panorama of rock and clay.

"What's the matter with you?" She obviously didn't see the dark wagon rolling in her direction.

He didn't stop to explain. Instead, he merely charged her, sweeping her to the side and tackling her to the ground right behind the boulder, knowing it was less than five feet from the edge. But it was enormous and there was no way the carriage would have any impact on it, even if it hit the rock head on.

He hoped.

Fortunately, the theory wasn't put to the test. Because about five seconds after he and Lottie had hit the ground—rolling over on the wet grass, both of them scraping themselves on the rocks and old dead tree limbs—the antique buggy went rolling past. Moving fast, having picked up speed as it rolled downhill, it missed the boulder by mere inches.

Shaking, rattling, it reached the edge of the lawn and barreled straight on, exactly where Lottie had been standing.

And went right over the cliff.

"ARE YOU SURE you're all right?" Simon asked as he and Lottie sat in front of the fireplace in his office a short time later. She was curled up under a blanket on the sofa, shivering, though he knew she wasn't cold.

She was terrified. "It would have killed me."

"You're fine," he murmured.

"That thing would have nailed me and taken me over with it. I would have seen it a moment too late and been hit dead-on."

Knowing he needed to calm her down, before her admittedly vivid imagination got too out of hand, he sat on the ottoman across from her, dropping his elbows onto his knees and leaning close. "You would have heard it in plenty of time, Lottie. The thing rattled like a freight train."

She just shook her head. "I wouldn't have, I was too busy, cursing you under my breath just like my great-aunt Carmela does whenever she's mad at someone. I wouldn't have heard a thing."

Nice to have a little forewarning about what she did when she was mad at someone. But Simon didn't waste time thinking about that now. He only wanted to calm her down, to reassure her that she was fine. Safe.

That he wouldn't let anything happen to her.

God, he would *never* let anything happen to her. He was still utterly terrified at just how close a call it had been.

"Where the hell did that thing come from, anyway?" Though her voice shook, a bit of toughness appeared in her expression.

"It's been just a backyard decoration for years. It's usually got blocks of wood stopping it from going anywhere. I have no idea how it could have started rolling."

She looked him in the eye for a long moment, and in her dark eyes, he saw a number of questions. Concerns. Worries.

One thing he did not see, however, was fear. Not of him, anyway.

He couldn't even begin to thank her for that trust. Nor could he begin to evaluate why he was so damned grateful for it when he'd been telling himself for months that he didn't care what anyone thought of him. "I swear to you," he murmured, "I would never do anything to put you at risk."

She waved her hand, grunting. "Of course you wouldn't. You can't possibly think I suspect you just tried to bump me off."

He didn't answer at first. No, he hadn't thought that…but it occurred to him that if his cleaning lady had been the one on the cliffs, that's exactly what she'd have thought. What most people would have thought.

But Lottie trusted him. End of story. God, had he ever been that trusting? That quick to evaluate someone and put all your faith in them, to never doubt?

"Damn, Simon, what is going *on* with you?" she asked, appearing shocked and dismayed by his continued silence. "You actually think I'd suspect you? What on earth happened to you to give you this awful outlook on yourself and on other people?"

He knew she wanted answers. He couldn't, however, give them to her. Instead, gently pulling her fingers open so he could look at her palm, he said, "Your hands are pretty cut up. You should go get these clean."

Sighing audibly, she shook her head, silently expressing her disappointment. Then she flipped his hand over, too. "Ditto." Dropping the blanket, she rose and rubbed her hands up and down her arms as if to ward off a chill. "I wish there was a bathtub in here. I'd love to soak in a bunch of bubbles in front of that fire rather than in that icebox on the third floor."

She'd mentioned the cold room a couple of times, but he hadn't had a chance to go up and check out the individual heating unit. He'd been too selfish, too self-absorbed to think about her comfort.

What a bastard.

"Look, there's another bedroom down here in the private

apartment. If you're not uncomfortable having a little less privacy, you're welcome to use it. I think it would be more comfortable than being up on the third floor."

Her eyes widened and she slowly nodded. "Thank you. That would be wonderful."

Wonderful? No. It would be sheer torture having her so close—close enough he'd probably be able to hear her breathing at night as she slept on the other side of a thin wall in the apartment. But he'd get over it.

"In the meantime, use my bathroom. My uncle had the private rooms renovated a couple of years ago and there's a double-sided gas fireplace, one side right at the foot of the tub." Even as he made the offer, he wondered how he was going to handle waiting around for the next hour, visualizing her standing in his bedroom, stepping out of her clothes. Walking naked to the bath and bending over to turn on the spigot. Reaching down to test the water. Settling in to the hot tub until only a layer of bubbles coated her wet body.

Only the smile on her face made him stop his instant impulse to take back his offer.

"That would be perfect," she said with a heartfelt sigh. Leaning down, she pressed her mouth to his temple, kissing him right beside the thin scar, his constant reminder, his penance. "Thank you. For everything. Whether you want to believe it or not, you saved my life."

Unable to resist, he caught the mass of rich, mahogany hair in his hand, twining his fingers in it and tugging her closer. He needed to feel her mouth, to breathe her in, if only to drive away the remaining coldness her close call had caused deep inside him.

She didn't hesitate, meeting his mouth with hers, parting her lips in a sweet sigh of surrender. Neither of them deepened the kiss or made it anything other than what it was…a gentle thank-you, a soft you're-welcome. An acknowledgment that something was happening between them.

And, on Simon's part, an admission that perhaps something more was going to happen.

Then she left the room, going upstairs to get her things. Simon walked out the other door of the office, which led to his bedroom. His bed was unmade, the covers tangled and strewn around—evidence of his restless nights, he supposed. He had a moment's impulse to straighten up, the intimacy of an unmade bed almost seeming unbearable in light of his feelings for the woman about to walk into his room.

But there wasn't time. If she walked in here and saw him making the bed, what else could she think except that he wanted her to help him *unmake* it?

Instead, he went into the bathroom, used the remote to fire up the gas fireplace, then turned on the hot water, letting it flow into the tub. Using a dimmer switch on the wall, he brought the lights down, wanting Lottie to have exactly the warm, relaxing bath she so needed after her harrowing experience.

Which meant he needed to get out of here. Because it wouldn't be relaxing if he was still here, hovering, picturing her clothes hitting the floor as she stepped into the tub.

But he hadn't even turned around when he realized he was no longer alone. He hadn't realized Lottie had come into the room behind him until he saw her hand reach around to dump a milky liquid into the water gushing from the tap. Frothy bubbles immediately appeared, and a strong scent of vanilla wafted up.

"You travel prepared," he murmured, not turning around, having to push the words out of his tight throat.

"I've just been waiting for the chance to get my hands on your...bathtub."

Lottie's voice was low, throaty, and Simon had to close his eyes and draw in a deep breath for strength. He needed to get out of here. Now. Before he did something really stupid.

"Help yourself to whatever you need," he said, walking away from her toward the linen closet. "Towels are in here." Grabbing one, he turned around, prepared to hand it to her.

But nothing, God in heaven, nothing could have prepared him for what he'd find.

Lottie stood there beside the tub, her hair loosely piled on her head with a few long curls trailing across her cheeks to brush her shoulders.

Her bare shoulders.

She was completely naked, her beautiful, curvy body perfectly illuminated by the flicker of light from the fireplace. Enveloped by steam, she was like some mythical being stepping out of the mist. Perfectly shaped, from her long, graceful neck, her delicate throat, to her smooth shoulders. Those unbelievable breasts topped with hard, rosy nipples. Her waist was slim, her hips generous. A tiny tuft of curls appeared between her creamy thighs, and the perfection continued straight down to her toes.

She was like the epitome of woman brought to life by an artist working with the most valuable, ethereal clay.

"I think I need someone to scrub my back," she murmured, her tone so sultry, her meaning so clear, it made his blood turn into lava in his veins.

She lifted her hand, reaching for him. "Will you?"

"Lottie…"

"You are not alone anymore. And I don't want to be alone anymore, either. Not when we can do so much for each other."

Lottie bent down and turned off the faucet, revealing more of that perfect body. The slimness of her waist, the generous curve of her hip. Rising, she smiled and drew in a deep breath. "I think my bath's ready."

He couldn't force a word past his lips.

Delicately stepping over the side of the large clawfoot tub, she hissed a little at the heat of the water. Slowly lowering herself, her hiss turned into a purr of delight.

Simon almost echoed it as he watched her begin to disappear beneath the bubbly surface, inch by inch. She stared at him, confidently, obviously seeing the sweat breaking out on his forehead as it became more and more impossible to hide his hunger.

"Umm, warm," she said as she stretched lethargically. She sunk lower, beneath the bubbles, her bent knees rising above them. Parted.

The tops of her round breasts remained just above the water as well, a few bubbles clinging to the taut nipples, begging to be kissed off.

She dropped a hand on her chest, sliding it down until it disappeared beneath the foamy white layer concealing most of her glorious form from his gaze.

"Yes, I'll definitely need someone to help me with my back," she whispered, licking her lips and never taking her eyes off him. "So tell me, Simon. Will you stay?" Lifting her hand, she trickled some soapy water on her upraised knee, lifting that endless length of toned leg high and resting her foot on the side of the tub.

"Please, Simon. Stay."

9

Lottie

I'VE BEEN ACCUSED of being many things in my life—bossy, hardheaded, loyal, mouthy and determined among them. But no one has ever accused me of being subtle.

This moment would surely put the exclamation point on that declaration.

As I sat in the bubbling, hot water, hiding my hint of nervousness behind sheer bravado born of outright hunger, I couldn't help wondering what was going through Simon's mind. Was he shocked? Surprised?

Please, not disgusted.

I didn't accept his offer of the use of his bathroom intending to strip naked and practically beg the man to make love to me. In fact, the thought hadn't even occurred to me until I was returning from my room, my bathrobe and toiletries in hand.

Seeing him standing there, testing the water, his thick, nearly black hair glimmering in the low light, made the vague idea an imperative compulsion. I'd stripped off my clothes, as if in a daze. Focusing only on how much—how very much—I wanted him, I'd put aside all question and doubt, embarrassment and modesty.

And now I waited, exposed and vulnerable, wearing my

desire on my face and making no effort to hide anything I was feeling.

Simon, to my great relief, was not very successful at hiding what he was feeling, either. Still standing a few feet away, at the foot of the tub, he looked down at me, his whole body clenched tight. From his rock-hard jaw to his stiff shoulders, his fisted hands and his rigid posture, he was the picture of a man striving for control.

"Stop fighting it," I urged, letting my fingertips trace a slow, lethargic trail up my thigh. I wanted to be touched by *him*, not myself, but I wasn't above using that sultry imagery to get him to acknowledge he wanted me, too. "Simon, please, stop pretending you don't feel the same thing I'm feeling."

"I'm not pretending it," he admitted, his tone thick. He cleared his throat. "I just don't know that we should act on this."

Sliding to the end of the tub, I shifted until I was on my knees, my arms across the edge. He was just a few inches away and as I rose higher, my hair brushed his hand. My mouth was close enough for him to feel my breaths falling warm on his stomach. My wet breasts glistened and shone.

"Yes, Simon," I murmured, reaching up to slowly unbutton his shirt, revealing his muscular chest inch by inch. "We should act on this."

He didn't resist. For a long moment, he remained silent, staring down at me as I finished unbuttoning and tugged the shirt free of his waistband. Then I reached for his belt.

"Lottie…"

"Shh. I *have* to act on this."

Casting a quick glance up, I saw his head was back, his eyes closed. The muscles of his chest flexed and rippled beneath the unfastened shirt and his taut stomach just cried out to be touched. Kissed. So I leaned forward, pressed my mouth there and licked my way down to the top of his trousers. I continued to taste him—savoring the salty, masculine flavor of his body—as I undid the belt and slowly tugged it free, loop by loop.

Tossing it to the floor, I unfastened his pants, nibbling my way lower to sample more skin as it was revealed. I scraped my teeth on a wiry, thin trail of hair that disappeared into the elastic waistband of his tight boxer briefs. Inhaling deeply, I moved my mouth lower, so I could exhale my hot breath right on that huge, rigid erection straining against the white cotton.

He still didn't speak. But his hands moved to my hair.

And I knew I'd won.

Almost shaking with my triumph—and my excitement—I tilted my head back to look up at him, seeing the blazing heat in his eyes as he stared down at me. "You are so incredibly beautiful." Moving one hand to my face so he could scrape the rough pad of his thumb across my lower lip, he added, "And I want you so much."

"So take me," I replied, sinking my teeth lightly into his thumb. "Have me."

He shrugged his shirt off, tossing it away and I almost slipped in the tub, my breath taken from me at just how perfectly made he was. His broad shoulders were even more emphasized by the leanness of his hips and waist, and there wasn't an ounce of excess anywhere on his hot, hard body.

Glancing at his bulging briefs, I quickly amended the thought. I suspected he definitely had something extra to offer in that area. Judging by the way the white cotton gapped away at the top, barely able to cover the man, I suspected it was a *lot* extra. And I just couldn't wait any longer to find out.

Starting to push his khakis down, I paused when he reached into his pocket. Seeing him grab a condom from it, I smiled. "I guess I wasn't the only one thinking this way."

He shook his head. "No. You weren't."

He said nothing else, and I went back to what I was doing. Getting the glorious man out of his pants.

When they were gone, I trailed my fingertips across his erection, almost shivering in anticipation. Simon continued running his fingers through my hair, tugging it until it tumbled down over my back and my breasts.

Scraping my nails lightly on his stomach, I watched his skin quiver in reaction, then I pulled the briefs down and off.

"Oh," I whimpered, my whole body shaking with heat and desire. The moisture between my legs was a hundred times hotter than the bathwater as I stared at the big, powerful erection just inches from my face.

I had to taste him. Oral sex wasn't something I'd had a lot of experience with—nor had I particularly cared for it, either—but I suddenly had this compulsion to thoroughly savor the man. Scraping the tip of my tongue across the base of his shaft, I moaned at his hot taste and musky scent. I thought I heard him groaning above me, but I couldn't focus on that. I could only think about exploring him, licking a path from the very base all the way up to the top of his cock.

Once there, however, I wanted nothing more than to suck deep. Pausing only to lick away a few drops of his body's glistening moisture, I opened my mouth on him. Knowing by the long shudders ratcheting through his body that he was definitely enjoying it, I sucked the entire silky smooth, bulbous tip between my lips and lathed him with my tongue.

"Holy…Lottie…"

I didn't stop what I was doing, lowering my mouth, twisting my head so I could take him deeper. I kept one hand on his lean hip, and slid the other along his thigh, then between his legs to cup his most vulnerable spot. He groaned again as I toyed with him, stroking and caressing while I continued to draw him deep into my mouth and then ever so slowly pull away.

When the enamel of the tub grew hard on my knees, I shifted a little. Simon used the moment to take control. Stepping away, he stripped off the rest of his clothes.

"You are absolutely perfect," I whispered hoarsely, meaning it when I saw his entire body for the first time. His strong legs were as muscular and toned as the rest of him. And his sex jutted out in bold male determination.

"Lie back," he ordered, staring at me from above.

I did. "Are you going to join me?" I asked as I slid back in the water, extending my legs out in front of me.

"Not yet."

Dropping a hand into the water, he gently pushed me until I was reclining against the curved end of the tub. Pulling a small, decorative bench out from under the window, he moved it behind the tub and sat down behind me. If I put my head back, it would be resting right on his erection.

I put my head back.

Simon didn't protest, but merely leaned over to place both hands on my shoulders, slowly kneading and massaging my body.

I almost purred at the strength of his touch as all my tension and worries disappeared. Sighing at the pleasure of it, I turned my head and lazily kissed the inside of his strong thigh.

My body was slick with the bubbles and his hands skimmed easily over my skin. But they didn't go quite where I wanted them. "Please," I whispered, knowing he knew what I wanted.

He did. He flattened his palms on my shoulders, then slowly moved farther down until they scraped over the tops of my breasts, which protruded from the top of the water. Taking them in his hands, he whispered something, low and guttural. Something that sounded like, "Perfect."

Yes. That described this moment. Perfect. With his hands on me, his muscular thigh brushing my cheek, the steam rising from the tub and the smell of vanilla blending with the hot scent of this man's skin, I was completely inundated by sensual pleasure.

He seemed to instantly know when I needed more. Because just at the moment I was ready to scream for him to increase the pressure—to stop the teasing, feather-light brushes of his fingertips against my nipples—he gave me what I hadn't even had to ask for. Catching the sensitive tips of my breasts between his fingers, he rolled them, toying with them until spasms of pleasure washed from there straight down my body. Beneath the water, my toes curled. My thighs quivered. My hips bucked.

An instant later, he bent farther and covered one breast with his mouth, sucking hard, sucking deep.

"Oh, yes," I groaned, wrapping the fingers of one hand in his hair. Raising my other arm, I draped it behind me, so it rested on Simon's strong shoulder. I dug into his muscular skin, squeezing and scratching as he pleasured me.

The position apparently wasn't close enough for either of us. Without a word, Simon gently slid away, careful of my head and hair. Rising from the bench, he pushed it aside. Then he dropped to his knees at the side of the tub. "You're sure about this, Lottie?" he asked, staring intently into my eyes.

I nodded, lifting a hand to his face, touching his lips, his nose and the thin scar by his eye. "I am absolutely sure."

That seemed to get rid of any last inhibitions. With a half smile on his lips, he lowered his mouth to mine and kissed me. It was sweet at first. And soft. Then his lips parted and our tongues met in a slow but hungry dance of give and take, demand and surrender.

With my heart pounding wildly and my body almost quivering in anticipation, I shifted and turned so I could wrap my arms around his neck. Simon responded by sliding one hand down my body, stroking the bottom of my breast, then cupping the indentation of my waist, the top of my hip. Finally he reached my thighs and slid between them, his fingers brushing lightly against my swollen, aching lips.

Gasping against his mouth, I arched toward his hand, wanting more. He complied, finding my clit and caressing it until I was almost crying at how good it felt. Keeping his thumb there to continue that pleasure, he moved his fingers down, exploring, playing. When he finally slid one finger and then another inside my tight body, I squeezed and clenched and came right there in the tub.

Not even able to keep kissing him, I let my body sag back while it shook with slow bolts of hot pleasure that seemed to stretch and extend, on and on, more intense than any orgasm I'd ever experienced.

"Oh, my God," I whispered when I was finally capable of speech.

Simon said nothing. Instead, he rose to his feet, then tugged me up. When I was standing, he bent and lifted me, one arm bracing my knees, the other behind my shoulders, carrying me over the side of the tub as if I were some petite fragile flower instead of a tall, buxom woman.

I liked it. Oh, yeah, I so liked it.

"I have to be in you," he said as he stepped over to the bench he'd vacated minutes before. "Let me in."

Sitting on the bench, he turned me around—did I mention the man's strength?—until I was facing him, sitting astride his thighs.

When I glanced down and saw that he'd already taken care of the birth control issue, I wanted to burst into grateful song. Instead I simply writhed on top of him, sliding up and down, wetting his shaft with my body's juices.

He resisted for a moment—long enough to drop his mouth to my breast and suck my nipple back into a throbbing tip of sensation. Then, with a low, helpless groan, he gripped my hips tightly and slowly began to ease into me.

I was dripping wet and more aroused than I'd ever been. But it had been a long time and he was of more than generous proportions, so I tensed a little. I savored the invasion—loved it—but I was also the tiniest bit tentative.

He seemed to understand. Lifting a hand to cup my face, he brought me close for a sweet, drugging kiss that made so many promises, none of which I'd asked for, or even expected. I knew he would never hurt me. Knew he'd stop if I asked him to. Knew I could set the pace, take control. Whatever I wanted.

Which made me only want him more. So wrapping my arms around his neck, I pushed against him, taking him all in one deep plunge that filled me to my core. It was like exploding and imploding at the same time, being filled and fulfilled. For the first time in my life I felt as if I was truly part of another person, joined in the most elemental way possible. I didn't mean just the physical.

With every slow, steady thrust he made, he was imprinting himself on me somewhere deep inside. Making a home, carving out a permanent position in my body, in my life and, I knew now, in my heart.

"Lottie?" he whispered as he kissed my throat and continued those sweet, mind-blowing thrusts that went from short and shallow to slow and deep, then back again. "I don't regret this."

I knew what he meant, and I knew why he'd said it. "Neither do I," I replied.

Wrapping my legs tightly around his waist, I kissed his cheek, his temple, his scar, letting him take us both higher and higher. And this time when I came in a shriek of pure bliss, he was right there with me.

I WASN'T COLD ANYMORE.

Sleeping in Simon's bed, wrapped in his arms, making love long into the night and again first thing in the morning, well, I didn't think I'd ever be cold again. In fact, it was amazing I hadn't completely gone up in flames.

Remember when I said I had only ever experienced meat-and-potatoes sex? Well, holy crap, last night had put me in the gourmet connoisseur category. I honestly didn't know the human body was capable of experiencing so much pleasure in that short a time frame. Nonstop, watch-out-my-head's-gonna-blow-off pleasure.

I had more orgasms in one night than I'd had in my whole life.

Even that wasn't the best part, though. The best part was that Simon hadn't pulled away this morning. He had not rolled over in the light of day, slipped out of bed, withdrawn into himself and ignored me. No, he hadn't actually been Mr. Cuddles, either. Still, he'd kissed me sweetly, asked if I was okay, then he'd offered to make *me* breakfast!

Shortly afterward, he'd gone back to work, with his office door closed as usual. I'd gone up into the attic again, as was becoming my habit, but at least three times, he'd come to the third floor and called up to check on me.

The man had a protective streak. The weird accident with the carriage last night seemed to have really brought it out and I honestly think he was afraid something bad was going to happen to me.

I still hadn't entirely gotten over that near miss, but I wasn't dwelling on it. And neither was he… He just wasn't going to let too much time go by without making sure I was okay.

I kind of liked being so cherished. Protected. Not in a bossy way, like my brothers had tried to do all my life. But in a good way, by a handsome, incredibly sexy man who had, truly, saved my life. Wow, that was a sobering thought.

I really could have died, couldn't I?

I didn't let myself think about it. What mattered wasn't what might have happened, it was what *had* happened.

As much as I wished I could just drag a few boxes of stuff down three flights of stairs and work with Simon in his office, I knew it wouldn't work. He might agree—just to be nice to the woman he'd had sex with in just about every position known to man the previous night. I knew, however, he wouldn't like the interruption.

Besides, I'd reached the point where I needed more than what I was finding in the attic. I really needed to go into town, to check out the land records office. The paperwork I'd found made me very curious about the deal between Josef Zangara and Robert Stubbs, and I wanted to find the actual record of it.

Unfortunately, however, I realized I had a problem. I'd used the broken-down-car excuse to stay here. Simon hadn't asked why the car service hadn't ever arrived, but I could practically guarantee he'd notice if my cheerful little PT Cruiser suddenly started right up.

But I had no other choice. So sending up a mental promise to go to confession when I got back to Chicago, I went to his office and knocked on the door. Sticking my head in, I asked, "Hey, I need to run down to town, do you need anything?"

At first I thought I was going to get away with it, that he wouldn't even remember the car. He appeared deep in thought, focused on his computer, not even lifting his eyes when I entered the room. "No." Then, as if suddenly remembering he had not a leg to stand on when it came to being standoffish with me, he looked up and gave me a sheepish look. "No, *thank* you."

Blowing him a kiss, I immediately slid toward the door, hoping to make a clean getaway, then Simon abruptly stood. "How are you going down to town when you car's not running?"

Busted. Man. It was one thing to plan to tell another little fib when I wasn't face-to-face with my intense, sometimes dangerous-looking lover. It was another to actually do it.

I guess it had been easier faking the breakdown because I'd never actually told Simon a lie. I'd told him the car wouldn't start. True, it wouldn't. Because I'd disabled it.

I hadn't *exactly* lied.

And I wasn't going to now. "It's running again. I just started it up."

His eyes practically glittered as he came out from behind the desk and approached me, walking slowly, sinuously.

Oh, the man could move.

"How surprising."

With a weak laugh, I said, "Yeah. I guess."

"Maybe the heavy rain did something to the engine the night you arrived," he murmured, coming closer still until his arm brushed mine.

"Umm…I don't know."

A tiny, nearly imperceptible smile tilted the corners of that incredible mouth and he never broke the stare, silently challenging me to keep up the facade. It was as if he *knew*.

But that was impossible. He would have tossed me out on my butt the other morning if he'd had any idea there was nothing wrong with my car. And if he'd found out later, he'd have been so mad, he'd *really* have tossed me out on my butt.

"Or maybe," he said, his hand slowly reaching for mine, in which I clutched the car keys, "you simply pushed this nice little button and got it running again."

My jaw dropping, I just stared as he tugged the keys out of my hand, holding the remote locking device up in front of my face.

"I saw the sticker on your window about the anti-theft system. And the brand name." Shaking his head and tsking under his breath, he added, "You're not the only one who knows how to do a little research, Lottie. A quick Internet search this morning told me all about the kill switch."

He…my God, he was on the verge of laughing. Which both relieved me and made me want to punch him for keeping me in suspense. "And you didn't say anything at first? You just let me dig myself in deeper. Jerk."

Dropping his arms across my shoulders, he tugged me close. "You're a sneaky woman, Lottie Santori. And if I'd figured it out sooner, I would have tossed you out on your gorgeous little ass."

Little? That was a stretch. But it was nice to think he thought so. Especially because, at one point last night, I'd begged him to take me from behind, so he'd had a pretty good view of that ass.

"I was trying to stall for time. To get you to see I wouldn't be any trouble, so you'd let me stay."

Throwing his head back, he laughed, long and deep, a laugh I'd never heard coming out of this man. One I liked very much.

"You, no trouble? Oh, that's a good one." Shaking his head and dropping his hands to cup my waist, he dragged me even closer, until our bodies met in all the good places. "Angel, you are trouble with a capital *T*. I imagine you're going to fit in quite well with that crazy little town at the bottom of my mountain."

Then he kissed me deep and wet and I forgot that I'd just been insulted. After he pulled away and told me to drive carefully, I went out to my car. Blushing a little as I remembered the man had caught me in a big, fat, desperate lie, I marveled again over how surprising he could be. Laughing when I'd have expected him to be angry. Making passionate love to me when he'd seemed to want nothing to do with me.

I wondered, deep down, if he might be as mysterious emotionally as he was in so many other ways. If, perhaps, my fears that the man would never open up and allow himself to genuinely feel anything for anyone could perhaps be wrong.

I hoped so. Because I was already feeling something for him. Something very strong, very deep and very unique.

I was falling in love with Simon Lebeaux. I had no doubt about it.

That cheerful thought and the happy mental pictures that went along with it occupied my mind during the drive down to town. Once I reached its outskirts, though, I began paying attention to my surroundings.

At the edge of Trouble, two enormous, paint-chipped old Victorian homes that had probably once been magnificent hovered like a pair of dark birds of prey. As I drove past them, I saw two elderly women sitting on rockers on the porch of one. They both eyed me suspiciously, turning their heads to stare at me well after my car had continued by.

"Small-town people," I muttered, already comparing the place to Chicago. I was a big-city girl, born and raised. Little towns like this made me itchy.

Trouble, especially, was a strange one. The narrow village seemed to be comprised of one main thoroughfare and a few offshooting streets. Oddly, some of the buildings downtown were quaint and in beautiful condition. An old-fashioned movie palace was obviously undergoing renovation. Construction trucks lined the curb out front and bricklayers were busy rebuilding a corner wall. I assumed there were even more of them inside bringing the tired-looking structure back to life.

There were other surprises too, the biggest being the juxtaposition of the beautiful, newly renovated buildings with some of the decrepit, sorry old ones. I couldn't even see into the dirty windows of a diner right on the main street. The grocery store sign was missing a few letters. Weirdest of all, the car dealership apparently doubled as a taxidermy shop. Because perched on top of every banged-up, dingy, dented Ford and Chevy parked in the knee-high grass was an odd menagerie of stuffed squirrels, raccoons and other small mammals.

"Freaky," I muttered.

The town did apparently like Halloween. Orange-and-black banners hung entirely across the street, from lamppost to lamppost, in a one block section of downtown. Being locked away up at Seaton House, I'd nearly forgotten the holiday was just a few days off.

Scarecrows sat on bales of hay outside a few stores. Bats and witches flew in black silhouettes across several plateglass windows. And just about every business establishment had a sign for a Halloween costume dance, being hosted by a Mr. Mortimer Potts, scheduled for this Saturday.

Parking in a public lot next to a small playground with shiny new slides and swings, I got out to walk around. The rain of the past several days had finally eased and sunshine washed the streets in light and the town's residents in smiles. Several nodded pleasantly and murmured hello as I passed.

"It's not so bad," I whispered, regretting my snarky attitude about the place. "Simon might actually like it."

Okay, that was probably a stretch.

Finding the courthouse, I went inside and was shown to the records office by a helpful receptionist. "Mr. Billows," the woman called as we approached an open door, with a cracked sign marked Records.

An ancient man's head popped out of the doorway. "Eh?"

"This young lady would like to see some of the land transfer records." Smiling pleasantly, the woman left me alone with the hundred-year-old city worker, whose gummy smile told me he was happy to have the company.

"Don't get many visitors," he said as he ushered me in. I thought for a moment I felt something brush my bottom, but figured I must have been mistaken. If I *had* just been goosed by a centenarian, I really didn't want to know about it anyway.

The old man looked as dusty as the piles of books stacked on every free surface in the place, but he was able to quickly retrieve the information I'd been after.

"You find what you're looking for?" he asked after I'd flipped through the 1938 journal for several minutes. He hadn't even protested when I pulled out my small digital camera and took pictures.

"Mmm-hmm," I murmured, nodding. Then, speaking mostly to myself, I said, "So Stubbs was able to buy Zangara out for thirty thousand dollars."

The old man appeared startled when he realized which record in the leather-bound journal I'd focused on. "Zangara. You know about Zangara?"

I nodded. "I'm doing some research on him—and on Seaton House—for my professor. He's writing a book on the case."

The old man's eyes bugged out, reflected a couple of times over by his thick glasses. "You're looking into the goings-on at Seaton House?"

"Well, the goings-on from the 1930s."

The man didn't look mollified. "Have you been up there, then?"

"I'm staying at the house," I admitted, lifting my chin pointedly. "The owner has been a tremendous help."

The old man sputtered, his jaw shaking as much as his palsied hands. Then, without a word, he grabbed the ledger book away from me and slammed it closed. "Out you go."

Stunned, I just stared.

"Out, out. It's my lunchtime."

I glanced at my watch. "It's three p.m."

"It's my dinnertime, then. Goodbye."

I couldn't voice a word of protest as the old-as-dirt guy put his hands on my back and literally shoved me out of the room. The door slammed shut behind me, punctuating the man's distress.

"Crazy," I whispered as I left the building. Did everyone in town have this horrible opinion about Simon? How could they when none of them appeared to even know him?

I was still muttering about it when I walked over to the pharmacy, deciding to see if they had any good vitamin supplements. Simon could use them.

"It's her, the one who's staying up there with *him*," I heard someone whisper. But the whisper was so loud, I suspected I was meant to overhear it.

Turning to follow the sound, I saw the stoop-shouldered cleaning woman who'd been so nasty the other morning. "Well, hello to you, too," I said, smiling pleasantly at her and her companion, a middle-aged woman wearing a purple ski cap. Indoors. On a nice autumn day. The cap was lumpy. Obviously covering a head full of curlers.

The pair of them whispered furiously, then the one in the hat trudged over. "It's true then? You're staying up there?"

"I am."

The woman looked around, but her friend merely shrugged and rolled her eyes, as if saying she'd already tried to warn me and I'd been too stubborn to listen. For that's what was about to come out of this one's mouth, I knew it.

"You shouldn't be up there, miss."

"Yes, yes, I've heard that there are a lot of nasty, untrue rumors about Mr. Lebeaux."

The woman shook her head, her expression dour. "Not just rumors, miss, I've seen the papers myself. I have a cousin down in Charleston who sent me clippings about the whole ugly mess."

I wasn't listening. La la la la, not listening.

"He's dangerous. And I wouldn't be able to sleep tonight if I didn't at least try to warn you."

Spare me from people spewing gossip in the guise of doing good.

"You have to know the truth."

Still not listening. Here are the vitamins. Big brand stuff, nothing natural. Too bad.

"Mr. Lebeaux was involved in some real ugliness down in South Carolina. That's how he got that scar on his face."

Okay, *mostly* not listening. I had wondered, so often, about that scar....

"It was right disgraceful. Sad what happened to him, of course, but not as bad as what *he* did."

I stiffened, realizing I didn't want to hear this from a gossipy stranger. Or a hateful cleaning woman who obviously had an ax to grind against her employer. I wanted to hear the truth—whatever it was—from Simon.

But before I could whirl around and dash out of the store, the woman rushed on. "He carries the scar out of shame, that's what I think. It's his scarlet letter. So all the world will know the truth about what he did to his fiancée."

That was enough. I turned and started to walk away. The woman grabbed my arm, though, not letting me leave.

"Please, if you don't believe me, do some looking on the computer over at the library. Because he's a dangerous man." Her fingers digging tight—tight enough to make me wince— she leaned close, so close I could smell cigarettes on her breath.

"Look and see for yourself. He threw a woman he supposedly loved off a tall building, not four months ago."

I froze.

"Make no mistake…Simon Lebeaux is a *murderer*."

10

Simon

SIMON HAD GOTTEN accustomed to Lottie being around, so spending the afternoon without her was surprisingly difficult. Having been alone for so long—by choice—he hadn't anticipated just how empty Seaton House would be without her.

He'd gotten used to her company in a very short time. Even when she was off somewhere in the attic or the basement, knowing she was around gave him a level of pleasure. Without her, the place seemed as quiet as the grave.

It wasn't until after he heard a clanging sound coming from the third floor that he remembered what *else* had disturbed him so much about being alone. In the days that Lottie had been here, there had been a few strange incidents. Her being locked in the attic and the carriage accident were the most obvious ones.

But there were also plausible explanations for both. Doors got stuck, despite what she thought about the knob. And the blocks holding the carriage wheels could have worked themselves loose with all the rain softening up the earth.

Beyond that, though, he hadn't experienced any of the unsettling, disturbing events that had plagued him for so long before her arrival. Which made the noise coming from above him all the more surprising.

Leaving his office, he went up to investigate. He could have predicted what he'd find…absolutely nothing. No unlatched shutter banging against the house. No water heater with rattling pipes. Just a long silent hallway with closed door after closed door, except the one to the room Lottie had been using. That door stood open.

Suddenly missing her, he decided to go in and move her things. As far as he was concerned, Lottie would be sleeping in his bed for the rest of her stay. Moving her in while she was gone seemed the most straightforward way to tell her he wasn't having any second thoughts about the previous night. And that he wanted whatever was happening between them to *keep* happening.

He didn't fool himself that it was anything other than great sex for as long as she was here. He was in no way ready to get seriously involved with someone. Especially not someone like Lottie, who embodied everything he, himself, was not these days. She was light and laughter. He was darkness and regret.

She wanted to heal him, he knew that. He also knew that aside from her physical attraction to him, she had a lot of protective feelings. Probably sympathy, pity. Certainly not the basis for anything more serious.

They had sex in common. That was all. It would be enough.

Going inside, he saw her half-unpacked suitcase. Clothes were strewn across the neatly made bed, and he quickly packed them up. Hoping she wouldn't mind him going through her personal items, he went over to the closed bathroom door, intending to get her toiletries. When he opened it, however, his nose was instantly assaulted by a thick, heavy perfume.

Instinctively flinching and staggering backward, he waved a hand in front of his face, wondering what the hell Lottie had been doing with the strong, heavy stuff. Her body certainly hadn't smelled like that last night or this afternoon when she'd left. Thinking about it, he realized he'd never noticed this particular fragrance on her at all.

And yet it was familiar. Instantly—disturbingly—familiar. Though his mind hadn't identified how he knew it, his body had reacted, tensing, almost recoiling. Not just because of how strong it was, but because of a vague, uneasy sensation associated with the smell itself.

Odd. Very, very odd.

One thing was sure, he needed to get out of here before the sickeningly sweet scent triggered a headache. Just as he headed for the door, he heard Lottie's voice, calling out from below. She'd come back just in time to catch him invading her privacy.

"What the hell," he murmured, leaving the bathroom and picking up her bulging suitcase and overnight case. She could get whatever she needed out of the bathroom later.

Going down the stairs to meet her, he prepared for *some* kind of reaction. She had to recognize her bags in his hands and he didn't know whether she'd throw her arms around his neck and kiss him or get indignant that he'd taken her willingness to sleep with him for granted.

She did neither. Instead, she immediately launched into a bunch of inane chatter.

He knew something was wrong. Her face was pale, pinched. She kept going on about the weather, the drive, the last of the autumn leaves blowing away across the road down the mountain.

Finally, when she made no effort to take off her coat and walk away from the front door, he murmured, "In case you're wondering, I was moving your things to my room."

She said nothing but merely glanced at the bags in his hands. Something was definitely wrong. Dropping her bags, he grabbed her hands, which were icy cold and quivering. "What happened? Lottie, tell me what's going on."

He thought she was going to say she'd been able to make no headway with the narrow-minded town officials. That it had been a wasted trip. So he was in no way prepared for what came out of her mouth.

"Tell me about the woman in Charleston."

HE TOLD HER.

The story about what had happened that night wasn't one he liked talking about. But since Lottie had heard some version of it—probably a highly untrue one—he knew he had no choice.

Simon would not have Lottie afraid of him for anything. And while she swore she wasn't, that her feelings hadn't changed, she also insisted that he tell her the truth.

Yesterday, he might not have. But after last night, he could no longer hide behind their casual relationship. It had become anything but casual in his bedroom.

The woman deserved to know the violent truth about the man she was sleeping with.

"You must realize, I assume, that I have to travel a lot for my work," he said as the two of them sat in his office. He'd led her here immediately after she'd asked for the story, figuring that though it was only five o'clock, they could probably both use a drink.

At least he could.

She had obviously felt the same and the two of them were sipping small, neat whiskeys as they faced one another on the couch.

"Of course," she murmured. "You have to spend time in a place to write about it well."

He nodded. "I like that part of my job, and my southern

cities series has really taken off. I started with New Orleans and Baton Rouge, obviously, then moved on to Savannah, Atlanta, then Charleston." Funny, really, since before that night, Charleston was becoming one of his favorites. "Anyway, I booked a room in one of the nicest downtown hotels and stayed there for two weeks, getting all the information I could."

Sipping his drink, he leaned back, trying to remember the details of that night, some of which had grown hazy during his recovery. "It was my last night in town and I went down to the hotel bar to have a drink and say goodbye to some of the staff who'd been so helpful." His throat tightened. "There was a woman there. A blonde. Sitting a few seats away."

"A stranger?" Lottie asked, interrupting for the first time. "Not someone you were involved with?"

"No. I'd never seen her before in my life."

She frowned. "Strike one for the rumor mill."

He really didn't want to know about the rumor mill.

"Sorry, please go on."

"I'm sure I don't have to spell it out. I'd been in town a few weeks, and I hadn't been seeing anyone for quite a while… She was very obvious about what she was offering."

Lottie's mouth tightened.

"I'm not exactly thrilled to admit I picked up an easy blonde in a bar, but it happened." Wondering just how much to say, he didn't see the point in holding anything back. "I wasn't the same man then, Lottie. I actually was somewhat social and enjoyed having fun. I wasn't exactly a playboy, but it wasn't my first bar pickup."

Though, it had definitely been his last.

She waved an unconcerned hand. "I'm not a saint, Simon. Please don't feel like you have to justify yourself."

Relieved, he continued to explain, telling her how the

woman had been the one to approach him, asking him to buy her a drink. How deliberate and provocative she'd been— which, of course, made sense given what had happened later. He'd been a mark to her, one she wasn't going to let get away.

"So you took her up to your room."

He nodded.

Her cheeks pinkening a bit, she softly asked, "Did you, umm…"

"No. I hadn't even touched her when she said she wanted to see the view of the city. So we stepped out onto the balcony. Then she claimed she needed to freshen up. She told me to wait right there for her, and went back into the room."

"Oh, no," Lottie said, obviously knowing where this was going.

"Yeah. I heard a door open and close but figured it was just the bathroom one. Before I even knew what was happening, she came back, followed by a young, burly guy with a gun in his hand."

She gasped. "They were rolling you."

"Exactly."

Lottie shook her head slowly, looking visibly distressed. "Simon, why didn't you just give them your money? Why on earth did you fight back?"

The same thing the cops had asked him. And he told her the same thing he'd told them. "I *didn't* fight back. I wasn't about to get shot in the face over a hundred bucks. I handed him my wallet and my watch. When he asked what else I had, I told him where to find the laptop." Smiling slightly, he admitted, "To tell you the truth, for a second there, I was more worried about whether I'd backed up the writing I'd done that day onto my memory stick than I was about losing a few possessions."

She managed a smile. A shaky one.

"I figured that would be the end of it. They'd get out and be long gone, figuring—probably correctly—that a tourist wasn't going to stick around town long enough to see them brought to justice."

"But they didn't leave?"

He shook his head. "No. That was when I realized I might be in a more dangerous situation than I'd thought. The guy ordered me to go to the edge of the balcony and turn around, facing away from him. I refused. Because I saw a look in his eye that I didn't like and realized his accomplice—the woman—had edged around beside me, instead of heading for the door."

Knowing he was reaching the most difficult part, he sipped his drink before continuing. "He lunged, and I knew at that second, he intended for me to go over the side. Make it look like a suicide or something. I guess that's why he didn't shoot at first."

A sniff and a sheen of moisture in Lottie's eyes told him how she was reacting. He put his hand on her thigh, squeezing lightly, and she covered it with her own, gripping him tight.

"Realizing this wasn't just some robbery I was going to walk away from with a frightening memory to share with friends, I fought back. He wanted me over that railing and I wasn't going. I was holding my own until the woman got involved. I didn't even see the knife in her hand—didn't realize she'd slashed at me until I tasted the blood."

"That bitch," Lottie said, visible tears now spilling out of her eyes. "I can't even imagine."

"I think that's what made it real—made me know for sure I was fighting for my life. So I managed to trip him. As he went down, he hit his head on the edge of a wrought-iron table that I'd sat at every day to have my breakfast."

"Was he…"

"Knocked out."

"But she wasn't."

"No." A muscle in his jaw clenched, causing the scar on the side of his face to throb. Just as it did every time he thought of the woman who'd put it there. "She was enraged, screaming at me for hurting him. I thought at the time he was her boyfriend but when the police checked their ID and found they had the same last name—Harrington—they figured they were married. We later found out they were brother and sister. Anyway, she was hysterical, thinking I'd killed him."

"Oh, there's moral authority, blaming a man for fighting for his own life."

Simon continued as if she hadn't spoken. "He'd dropped his gun when he fell. She picked it up."

"She was the one who shot you," Lottie whispered.

He nodded, rubbing at the scar on his chest, remembering the pain when the bullet had pierced his body. "Not in a really critical spot—she missed my heart by a couple of inches. So I wasn't entirely out of commission. I lunged at her and we fought over the gun." His voice quivering the slightest bit at the memory of how it had felt, in that moment, he proceeded to the ugly end.

"She was strong—I was getting dizzy from losing so much blood—and I knew she was about to shoot me again. So I tackled her, trying to knock the gun out of her hand."

Staring into Lottie's gentle brown eyes, he finally admitted, "And she went over the railing."

SIMON HADN'T KNOWN exactly what to expect from Lottie after she'd heard the whole ugly story. In his mind, the images were so horrible, so bloody and vicious, he couldn't help wondering if she'd retreat from him. What woman would feel okay finding out her lover had been responsible for the brutal death of another woman?

He should have known better. After a long moment in which Lottie absorbed his words, she slowly sipped the rest of her drink, and dried her tears. Shifting closer to him on the couch, she lifted her hand to his face. The soft tip of her index finger traced the scar from his cheekbone up to his forehead, then she twined her fingers in his hair and pulled him close. Just before touching her lips to his, she murmured, "Thank you for telling me."

Her mouth was sweet and welcoming. She held nothing back, being as loving as she'd been before he'd told her the whole truth about himself.

Well, almost the whole truth. He hadn't told her about the strange things he'd experienced here at Seaton House. Bad enough the woman found out he'd killed someone—he didn't want her thinking he was a nutcase, too.

"I want you, Simon," she murmured against his lips. "I want you so much."

Almost groaning in pure relief, he dropped his hands to her waist and tugged her over onto his lap. She curled into him, tilting her head to kiss him again, deeply and passionately.

The warmth of her mouth and the softness of her body pressing against his soon had him forgetting everything else but her. Them. What they'd made each other feel last night. What he wanted to feel again, now.

Slowly lifting her mouth from his and smiling at him, Lottie slid off his lap and walked toward the fireplace. He'd started a fire in it while she was gone, both for added warmth for himself, and because he really liked the way she looked getting warm in front of it.

She wasn't getting warm now, though. She was getting hot.

Not saying a word, she tugged her red sweater free from her jeans, and slowly lifted it. Seeing the lacy red bra beneath, Simon had to suck in a quick, appreciative breath.

Disentangling her hair from the sweater, she finally tossed the thing away, then ran her hands through those thick, long brown curls, shaking her head hard so they tumbled riotously over her upper body.

She didn't seem to mind that he wasn't getting up to join her. He stayed sprawled on the couch, watching with lazy appreciation as she kicked off her shoes, then unsnapped her jeans. Rolling them down slowly—slowly enough that he knew she was intentionally heightening his anticipation—she finally pushed them all the way off. Her tiny red panties matched the bra. They were minuscule, just a red thatch of material barely covering her dark curls, and a few loops of satin cruising over her hips.

"Turn around," he ordered, wanting to see more.

She did. He groaned, low and long, at the gorgeous ass revealed by the thong panties. Hearing him, she looked over her shoulder and said, "Are you going to stay over there watching, or are you going to join me?"

Shifting in his tight jeans, he smiled lazily. "Depends on what you're going to do next."

"What do you *want* me to do next?"

Oh, just about everything. He started with the most basic. "Touch yourself."

She turned to face him, her lips curling up at the corners. Bringing one hand to her throat, she trailed the tips of her fingers down, skirting lightly over the curves of her breasts that pushed high above the seam of the bra, down to her belly.

When her fingers disappeared beneath the elastic hem of her panties and streaked through her curls, he heard her emit a little gasp of pleasure.

Her eyes closed. Licking her lips, she dropped her head back as she continued to delicately stroke herself, her hand hidden by the red fabric but her actions entirely clear just the same.

When she moved, he hoped she was going to kick off the panties and show him exactly how she liked to be touched. But instead she reached around and unfastened her bra, letting it slowly slide down her arms to the floor.

Now Simon groaned. Her breasts had been gorgeous, glistening and wet in the low light last night. Now, in the brightly lit room, he felt certain he'd never seen a more beautifully shaped woman. He already knew how much she liked having her nipples sucked and the way she began to rub her palms over them, then tweak them, told him even more.

"Lose the panties," he said, unable to stand much more of this but wanting to stay here—a few feet away—to appreciate her for a minute longer.

She did, sliding her hands down her sides and hooking her fingers in the waistband. They fell to the floor, leaving her completely unclothed, bare and beautiful. There was no shyness in her, no worries about the number of lights on in the room. Not that she had a *thing* to worry about.

Finally, unable to stand any more of this self-imposed torture, he rose and walked to her. "You are absolutely breathtaking, do you know that?"

She said nothing, not denying it because she had to see by his expression that he meant what he said. When he reached her, she wrapped her arms around his neck and brought him close. Licking his lips, she made herself at home with his mouth. She didn't let the kiss end even as he unbuttoned his shirt and twisted out of his clothes.

Only when he was completely naked did she pull away, glancing down at him. She swayed a little, putting a hand on his shoulder to steady herself. "You know, I'd say it takes one to know one but it sounds so third grade."

Laughing—charmed by her, as always—he dropped to his knees. She tried to come down to meet him on the floor, but he wouldn't allow it, holding her hips to keep her where she was. When he pressed a hot, open-mouthed kiss on her stomach, she obviously figured out why. "Simon…"

"I didn't get to taste you the way I wanted to last night," he murmured, kissing his way down her belly, sampling the indentation of her navel, then following her hip bone with the tip of his tongue.

She jerked a little when his cheek brushed against her soft nest. Jerked right toward his face, which was exactly where he wanted her to be. Still holding her hips, he tugged her closer, toward his waiting mouth, loving her smell and the glisten of arousal on her most secret flesh.

Unable to wait another second, he opened his mouth on her, licking between her folds. She cried out, dropping her hands to his shoulders and digging her nails into him. Wanting to smile at how responsive she was, he instead moved a hand to her thigh, silently ordering her to spread her legs to give him better access. Once she had, he went back to what he'd been doing, covering her clit with his tongue, scraping it gently with his teeth.

"Oh, God, I won't be able to take much of this," she said through hoarse gasping breaths. "My legs will give out."

He couldn't have that. So again, without saying anything, he gently guided her to the leather chair beside the fireplace and pushed her to sit down. "Simon?" she asked, looking a little confused.

That confusion changed to shocked excitement when he lifted both her legs and placed them on the arms of the chair, opening her—exposing her completely.

She tried to close her legs.

"Don't," he ordered, keeping his hands on her knees as he looked his fill at the beautiful folds and glistening curls. "Don't you dare stop me."

"Uh, okay," she said with a whimper, sounding almost desperate.

He knew how to end her desperation. Bending to her, he licked her from back to front in one long, slow slide. She jerked hard, letting out a tiny screech, but Simon was only beginning. He wanted her to be saturated with pleasure, until she came in his mouth. So dipping down again, he slid his tongue into her wet channel, making love to her the way he would with his fingers and his cock in just a few minutes.

Finally, when he saw the way her muscles were clenching and he heard the sweet, helpless groans of pleasure coming from her mouth, he moved in to take her over the top. Sliding a finger inside her, he lathed her tight little clit, staying with her for the ride as she cried out her ultimate satisfaction.

Unable to wait, he didn't even give her a chance to recover. Grabbing a condom out of his jeans pocket, he sheathed himself, then slid up her body and between her still parted thighs.

"Yes, oh, yes," she murmured as she wrapped her arms around his neck and her legs around his hips.

She thrust up and he plunged down and they burst together in a hot, hard frenzy of pleasure. They pounded together for a few deep, hungry thrusts, then slowed down to savor the moment.

Worried about putting too much strain on her, he wrapped his arms around her waist and lifted her, keeping his body tightly joined with hers. Lowering her to the thick carpet in front of the fireplace, he followed her down.

"Have I told you I hadn't had a lot of experience with… this…before?"

He froze for a second, wondering if she was saying she'd been a virgin. It seemed impossible in this day and age, especially with a woman as sexy as Lottie.

She apparently saw his shock because, laughing softly and

cupping his face, she continued. "I mean, I've never done a lot beyond the basics. So I just never knew—I didn't realize—in spite of reading sexy books or watching dirty movies."

One eyebrow shooting up, he gave her a look of surprise. "Dirty movies?"

"Don't get so excited, I don't have them with me."

Sliding deep, he moaned at her heat, the tightness of her wet body. "We don't need them."

She shook her head. "Definitely not. But my point was, I've never known how wonderful it could really be." Kissing him sweetly on the mouth, she murmured, "So thank you."

Thank you. With the tension building as he thrust hard, then tormented her with shallow little strokes, he almost started to laugh. The woman was thanking him during sex.

He'd been thanked afterward. But never during the, uh, heat of the moment.

"You're one of a kind, Lottie Santori," he said as he kissed her face, her neck, her throat.

Then he wasn't capable of saying anything because the familiar heated sensations had begun rocking his body hard. Everything centered low, deep inside him, and Lottie's shallow gasps of delight told him she was coming along with him.

Finally, groaning as every last bit of physical pleasure was wrung from him, he buried his face in her hair, whispered her name, and wondered how on earth he was ever going to let her go.

11

Lottie

I DIDN'T KNOW it was possible to be so happy and yet so worried at the same time.

Physically, of course, I was completely and totally immersed in sensual fulfillment. The way Simon made love to me was like something out of a fantasy, a woman's erotic journal that she never expected to show to anyone much less actually experience in reality.

He gave me everything I'd ever dreamed of having physically. And since he'd opened up to me about what had really happened to him, I felt much closer to him emotionally.

One thing was sure—knowing what he'd been through had only deepened my feelings for the man. I wanted to crush anyone who hurt him, to ease away his scars and his bad memories and make his life go back to the way it had been before such ugliness had intruded into it.

I also wanted the world to see him the way I saw him—as an innocent, brave man forced to do something he personally found repulsive in order to stay alive.

He wasn't a killer. Certainly not a murderer, like those hateful old people from the town below seemed to think.

I wanted them to know the real him so much that I decided I was going to get him to go down to Trouble and socialize with some of its residents. Of course, the moment I'd mentioned the two of us going to the Halloween party at the fire hall tomorrow night, he'd laughed so hard I almost smacked him. He'd never even answered, just continued to chuckle as he walked out of the room, shaking his head. Like I'd made a big fat joke.

"You *are* going to that party, buddy," I whispered Friday afternoon as I sat in the basement, looking through his uncle's papers. I wasn't finished in the attic, but something had been bugging me. I couldn't even say what it was, but I knew there was something I'd missed, or overlooked, about the more recent activities at Seaton House.

Damned if I could figure it out, though. I'd been down here for hours and so far hadn't discovered a thing.

Maybe it was because my head wasn't in the game. I couldn't keep focused on my work because my overactive, vivid imagination—remember it?—kept replaying Simon's awful experience in my brain.

I am not a bloodthirsty person, and I generally don't believe in the concept of an eye for an eye. But despite all my protestations that I'm civilized and liberal-minded, I genuinely could not bring myself to care that the woman who'd attacked him was dead.

Awful, right? Inhuman?

Maybe. But it was true. In those moments on that balcony, it had been her or Simon. And I was not the least bit sorry that Simon was the one who'd walked away. Bloody and injured…but alive.

It could have ended so differently—that's what had me so freaked out about it, a full twenty-four hours after he'd told me the story. My brother Mark is a cop, a detective with the Chicago P.D. So I know a little something about crime and criminals and the way they operate. The whole family, including Mark's new wife, Noelle, whom he'd married two months ago, lived in terror whenever we heard something on the news about the cops taking down a violent criminal, or interrupting a robbery or something.

I'd heard my brother talk enough to know that someone bent only on robbery wasn't going to risk his neck if things went bad. They were usually after a quick infusion of cash for some other illegal purpose—often drugs. And they quite often bluffed about having a weapon during their holdups, since committing a crime while armed was a much more serious offense.

These two people, the sister and brother—Harrington, he'd said—had planned out their crime. They'd chosen Simon as their target, gained entrance into his room and obtained everything of value without any genuine protest from Simon. They could have gotten away without upping the ante of their crime by assaulting him.

But they hadn't. Simon had said the man wanted to kill him and make it look like a suicide or an accident. I believed him.

Why? That was the question that wouldn't leave my mind. Why Simon? Why try and kill him over a hundred dollars and a laptop? It just made no sense. They could have tied him up so he wouldn't be discovered until the next morning and hit the road, never to be seen again.

It was a mystery, a puzzle. I like those, so I couldn't let it go. Though certain Simon wouldn't want me poking around in his troubled past, I felt the need to know more. To do my job—investigating—and see what I could come up with.

Before going back upstairs, I grabbed a box of materials I wanted to go through again. It wasn't that heavy. Besides, hoisting it up a flight of stairs was better than having to come back down here and breathe this musty air again today.

Once upstairs, I took the box into the empty room that had once been the hotel's restaurant. Small two- and four-person tables still dotted the place, with chairs sitting upside down on top of them. Not wanting to disturb Simon in his office, I left the box in the corner, flipped on the lights and carried my laptop over to one of the tables.

Setting up a little work station for myself, I got online and started digging around in the archives of the Charleston papers. It wasn't hard to find the articles about the case. A Google search of Simon's name quickly brought up pages of references on the books and articles he'd done, but in the top ten findings was a recent story about the robbery-gone-bad.

I read the article with interest, looking at the grainy mug shot of the male suspect. Interesting. He'd been charged not just with armed robbery and the attempted murder of Simon, but also with his own sister's murder. I wasn't sure of all the legalities, but it appeared that because she'd been his accomplice in a felony and had died while committing the crime, he was culpable for it under the felony murder laws.

"Ironic," I whispered as I scrolled through the article.

The man was awaiting trial, having been denied bail because investigators had been unable to determine a permanent address for him and he'd been uncooperative about his background.

He and his sister—also pictured…a license photo, apparently—had not been from Charleston. They'd had ID from other states but when police had tried to track down the addresses listed, they'd found empty lots or mailbox companies.

"Why?" I whispered, more confused than I was before. If the pair had been career criminals, surely the police would have been able to find some history of felonies dating before that night. They weren't locals acting on an opportunity. As crazy as it seemed to me, it almost appeared that they'd gone to Charleston and targeted Simon *on purpose*.

Unable to learn much more, I decided to do something I'd

*neve*r thought I'd do. My brother Mark was a protective pain in the butt, but he was still my big brother and there wasn't anything he wouldn't do for me. And, of course, vice versa.

It was time to call in some help.

Going outside and walking around the house until I could find a spot where a few bars appeared on my cell phone, I dialed his number.

"Detective Santori," he answered.

"Private Citizen Santori."

"Lottie! Hey, girl, where are you? Why the hell haven't you called? The folks are worried."

"I've called, they just don't know how to check their damn answering machine."

Mark didn't respond for a second, then he chuckled. "You're probably right."

"How's Noelle?" I asked, wanting to stall a bit more before admitting why I was calling. It wouldn't be good to appear too desperate, I'd learned from experience. Growing up, the more I'd wanted something, the more my brothers had made me work for it.

"She's great," he said, his voice getting soft and mushy the way all my brothers' voices did when they talked about their wives. Or, in Nick's case, when he talked about his latest Marine skirmish or machine gun or something. Ick.

"She's getting an award from a national family organization for the Give a Kid a Christmas program she saved at the shelter last year."

"Wow, that's fantastic." Then, knowing my brother, I added, "Don't do something stupid like get involved in a case and forget to show up!"

"Impossible. The ceremony's in D.C. I'm taking a few days off and we're going on a minivacation. So how's the job going? Everything okay at the murder house?"

Mark had been interested in my trip because of the crime angle, and I quickly gave him a rundown of what had been happening. Skipping, of course, any description whatsoever of my host. Or any details about our wild, sexual affair.

He obviously read between the lines. "Wait a second. You're telling me the hotel is no longer even open and you're staying there with the owner and nobody else? Who the hell is this guy?"

"He's a nice man who could use some help," I replied, determined to get through this without getting into a shouting match with my nosy sibling. "I need you to do something for me, okay? Simon—Mr. Lebeaux—was attacked during a robbery that went bad in Charleston in June."

"Mmm-hmm," Mark murmured. I heard a few clicks and knew he was sitting at his desk, already pulling up any information he could find on my lover. Not because I'd asked him to help, but because he wanted to know more about the stranger I was living with. Alone. In the middle of nowhere.

"He's young," Mark said, his voice disapproving.

"He's also totally hot," I snapped back, "but that's not the point."

"Christ, he killed a woman? Get out of there, Lottie, now."

I gritted my teeth. "Read the whole report. He was attacked, Mark. Brutally. And he has the scars to prove it."

Another few moments of silence. Then came a grunt. "Okay. It was self-defense."

That was probably as good as I was going to get. "The case is strange. Even I can see it." Rubbing the corners of my eyes with my thumb and forefinger, I added, "They went into his room that night to kill him, not to rob him. Yet the media makes it look like the police know nothing about these people, not even where they were really from. How does that happen? Does it make sense to you?"

"People kill people every day."

"Yes, I know," I said impatiently, "but this is different. Please, just check into it, would you? See if you can use your all-cops-are-brothers network to find out more?"

"Why? What does this have to do with the old murder case? Isn't that why you're there?"

"That's why I came." I knew that while Mark was protective, he wasn't a Neanderthal like Tony, the oldest. Nor was he as obnoxious alone as when Nick, his twin, was around.

Plus, my brother had had the sense to marry a terrific, down-to-earth woman he'd known for eight months. And the two of them practically ignited whenever they looked at each other.

He had to know a little something about falling fast for someone.

"I care about him, Mark. I genuinely do. This thing has up-rooted his whole life and he's still trying to get over it."

"I don't like this. Whether it was self-defense or not, the man was still involved in something pretty damn sordid."

Argh. Finally knowing I had no choice, I relied on an old standby for dealing with one of the boys. "If you see your way clear to doing this for me, then maybe I'll see my way clear to keeping quiet to the folks about the fact that a bullet came within a couple of inches of your head at that armored car robbery last year."

He sucked in a shocked breath. "How the hell did you…"

"Someone I went to college with is now on the force."

"*Who?*"

"Yeah, right." I rolled my eyes. "Do we have a deal?"

"You're a pain in the ass."

Uh-huh. Tell me something I didn't know.

"Fine," he said, and I could have sworn I heard a note of reluctant admiration in his voice. "I'll find out what I can and be in touch."

By Saturday afternoon, I knew there was only one way I was going to get Simon to go to the Halloween party with me.

Seduction.

I'd mentioned the dance again the previous night and while he hadn't laughed, he'd very firmly rejected the idea. Socializing with a bunch of people who thought him a serial killer wasn't his idea of a good time.

Couldn't say I blamed him. But that, in my opinion, was all the more reason to go. To make people see that he was in no way dangerous and certainly not a killer. Therefore, he had to go to this dance.

I spent the morning and part of Saturday afternoon going through some more dusty old trunks and boxes. Today, however, I was looking for something other than documents.

Funny, as a kid, I would have absolutely loved stumbling into an attic like the one in Seaton House. Attics nowadays were boring. Pink puffy insulation and tattered boxes of Christmas decorations with crusty masking tape on the sides.

This one, though, once I'd gotten past the creepiness and the fear of being locked in, had proved to be a treasure trove. I'd found a half-dozen huge old sea chests, all of them filled with clothes ranging from recent pieces, apparently kept in lost and found, to antique ones that might have belonged to people who'd once lived in this house. If Simon ever needed money, he could throw this stuff on eBay and make a fortune from vintage clothes lovers.

This ensemble, in particular, was something else.

Staring at myself in the mirror on his closet door later that afternoon, I smiled, then giggled. Because I looked exactly like what Simon had thought I was on the night I'd arrived.

I looked like a hooker.

A very old-fashioned one, but a hooker nonetheless.

The antique lace-up corset, chemise and knickers were

obviously meant to be worn as underclothes. But without anything over them, they looked pretty damned hot. Especially given my, umm, overample curves. My boobs were squished so tight and plumped up so high they were practically touching my chin.

The lacy underwear hugged my generous hips and cupped my Italian girl butt. Though yellowed, they'd held up in the wash and looked pretty presentable. They definitely didn't appear ready to split apart at the seams, despite the pressure my curves put on them. And the black, ankle-high granny boots were painful in the extreme, but there was something so naughty about them I just didn't want to take them off.

Going heavy on the makeup and wild with the curling iron and hair spray, I got myself so tarted up I would have been thrown off the Vegas strip. Then, putting as much strut in my step as I could, I walked out of Simon's bedroom, into the office, tiptoeing up behind him as he sat at the desk.

Bending down to blow in his ear and kiss his neck, I whispered, "Hey, lover."

He jerked so hard, he almost cracked his head on my jaw. "Wha...oh, God, Lottie," he said as he turned around and saw me.

"I'm so sorry I startled you," I said, seeing the tightness in his whole body. I was an idiot. Of course the man was skittish about people sneaking up behind him. Who wouldn't be after experiencing what he had? "I am so sorry," I repeated. "I was just trying to surprise you."

That clenching in his jaw finally stopped and he drew in a deep breath. He also really *looked* at me for the first time. One of his eyebrows lifted as he took in my heavily made-up face and teased-up hair. And then he got a glimpse of the amount of *me* bursting out of the corset.... "What in hell are you supposed to be?"

"Remember that first night when I arrived? You thought I was a working girl? Well…think back a hundred years or so."

Finally, when I'd been afraid he would just decide I was nuts and sigh that he'd ever gotten involved with a fruitcake, he began to smile. "If you'd shown up like that the other night, I might not have kicked you out."

Twisting his seat around so he faced me, I climbed onto his lap. "You didn't kick me out, remember?"

"Uh-huh. You tricked your way into staying."

"As I recall, you invited me to stay that first night."

He snorted. "Uh, right, invited. You are about as thick-skinned as they come. I did everything but throw your bags out on the lawn."

Wiggling a little and wrapping an arm around his shoulders, I nibbled on his earlobe. "Aren't you glad you changed your mind?"

"Very glad." He was eye level with my breasts and the heat in his gaze told me he liked what he saw. Liked it a lot. Which meant it was time to press my advantage. "So if you're glad I'm here, you must want to make me happy, don't you?"

"Didn't I make you happy twice last night?"

"And once this morning," I said, nearly purring with contentment at the memories. Leaning closer so I could kiss his neck, I pressed my cleavage near his mouth and was rewarded with the scrape of his tongue along the hem of the corset. "But there's something else I want you to do for me."

"Anything," he mumbled, continuing to taste his way along my breasts, his tongue flicking out, beneath the fabric, teasing me with delicate strokes on my nipples.

"I want you to take me out."

Another kiss, another nibble, another flick. "Mmm-hmm."

"Mmm-hmm? That means you'll do it? You'll take me?"

"I will absolutely take you," he said as he began to unlace

the corset, his stare nowhere near my face so he couldn't see my triumphant expression.

"Excellent. Then it's all settled. You can go dig through the same chests and find something to wear. The dance starts at seven, so you should probably hurry up and do it now."

I hopped off his lap, knowing his playful mood was going to evaporate once my words sunk in.

I was right. "What the hell did you just do to me?"

Nibbling on my lower lip, I admitted, "I think I just seduced you into giving me what I want."

He shook his head, as if in a daze. "You mean…you tricked me? So I'd take you to some stupid costume party with a bunch of strangers who think I'm a psycho?"

"Oh, come on, don't be so melodramatic. I didn't lie to you or force you. You agreed of your own free will."

"Free will. I don't think the free will in the northern half of my body had anything to do with it."

"Well, your southern one has been calling the shots a lot, lately, so let's go with that, okay?" I said, hearing laughter bubble out of my mouth. "Besides, Simon, what better night to go out among people who think you're a psycho than on Halloween?"

"Halloween's not until Tuesday."

"I have to leave Tuesday."

We both fell silent, looking at one another. My laughter faded, as did the smile I would have sworn had begun to lurk about his lips. I didn't want to think about leaving here. I didn't want *him* to want to think about it, either.

The moment dragged on, neither of us, obviously, knowing what to say. Then, finally, with a heavy sigh, Simon said, "Fine. We'll go to the stupid party."

When I did a little happy dance, he rose to his feet and stared at me. Hard. "But we go on my terms."

His terms? Hmm. That sounded scary. But I was too glad to ask questions.

Whether Simon liked it or not, he was going to go out into the world and return to life. He'd be the charming man I knew he could be and crush the ridiculous rumors flying around about him. Then we'd come back up here and we wouldn't leave his bed until Tuesday when it was time for me to get in to my car and drive away forever.

Suddenly, with that thought, my triumph and happiness about tonight oozed away. And I stood there feeling utterly, completely empty.

"I suppose I have some work to do," Simon said as he walked around the desk toward the door. Before he left the room, however, he looked over at me, a dangerous twinkle in those dark eyes. "Remember. My terms."

Forcing myself to throw off the dark concerns of what was to come, I nodded. "Your terms."

TWO HOURS LATER, I realized I should have been a whole lot more worried about Simon's *terms*.

"Oh, my," I whispered as I watched him descend the stairs.

I honestly wasn't sure what I had been suspecting. I just knew I was in no way prepared for this. My curiosity had been killing me the whole time he'd been in the attic doing whatever it was he'd been doing. Telling me to leave him alone every time I'd gone to the base of the stairs and shouted up to see if he was all right, he'd insisted he'd be ready to leave by seven. He'd even showered and dressed in one of the third-floor rooms, just to make sure I wouldn't peek.

"Well," I muttered as he reached the bottom of the steps, "I'd definitely call that *your* terms."

When I saw Simon dressed in his "costume" for the dance, I had to admit just how outrageous his terms were.

Part of me wanted to shriek in fear. Another, stronger part, wanted to howl with laughter. Instead I just stood there stunned, wondering how on earth the residents of Trouble would react.

Finally, though, I couldn't help applauding his ingenuity. I slowly began to clap. "Mr. Zangara, I presume?" I said as he reached the foyer and strode toward me in the old-fashioned black frock coat and trousers. The striped vest and white shirt beneath screamed 1930s wealth, which was, of course, the first hint of his persona.

"Where on earth did you get that thing on your face?" I asked, glancing toward the dead giveaway—the long, handle-bar mustache drooping down each side of his mouth.

"Old wig."

"And how's it staying on? Heaven help you if you have to sneeze."

"Spirit glue. Did you see the big case of theatrical makeup up there?"

I had but since I'd come equipped with my own makeup and quite enough hair, I hadn't availed myself of any of the items in it.

Damn but the man was creative. Shaking my head and chuckling, I noted the slicked-back, brilliantine-shiny hair, the derby hat, the gold-fobbed walking stick. Right down to the antique black shoes on his feet.

"Think anyone's going to realize who you're supposed to be?" I asked, knowing better than to try to talk him out of this. He said he was going to Trouble on his terms and darned if he wasn't doing it.

"I don't particularly care," he said with an even—if slightly dangerous—smile. "Ready?"

Taking his arm and nodding, I let him lead me outside. As he opened the door to the car and helped me in, he murmured,

"Lottie, sweetheart, if any man comes within a foot of that cleavage of yours, I'm breaking his arms."

Grabbing his neckcloth and tugging him down, I met his mouth in a quick kiss. "Simon, darling, if any woman lays a hand on your...stick...I'm scratching her eyes out."

He pressed a quick, hot kiss on my mouth, then shut the door, leaving me to wonder. Was this laughing, flirtatious, mock-jealous man dressed in a ridiculous costume really the same angry stranger I'd met a week ago? I found it hard to believe, seeing only glimmers of the dark figure who'd tried to throw me out in the storm.

Simon was charming, protective, funny. Even as we got closer to town and I saw the way he stiffened in his seat, he still kept smiling, harassing me about my costume and offering to let me wear his coat all night.

"I'm quite fine in my coat, thank you," I said primly.

"Good. Why don't you keep it on the whole time?"

"I don't think so," I said, partly to flirt with him and partly because I fully intended to keep the man's attention on me all evening. Not on any other attractive females who might be at the event. Once they realized he was not some dangerous killer, I had a feeling Simon was going to be very popular with the ladies.

When we got to the decorated fire hall, I heard the loud music and laughter coming from inside. Simon had grown more quiet as we'd approached. "It'll be fine."

He shrugged, as if he didn't care. But I knew he had to. It couldn't have been easy living in self-imposed exile for so many months. Reentering the world of the living was going to require some trust. Trust that had been shot and cut out of him one hot June night.

Walking to the entrance, I grabbed his hand and twined my fingers in his. "You're totally hot for a serial killer."

He laughed softly. "And I would so pay big bucks for a chance with you."

Waggling my eyebrows and licking my lips salaciously, I tossed my curly hair. "Well, honey, for a man who looks like you, I might just be tempted to give it away for free."

We were still grinning as we walked into the place. That was good. Because it made it a little easier to deal with the fact that everyone within sight stopped talking the moment they spotted us.

Simon, obviously more worried about me than he was about himself, dropped a possessive arm over my shoulder. As if worrying that I, Lottie Santori of the alligator-thick skin, could get my feelings hurt over being snubbed by some yokels wearing witch hats and angel wings.

I was about to make some kind of big "here we are, you narrow-minded, superstitious people" announcement, but suddenly a man appeared, walking toward us through the crowd, which parted for him with every step. Some eyed him with admiration, some with disdain. Some even with fear.

He was tall—very tall, probably six-five—and lean to the point of skinniness. Despite having a youthful-looking face and brilliant blue eyes, his shoulder-length hair was snow-white.

With his build, he would have looked appropriate dressed as a scarecrow, but he instead wore an old-fashioned big-game hunter getup, like I'd seen in old African safari movies.

"Mortimer," Simon said softly.

Glancing at him, I saw a smile on his face and realized this was friend, not foe. When the older gentleman reached our side and clapped both Simon's shoulders in enthusiastic welcome, I knew it for sure. And I immediately loved him for it.

"Simon! How marvelous that you came. Couldn't be happier to see you, my boy."

"It's good to see you, too, Mr. Potts."

"Mortimer, please," the man insisted with an airy wave of his hand. "Your costume is perfect. I do wish my manservant had had time to find me one. Unfortunately, we've been busy with the renovations and I was forced to come without one."

"He's not wearing a costume?" I muttered under my breath.

Feeling Simon tighten his grip on my hand, I shut my mouth. Then the old gentleman turned to face me and I swear to God, the guy gave me a look that said even though there was white hair on top of his head, he was still randy male from there down.

"Oh, you devil," he said, obviously speaking to my date, though he never took his eyes off my face. "My dear, you have brightened up the room with your presence."

Simon quickly introduced us and we chatted with Mr. Potts for a few minutes. Around us, I noticed conversations beginning again. And then, surprisingly, people began approaching. A couple of them had obviously met Simon and carefully bid him welcome, and he managed to keep his expression pleasant, actually engaging in small talk.

Soon more of the partyers drifted over, some introducing themselves, some relying on Mortimer for introductions. But the ice had definitely been broken.

I didn't think anyone had figured out who Simon was supposed to be. Fortunately, the old guy from the records office—who'd immediately recognized Zangara's name—was nowhere around.

Simon was relaxed, laughing freely, being the charming, friendly man I'd come to know. And by the end of the night, everyone in this room would know it, too.

The women, it appeared, were already figuring it out. Much to my chagrin, my prediction about how popular he'd be with the ladies proved correct. Despite the clothes and silly mustache, Simon couldn't turn around without tripping over some simpering young twit in an angel or Greek goddess costume.

Well, good. He's popular. He's enjoying himself.

But as I saw one woman in a devil costume get a little too close with her low-cut red dress, I couldn't help wishing—just a tiny bit—that I'd kept the man all to myself.

12

Simon

IF IT DIDN'T SEEM so ridiculous—because he honestly couldn't even *see* another woman when Lottie was in the room— Simon would have thought she was jealous. As they left the firehouse, having stayed until the end of the party so Lottie could shake her hot backside to one last song—Lord have *mercy,* the woman could move—he noticed the way she frowned at a couple of women who came up to say good-night.

When they got in the car and started driving back toward Seaton House, she remained quiet, peering out the window into the dark night, seeming to be enraptured by the lights going off one by one as Trouble rolled up its sidewalks for the night.

Reaching over, he put his hand on hers. "You okay?"

She said nothing for a second, then she turned in her seat. "No. I'm feeling like crap."

Surprised, he just waited.

"I was jealous tonight."

He knew better than to smile.

"Jealous of every woman who flirted with you or asked you to dance. I swear to God if that woman in the Aphrodite costume had asked you one more time if you could help her refasten her strap that kept *accidentally* popping open, I was going to find the nearest urn and *really* go Grecian on the bitch."

Unable to help it, Simon started to laugh softly. He liked Lottie in this fierce mood and damned if he didn't like her being jealous over him. Because it meant she felt something for him. Something beyond physical attraction.

A voice of reason quickly told him what. *It's protectiveness.* She was worried about him, that was all. Other than sex, all they really had between them was her desire to nurture and an old murder case.

"I wasn't even aware there were any other women in the room tonight," he admitted, no longer laughing. "You were— and are—the most beautiful woman I've ever seen."

She seemed a little mollified. As they reached the turnoff for the private mountain road leading up to Seaton House, she unfastened her seat belt and shifted around. Wriggling closer, she put her hand on his chest and her head on his shoulder. "You really think I'm beautiful? Because honestly, in this outfit, I realized I have the Santori women's butt. I'm lucky I didn't split a seam."

His mood immediately lifted as it so often did when something outrageous and unexpected came out of her mouth. He began to smile. Sliding his arm behind her, he reached down to squeeze her ass. "This butt is amazing. Everything about you is amazing."

She wriggled against his hand, her breaths audibly picking up their pace. Simon didn't move his hand, especially when she pushed back against it. With a little shiver of excitement, she leaned closer, rising to her knees and parting her legs.

"Do you know how much I love touching you?" he asked.

"Do you know how much I love having your hands on me?"

Shifting in his seat as his body reacted to her hot breaths against his neck and the warmth dampening her clothes, he couldn't resist touching her more. Stroking his fingers back and forth across her cleft, he listened to her desperate whimpers in his ear.

Shifting even more, she reached down, stroking his chest and his stomach, then moved her hand to his lap. "Oh, God," she whispered, tracing the outline of his rock-hard cock through his pants. "I have to feel that."

"We'll be home soon," he said, forcing the words out of his suddenly tight throat. He wanted nothing more than Lottie's touch, but he feared he might drive off the mountain if he got it right now.

But she obviously didn't want to hear that. Reaching for his waistband, she began to slowly unbutton the fly of the old-fashioned trousers. "Mmm, easy access. I don't have to worry about catching anything on a zipper."

"Lottie…" he said, shaking his head, not sure whether he really had the strength to resist if she persisted.

She persisted. Slowly tugging the dress shirt up and out of the way, she worked her hand into the opening of his briefs and encircled his cock. "I really like what you can do with this thing."

Choking out a desperate laugh, he said, "I *really* like it, too, sweetheart, but I don't particularly want to drive off the side of a mountain and be found with my dick hanging out of my pants."

Laughing softly she continued touching, up and down, squeezing and stroking him to full, throbbing arousal. She soon had him almost shaking, and almost flooring the gas so they could get back to the house and have safe, wild sex—in the car if necessary.

When she lowered her head and replaced her hand with her mouth, he muttered a soft curse and clenched his hands around the steering wheel.

"Keep your eyes on the road, *sweetheart*," she whispered,

her lips brushing the head of his cock. Her tongue flicked out, wetting him, then she sucked him into her mouth.

He leaned back as far as he could in the seat, keeping his eyes on the road even though his mind was anywhere else. Lottie's warm, wet mouth was like heaven and for a few moments he just gave himself over to sensation.

Though he knew he should keep both hands on the wheel, he couldn't resist dropping one hand to her head, twining his fingers in that thick hair. She moved, up and down, taking as much of him as she could, then releasing him to press light kisses on the tip of his shaft, only to plunge down again.

Simon thought he would go out of his mind with the anticipation—and the sheer physical pleasure of it.

Seeing the sign for the parking lot entrance, he sent up a silent prayer of thanks. Both that they'd made it up the mountain alive and intact, and that within sixty seconds or so, he was going to be plunging into Lottie's tight, wet body and finishing this right where he wanted to.

But as he pulled into the private driveway that led to the garage in the back of the house, something caught his attention. He would have sworn that absolutely nothing could distract him from what Lottie was making him feel. However the scene before his eyes was so startling, he sat upright and hit the brake. Hard.

Lottie must have thought he was stopping for another reason because she sucked harder, pumped faster. Cupping his balls in her hand, she carefully squeezed, as if wanting him to shoot off in her mouth.

He might have. If he weren't so certain he'd finally lost his mind. And not just out of pleasure.

Because a few dozen yards away, near the spot where the wagon had gone over the cliffs, stood a woman. Her hair was blond—falling over her shoulders. A strange light was coming out from behind the large boulder where he and Lottie had taken refuge a few days ago during the carriage incident.

The light illuminated the figure and even though she was far away, he could make out the short red skirt she wore. And the white top. Only, it wasn't completely white. Under the mysterious, glowing light, he could see splotches of red. Like paint splattered on a drop cloth.

"Or blood," he whispered. Blood splashing onto a white blouse. "No. It can't be."

Lottie, still down below the dashboard, mumbled something that sounded like, "Don't stop me."

Looking down, he realized he was still hard, she was still blowing him, but he felt almost removed from the situation. He was in a daze, shocked by what he had seen.

A blonde in a bloody blouse and a red skirt.

It can't be.

The impact finally hit him and he felt like someone coming out of unconsciousness. His body caught up with what his eyes had seen. Though Lottie had made him feel incredible, his body was no longer in control. His mind was.

She obviously noticed. She looked up, confusion on her face. "Simon? Is something wrong?"

Cupping her cheek, he tugged her up. "It's fine," he murmured, knowing it wasn't fine. He wasn't fine. Laughing almost desperately, he said, "I need you to look at something and tell me if I'm losing my mind or not."

She didn't make any sassy comeback about how good a look she was getting at *something* right there where she was. Instead, immediately sitting up, she stared in his eyes and gently asked, "What's wrong? What is it?"

"I saw something," he whispered, looking ahead again, out the windshield, though he knew what he would see.

Absolutely nothing.

"What did you see?" Following his stare, she swung her head around and looked toward the back lawn. "Was something there?"

Shaking his head slowly as the dull throbbing of a headache began to build in his temple, he murmured, "I don't know. I honestly don't know."

AN HOUR LATER, sitting in the office after chewing a couple of aspirin and washing them down with coffee, Simon stared into the fire roaring in the fireplace. Lottie had lit it while he'd been in the bedroom taking off his costume. Then she'd gone to undress, leaving him alone with his thoughts, not starting the conversation he knew they were about to have.

In the car, after admitting she'd seen nothing unusual on the cliffs, she'd gotten very quiet, not pressing for answers. Once he'd gotten his pants back together, they'd walked inside pressed closely together. Now, staying at bay, she seemed to be giving him time to regroup.

Regroup. Get a grip. Figure out what the hell was wrong with him.

Something was. He couldn't pretend any longer. During all the time Lottie had been here, he'd been able to shove away his misgivings, ignore the tension or the occasional hairs standing up on the back of his neck. There'd been no major headaches, no more weird pictures on his laptop, no smells. But in the back of his mind, he'd noticed a few things. Drafts in empty rooms. Sounds in empty hallways. Plus the strange things that had happened to Lottie.

He'd been putting off dealing with what had been going on here for the past three months. But tonight, seeing that figure on the cliffs—a figure who looked so disturbingly familiar—he knew he had to find out what was happening to him.

If he was really losing his mind. Or if there was some other explanation he hadn't yet grasped.

"You sure you don't want hot cocoa?" Lottie asked as she came into the room, her hands curled around a steaming mug piled high with whipped cream. "Coffee's going to keep you up."

"I don't think I could sleep anyway."

She sat beside him, carefully sipping her hot drink. Still silent, offering only a quiet layer of support that he could take advantage of the moment he was ready.

Now, he supposed was as good a time as any.

"Have you ever questioned things you see, wondered if they're really there or if your eyes are playing tricks on you?"

She shrugged. "Sometimes. A twenty on the table when I'm expecting a five-dollar tip at the restaurant. That kind of thing."

"I mean something a little more...dramatic." *Like ghosts*.

She didn't answer, instead leaning over to set her mug on the table. "What did you see, Simon?" she asked, her voice barely above a whisper.

He hesitated for a brief moment. This was the point of no return, and if it were anyone other than Lottie sitting beside him, he wouldn't have been able to go on.

But it was Lottie. And he trusted her like he'd never trusted anyone before in his life. "I saw *her*. Standing next to the cliffs."

Turning to face him, she bent one leg and tucked it beneath her on the couch. "Who?"

"The woman from Charleston."

Her shocked inhalation told him she hadn't expected *that*.

"Look, I know she's dead. I don't believe in ghosts. But I swear, Lottie, for a few seconds, she was *there*."

"Maybe the wind, the trees?"

"It wasn't a shadow or a weird reflection."

"It was pretty dark out. How could you be sure it looked like her?"

"There was a strange light shining on her."

She bit her bottom lip before saying, "You were a little… distracted."

Forcing a smile, he slowly nodded. "Yeah, thanks for that. I fully intend to get back to what we were doing sooner or later."

"I vote for sooner." Then her smile faded and she got serious again. "But I mean, it's possible, isn't it, that you were just caught up in a moment and your eyes were playing tricks on you? Because you weren't exactly concentrating on what you were looking at."

Sure. It was possible. When taken with all the other odd things that had happened around here, however, he somehow doubted it.

Lottie didn't know about those things, however, so he slowly began to tell her. Starting with the first incident, about ten days after he'd taken up residence in Seaton House, when every window in every room on the third floor had been opened.

"That's freaking weird," she muttered.

"It was just the start."

Going into more detail, he told her about empty beds that bore the indentation of human bodies, the sounds, the locked doors that suddenly unlocked, and vice versa. She narrowed her eyes in deep concentration, not for a second looking as though she doubted him.

When he brought up the smells, she immediately said, "I remember. When I came in your office that day, you were so shocked that I smelled it, too."

"Yeah, I was. Before that I'd figured it was some weird chemical warning from my brain about an impending migraine."

"So it happened often?"

"Yes. Every time preceding a pretty bad episode."

"Mmm…"

He wasn't nearly finished, however. It was time to admit the rest, however crazy it might seem. "Tonight, on the cliffs, it wasn't the first time I've seen her."

"*What?*"

"That day when you came in here and I'd smelled that odor, I thought I saw a blond woman walking by the window out on the veranda." Thinking back to the night she'd arrived, which almost seemed another lifetime ago, he added, "And the night you showed up in the storm—I was in here trying to fight off a migraine."

He swallowed, remembering those moments when he'd felt absolutely certain that he was going insane. "I opened my eyes and saw crime-scene photos of the body on my laptop screen. I closed my eyes and they were gone a few minutes later." Vividly reliving those moments, he glanced toward his computer, sitting on the desk. "At first, I thought I'd just dreamed the whole thing. But when I saw my own handprint on the screen from where I'd tried to block it out, knew I'd been awake."

Lottie's mouth was open, her eyes widened in shock. He didn't blame her. Taken individually, the incidents were strange but easy to brush aside. Especially by anybody who simply didn't accept supernatural explanations.

Like him.

But heard all together—*experienced* all together, as they had been by Simon over the past few months—it was a hell of a lot harder to laugh off.

Lottie obviously agreed because she was still silent, her eyes flashing, her jaw clenching. She looked over his shoulder, into the distance, her mouth moving a little as if she were speaking under her breath.

"What?"

"The attic…when I got locked in the attic."

"I know. That was the first thought that crossed my mind."

"And the buggy?"

"Sounds crazy, doesn't it? It *feels* crazy to even be wondering about this shit."

Lottie leaned back, dropping her head on the headrest and staring up at the ceiling. "You haven't, by any chance, made my bed while I've been here, have you? Or sprayed some perfume around my room?"

Instantly curious, he shook his head. "Absolutely not. I don't even bother to make my own usually." Then, remembering when he'd gone up to move her things down, he added, "As for the perfume, I smelled it and thought you'd decided to take a bath in the stuff."

She nodded, still looking straight up, not over at him. "Other than there being too much of it, did you like the smell?"

He didn't want to offend her, but he had to be honest. "Not particularly."

"Neither did I."

"It wasn't yours?"

"No." She was still quietly contemplative, a million thoughts apparently leaping around in that beautiful head of hers. "Simon, do you remember what it smelled like?"

Nodding absently, he lifted his feet and placed them on the coffee table, leaning back in the couch to stare up at the ceiling, which seemed so fascinating to her. No brilliant answers came to mind. But when he closed his eyes and focused on the perfume, he remembered that it had smelled familiar.

And suddenly, he remembered why.

"Jesus. This sounds crazy, but I think—it might have been *her* perfume."

"The woman from Charleston," she said, sounding completely matter-of-fact, as if she'd expected the answer.

"Yes."

"I thought as much."

That surprised him more than anything Lottie had said yet.

The rational part of his mind knew none of this could be supernatural. There were no such things as ghosts—he wasn't being haunted by the restless spirit of a woman he'd killed. But the utter strangeness of it had him confused. Even a bit in shock.

Maybe if he'd been his old self—completely recovered, the confident, laid-back guy he'd always been before June 20th, he would have laughed it off. Or at least not started questioning his own senses.

He wasn't that man anymore, though. He'd seen the darkest that the human race had to offer. His trial by fire had introduced a new reality into his life because he'd seen close-up, vivid proof that evil really did exist. He'd personally come to grasp the concept that someone could attack and murder another human being with no provocation or reason.

It made him question everything—*everything*—he'd ever thought about life and humanity. And if that didn't change a person, he didn't know what would.

So this new Simon was a little too ready to accept ugly possibilities. Like the idea that he was losing his mind.

No. Lottie has seen some of this. I am not crazy.

Finally, after a few more minutes of silent contemplation, Lottie sighed deeply and lifted her head. Her face creased in a frown, she scooted closer on the couch, so their thighs touched, as did their arms.

Reaching up to cup his cheek, she rubbed the tip of her finger across his scar, as she always did—whether she realized it or not. "It's going to be okay."

He couldn't contain a bitter laugh. "You think so? How? Is somebody going to come along and put me in a special coat and a room with rubber walls and give me pills to make me feel all better?"

She shook her head, leaning close to press a gentle kiss on his mouth. "No, love. You see, I think I know what's going on. We just need to figure out what to do about it."

Call the psych ward. He tensed in anticipation of the words. When they didn't come, he gruffly asked, "What, exactly, do you think is going on?"

She took his hands in hers, staring him in the face, her expression entirely earnest. Finally, with a bit of fire flashing in those brown eyes, she said something he'd never expected to hear.

"Simon, honey? Someone is fucking with you."

13

Lottie

I'VE SAID IT BEFORE, I'm not a violent person. Sure, I have my moments of Italian temper, particularly where my brothers are concerned. Or when somebody cuts me off in traffic or talks loud on a cell phone in a public place. Yes, those tee me off. But I've certainly never wanted to do serious physical harm to another person.

Anything's possible, right? Because oh, man, when I figured out what had been happening to Simon, I was ready to crush someone. Rip them apart with my bare hands.

He, God love him, didn't believe it at first. The man has been carrying so much guilt and regret around that it almost seemed easier for him to accept he was being meted out some psychological punishment for his perceived crime rather than thinking someone had been playing vicious, ruthless mind games with him.

I could certainly see his skepticism. It sounded pretty bizarre, I know. Still, it was the only thing that made sense when looking at the big picture. And gradually, by hitting every single point, going over every odd moment he and I had *both* experienced, I'd brought him round.

Did I say *I* was mad?

"I don't think I have ever been more furious in my life,"

he snarled as he paced back and forth in front of the fireplace, practically wearing a hole in the carpet. "I can't believe this. Someone here, sneaking in and out of this place, *spying* on my every move?"

Oh, God, I hoped not his every move. The thought that someone might have seen us during an intimate moment made my flesh crawl. Simon obviously had the same concern because he whirled around, then crouched down in front of me. "The doors were closed."

"The bastard's getting around somehow. Who knows what secret peepholes he has in here?"

Thrusting a frustrated hand through his hair, he straightened up and resumed his pacing. "You really, genuinely believe this is what's been happening?" he asked, not for the first time.

"It makes sense," I said, hearing my own disgust. "The open windows, the beds, things being moved around, noises… how easy is that? I mean, you're down here locked in your office all by yourself most days, you wouldn't hear a herd of donkeys running around on the third floor. Before I came, I bet there were days when you never even left your room."

He nodded slightly in acknowledgment.

"Someone could have gotten inside through one of these lousy old locks—hell, someone who once worked in the hotel might have a key! Then they just went and did their mischief, made some noise so you'd come investigate and find some weird, inexplicable situation. Voilà, you're obviously psycho."

He threw himself down in the chair beside the fireplace, his long legs kicked out in front of him. His fingers were clenched into tight fists on the armrests and fury was crashing over the man in near visible waves. "The woman?"

"The guy has an accomplice. Somebody did a little research into you, got a hold of some pictures—which is incredibly easy on the Internet now. And then he recreated a few moments to freak you out...." Rolling my eyes, I added, "If it weren't so late I'd suggest going out and looking around along the cliffs. I bet we'd find very *real* footprints."

"The rest...the smells? The pictures?"

"I'm no expert," I said, voicing what I'd begun to suspect about some of the other weird goings-on. "But I know my great-aunt Cecelia has suffered migraines all her life. They are quite often triggered by cloying, sweet smells. Odors piped in through the air vents might very well have been intended to cause your migraines."

He muttered a string of curses that even my foul-mouthed older brothers would have been impressed with.

"How could they know I have migraines?" he finally asked when he'd gotten just about every cuss word known to man out of his system.

"If they've been prowling around your house, they could have seen you dealing with one. Those curtains are never closed. How easy would it be for someone to peek in here and see you lying down with a cloth on your head?"

A muscle in his cheek kept flexing. "Yes. Possible."

"As for the thing with the computer, jeez, Simon, I told you when I first got here that your network was way too easy to get into. No firewall whatsoever."

"You can't just make an attachment show up on someone else's computer by sending an e-mail," he said, immediately shaking his head. "There's no way somebody crept in here and opened up a file while I was lying right beside the damn laptop."

I thought about it for a minute, trying to remember some of the details from the computer classes I'd taken in college. "Look, sometimes in class when I was working on a program or presentation and ended up totally screwing it up, my professor would be able to take control over my system from his own computer. I'd sit back in my chair and watch the cursor moving around the screen like the stylus on a Ouija board and he'd fix whatever the heck I'd done wrong."

Simon didn't appear convinced.

"I'm not entirely sure *how*, but it can be done. I've seen it. And someone with a little computer knowledge probably wouldn't have much trouble, especially if they got their hands on your laptop one day when you were in the shower or something."

Simon stopped arguing, obviously seeing the plausibility of the scenario I'd described. It *was* plausible. Outrageous and vicious and vindictive…but plausible.

"It makes sense," I said softly, completely certain I was right. "We have three choices. Either you're crazy, there is a ghost at work in this house, or some sick person is getting kicks out of trying to get under your skin. I vote for option three."

He glanced up, meeting my eyes from a few feet away, and slowly nodded. "Yeah. I hate to think I've had some filth in and out of my house, spying on my private life for three months, but it absolutely makes the most sense." His mouth pulling tight and his thick lashes lowering halfway over his eyes, he added, "Someone's 'gaslighting' me, like in that old movie. But who? And *why?*"

His anger had eased, and had probably been replaced by embarrassment…even pain. Which made perfect sense. Who would want to think someone could be so twisted and hateful? I was feeling violated after being here a short time—I couldn't imagine how he had to feel.

"I don't know who, but I might have an idea why. It seems to me that somebody's trying to get you—and now me, judging by the thing with the attic, and the carriage—out of this house. Anyone feel they have a claim on it?"

"Uncle Roger had no other living relatives."

Scratch that. "Okay, how about potential buyers? Has anyone been after you to sell it?"

"The day the will was read, my uncle's attorney told me there were interested parties who'd approached Uncle Roger before he died. I told him to forget it, just as Uncle Roger apparently had, several times."

That sent a chill up my spine, though at first I wasn't sure why. "Did they persist?"

Rubbing a weary hand on his forehead, he nodded. "Yeah. The lawyer's called a couple of times, asking if I've changed my mind."

I almost said *aha* in triumph. We were on to something. I knew it. Hey, I did this for a living. "So we contact the attorney and get the name of the buyer."

Simon reached for the phone, which startled me into a laugh. "Uh, babe, you do realize it's three a.m., right?"

"Oh. Right."

Suddenly feeling that late hour in every bit of my body, I rose to my feet and stretched. "I think I've had about as much as I can take for the night."

Simon nodded and stood beside me. "You think you'll be okay sleeping here tonight?"

I knew what he meant, of course. It was possible—unlikely, given the late hour—but still possible that someone was lurking somewhere in Seaton House. The very thought of it made me sick. "Well, if they are, they know we're on to them now." I raised my voice. "And that they better get the hell out before we find them and have them thrown in jail for a few decades."

An exaggeration, I was sure. But worth a shot.

Simon laughed softly, the tension seeming to ease from his shoulders for the first time in hours. "The bedroom has one door and it locks."

"And you have a big dresser we can shove in front of it, right?"

Laughing, he dropped his arm across my shoulders and led me into his room. Once we were inside, with the door locked, I glanced at the dresser and cocked an eyebrow.

"You were kidding, right?"

I shook my head.

"You want me to break my back and be no good to you at all?"

"I'll be on top."

He grabbed me around the waist and pulled me tight. "That sounds fantastic. But how about we use the chair instead?"

I eyed the chair, piled high with his clothes from the costume party, and grunted. "That won't keep anyone out."

"Oh, I'm not worried about keeping someone out. If someone gets in, you can bet I'll be waiting for him. The chair will, however, make some noise, guaranteeing nobody can sneak in on us."

I didn't want to think about Simon being put in the position of having to defend himself against anyone ever again. Hopefully though, it wouldn't come to that. Whoever had been tormenting him was a damned coward as far as I was concerned, lurking in the shadows, playing vicious tricks. A scavenger—a hyena—picking him off piece by piece then scurrying away like a rodent. He wouldn't face Simon head-on.

So, nodding, I said, "Okay. You can save your back, we'll use the chair." And as he picked it up to place it beneath the chair, I added, "But I still get to be on top."

WE SLEPT LATE the next morning, which obviously wasn't any big surprise. Making love and then sleeping wrapped in each other's arms seemed the best way to thrust the ugliness of our discovery out of both our minds. But judging by the look on Simon's face late the next morning when we finally ventured from the bedroom, his thoughts had gone right back to our previous night's conversation. "Do lawyers keep Sunday hours?" he asked.

"I doubt it," I said as I finished flipping some pancakes onto a heavily laden platter.

"Tough," he said, "I'm calling."

"Yeah. I figured you would. But eat first, okay?"

"You calling me skinny again?"

"Oh, no, you are in perfect shape. But after all the late-night exercise, I think you need to regain your strength."

Appearing mollified, he helped himself to a heap of pancakes and proceeded to devour them. Oh, I loved a man with an appetite.

Picking at my own food, I thought about my conversation with my brother the other day. I didn't think what was going on at Seaton House had anything to do with Simon's incident in Charleston. However, despite my assurances to Simon that anyone could have gotten those pictures of his attacker, I was a little curious about it. Deciding to call Mark while Simon went after the attorney, I mentally went over a list of points I wanted to cover.

I didn't worry about bothering my brother on a Sunday because I knew, by one, he and Noelle would be at the folks' house. This was the Sunday before Halloween, a good excuse for a gathering. The men would be watching football, the women would be hanging out in the kitchen. Mama would supervise, making homemade pasta, meatballs and *brachiole*. Gloria would be chasing after my nephews, two little boys who were Tony's pride and joy. Meg would probably be holding baby Maria's fingers and encouraging her to take her first steps with Joe watching over her shoulder. Lucas would arrive with his bride, Rachel, who would undoubtedly have a delicious, fattening southern dish in hand.

My family. I missed them. The whole loud, boisterous bunch of them. And I couldn't help wondering what it would be like to walk into the house with Simon on my arm. Seeing him shake my father's hand, sample Mama's cooking. Talk sports with my brothers and tantalize my sisters-in-law with his dark sexy looks and that mysterious scar.

He'd win them over, of course. They'd love him. Just like I do. *I do.*

I really needed to stop thinking about it. Especially because I was still supposed to be going home soon and the thought that Simon might actually come with me to meet my family seemed utterly impossible. And, right now, the idea of leaving him filled me with more anguish than anything I'd ever experienced.

Then again, I suddenly realized, there was absolutely nothing that would compel me to walk out of here without making sure whoever had been tormenting him was caught, that Simon would be okay and be able to get on with his life.

So, no, I might not be leaving here on Tuesday at all. Maybe I'd have to take the rest of the semester off. Get my brothers to go over to my apartment, pack it up and put my stuff in storage. Maybe I'd stay.

If he *wanted* me to.

Once we'd finished breakfast, Simon said, "Look, while I make this call, why don't you get in your car and go into town and do some shopping or something."

I frowned. "On a Sunday? That town doesn't look like it has stores that are even open on Saturdays."

"So go to church."

"I'm staying."

He shook his head, taking my arm. "I want to search this house, top to bottom, and I really don't want you here in case I bump into our *ghost*."

Oh, sure, right, like I was going to leave him alone for *that*. "Searching will go much faster if there are two of us."

"Lottie…"

"Simon! I am not leaving," I said, poking him in the chest with my index finger, my eyes narrowed. "There is absolutely nothing you can do or say that will make me, so you might as well shut up, go make your phone call and meet me in the foyer in a half hour so *we* can begin searching."

Staring at one another, we engaged in a silent battle of wills. But he obviously had a lot more sense than any of my brothers, because he realized right away he wasn't going to be able to change my mind. "All right. Half an hour."

I rose on tiptoes and kissed his mouth. "Deal."

Once he'd gone into his office to try to track down the attorney, I went outside in search of a cell phone signal. By some weird twist of fate, as soon as I saw a couple of bars on the phone's screen, it began to ring.

Spying the number on the caller ID, I started to laugh. "Hey, how'd you know I was picking up the phone to call you?"

Mark probably didn't hear me, since he immediately snapped, "I've been trying to reach you all morning, why the hell haven't you had your cell phone on?"

"I did. There just isn't any decent reception unless I stand on my head with three plates on my nose."

Chuckling, he said, "Look, the whole family's in the house."

"I figured."

"So I'll be quick before somebody realizes I have you on the line and grabs the phone away."

I'd been missing my family, but I didn't want to get involved in a marathon Santori phone-fest. Mark would understand. Every one of us had been on the receiving end of the never ending pass-the-phone parties at some time or another.

I did not want to waste an hour having the same conversation with every person in the family. Including, most likely, the little ones. "Look," I said, "I'll call back to talk to the folks later, but I need to talk to you. I have a question you might be able to answer."

I asked him about the accessibility of the crime-scene photos. And whether someone could possibly have gotten their hands on an evidence list that might name the kind of perfume in the dead woman's purse.

His answer didn't surprise me. "That's a tough one. I mean, sure, the pictures could have gotten out. Or maybe some sicko took his own shots of the scene before the first responders secured it."

Hard to imagine someone yanking out a camera and taking pictures of a woman lying in her own blood, especially if they weren't sure whether she was dead or not. Then I thought about Princess Diana and realized it was entirely too possible.

"But the evidence list? I don't know, that's a little more tricky," he admitted. "Which doesn't mean someone sitting in the bar that night couldn't have smelled the woman's perfume and recognized it. And, of course, anyone who knew her might have known what she wore." Then, obviously really thinking about my questions, he asked, "Why, Lottie? Why do you want to know this stuff?"

I thought about telling him everything, but knew he would just freak out. Being hundreds of miles away, he'd feel helpless and would order me to leave, abandoning Simon to whoever had been stalking him. And if I refused, I wouldn't put it past him to walk into the house, tap Joe, Lucas and Tony on the shoulders and march them all out to his car for a little ride. To Pennsylvania.

That definitely nixed any idea of telling him the truth. Having four of my five brothers here *would* prove very beneficial in helping us search this house from top to bottom, which I intended to do as soon as I was finished my call. But they'd also be assholes to Simon the minute they realized I was sleeping with him. So I didn't tell him.

"Just something that came up," I said. Wanting to stop him from asking more questions, I continued. "Now, why were you trying to call me?"

"Uh, didn't you ask me to look into this case for you?"

Well, duh. I'd gotten so worked up over what was happening to Simon now—on who was using his tragedy against him—that I'd almost forgotten wanting to know more about the details of that tragedy. "Of course. Sorry. What did you find out?"

He quickly went over the stuff I already knew, but then surprised me by saying, "The lead investigator did tell me they've learned a little more about the suspects. A family member came to claim the woman's cremated remains several weeks after she died. I guess her brother was thought to be the only next of kin, but someone else stepped forward."

"Who was it?"

"The person skipped out before investigators could talk to them. The police did get a name and location, though, from the mortuary records."

Hmm.

"Who was the family member?"

He shuffled some papers. "A Lou Harrington from Philadelphia."

Hmm again. Brother Lou? Cousin Louie? Uncle Luigi? Not enough information.

"Anyway, beyond that, the jailed suspect still isn't cooperating. Philadelphia police have looked into it and don't

have any criminal background on either one of the attackers."
Mark cleared his throat.

"What?"

"Well, the investigator I talked to did have some things to
say about the victim."

I immediately tensed. "Oh?"

"Yeah. Mainly what a poor son of a bitch he was to stumble
onto these two, because they really messed him up. That balcony apparently looked like a slaughter had taken place, but
all the blood was the intended victim's."

Hot moisture rose to my eyes but I blinked it away. Simon
wasn't hurting physically anymore. And dammit, soon he
wouldn't be hurting emotionally. I'd see to that if it was the
only important thing I ever did in my life.

"He also said the bartender and hotel staff had noticed the
woman hanging around a couple of nights before that one,
never talking to anyone. But the minute this Lebeaux guy
came in, she was all over him."

"She—they—targeted *him*," I said, never doubting it. "Not
just any wealthy-looking hotel guest would do."

"Looks that way."

Big hmm. The hairs on the back of my neck were standing
up and if I had a mirror handy, I knew I'd see my pulse throbbing in my temple. Because I sure felt it.

"Lottie, just thought I'd mention…the staff also told the
investigators that Lebeaux hadn't been, you know, trolling the
bar during his stay. They never saw him with a woman until
that night and she was definitely the aggressor."

Hearing a note of gruffness in Mark's voice, I suddenly realized why he'd told me that. He knew. He somehow knew,
without me saying, that I was involved with Simon. And
though he was far away, it almost seemed as if he were offering his approval, and his support. Have I mentioned I really
do love my brothers?

"Thanks, Mark. Give Noelle a hug for me."

"I give her plenty of my own, but I'm always happy to give her one more."

Laughing, I promised to call later. And I promised to be careful. Then I disconnected the call and went inside to find Simon. It was time to search Seaton House and get to the bottom of what was happening within its walls.

14

Simon

WITH THE SKELETON KEY in hand, they searched the entire house. Every room. Every closet. From the attic to the basement. It took most of the day, but by Sunday night, Simon felt sure they'd exhausted all possibilities within the building itself.

That didn't mean someone hadn't been doing exactly what Lottie theorized—it just meant they hadn't taken up residence in his house. There were a few outbuildings—the free standing garage, a gardener's shed and a small building where Roger had kept the outdoor lawn equipment. But it was getting dark, so they'd have to search those tomorrow.

There were other things that had to wait until tomorrow as well, including word from his uncle's attorney, who hadn't, despite Simon's best efforts, been reachable today. So by that night, he was feeling irritated and frustrated.

"Look, we've searched the whole place, we know we're secure for tonight," Lottie murmured as they lay sprawled on his bed. They'd both collapsed there, fully clothed, tired from their long, dusty day of creeping over every inch of the place. "We'll find out more tomorrow and search the grounds."

"I just wish there was more to do tonight."

"You could do me tonight."

He tugged her onto his chest. "I fully intend to." Smiling, he added, "But first, I'm absolutely starving."

Some women might take offense at being put in second place after a meal, but not Lottie. She immediately shot up. "Excellent. I'll make us something fabulous."

Laughing, he tried to pull her back down. "I didn't mean right this minute."

There was no stopping her, though. Following her into the kitchen, he watched her dive into the fridge and start pulling out enough food to feed an army. Or a big Italian family.

"Anything I can do to help?"

"Absolutely not."

Restless, he paced the kitchen. "I'd feel better if I had something to do," he muttered, talking more to himself than her.

She paused, turned around and said, "I know. Listen, I had another thought. Something else we could research without waiting for the lawyer."

"Tell me. I need a distraction."

"I brought a box of papers up from the basement and left it in the old restaurant. There are a lot of guest ledgers, registration records and correspondence. It's recent stuff, like from the last year or two."

He immediately followed. "If someone was really interested in the hotel, they might have approached Uncle Roger directly."

She nodded. "Very good, you're catching on to this investigative stuff."

"I'm a fast learner."

"Unlike me, who didn't decide until I'd nearly finished college what I wanted to be when I grew up." Getting back to work, she rinsed a few tomatoes in the sink. "You might also want to look through the ledgers to see if there's anyone who stayed here a lot, particularly last spring when someone was trying to get your uncle to sell. They might have come as a hotel guest a few times before deciding to try to buy the property."

Damn she was smart. And gorgeous. And sweet.

And he was falling for her. Staring at her back across the kitchen as she started chopping vegetables, he froze, unable to move as the truth washed over him.

He was no longer developing feelings for her. He was in love with her.

"What are you waiting for?" she asked, looking at him over her shoulder.

"Eyes front, lady, watch that knife," he said, seeing her continue to slice into a ripe tomato with a sharp blade.

"Fine, but get out of my kitchen and make yourself useful."

Laughing, he left the room to do exactly that.

He found the box right where Lottie had left it. Pulling it over to the nearest table, he made a mental note to give her hell for carrying the thing up by herself. It was not light.

For the next hour, he went through every piece of paper, organizing them all by date where possible. Lottie wasn't the only one who knew how to do a little research. One of these days, he was going to have to remind her what he did for a living.

One of these days.

Like, tomorrow? Wasn't that, after all, the only day he had left with her? She was leaving on Tuesday, driving out of his life as quickly as she had driven into it.

Ask her not to go.

He thought about it, but quickly realized he couldn't. Yeah, he was a selfish bastard. He'd proved that in any number of ways since he'd known her. But asking her to stay here meant asking her to babysit a screwed-up man. One who'd obviously been so emotionally whacked-out, he'd practically invited someone to terrorize him in his own home.

She would probably do it. Lottie's tenderness, her concern for him—her *pity*—meant she'd probably give him whatever he asked.

Which was why he'd never ask.

He didn't want her to stay on those terms. He didn't want her pitying him, thinking she needed to save him from the dark morass he'd allowed his life to become.

No.

If she stayed, it would have to be because she saw—and loved—the real man. The man he'd been before. The man he *would* become again. Maybe not by Tuesday, but someday soon, he *would* be the kind of man she'd be proud to be with.

After this is over....

Thrusting all those thoughts out of his mind, he got back to the task at hand. He had to push away the sadness whenever he stumbled across something handwritten by his uncle, knowing Roger would have wanted him to get to the bottom of this nonsense. The hotel had been in the family for decades. If someone was trying to make a grab for it by using some stupid psychological game, Uncle Roger would be the first one to insist that Simon nail the bastard.

Starting with the older paperwork, he realized it would take too much time, so he moved forward, to this past spring, as Lottie had suggested. It wasn't long before he stumbled across a note his uncle had jotted down on his daily planner. A note about a meeting with his attorney regarding the offer on Seaton House. He set the note aside, knowing he was on the right track.

It was soon joined by several more items, including the guest records from the final few months the hotel had been in business. A few names showed up more than once, but one visitor had come back to Seaton House six times between March and June.

When he saw the notation on the final visit, Simon frowned. Though no smell preceded it, he felt a throbbing begin in the base of his skull, as if he were about to get one of his headaches. But he knew it wasn't a migraine. Something else was making his blood pound harder in his veins and tension flood through his body.

He'd been looking for a suspect in the recent events targeting him. But what he greatly feared he found was something much—*much*—worse.

Almost dazed as the possibilities flooded into his head, clicking into place, he closed the books, rose from the table and walked back to the kitchen.

Lottie, looking so sweet and sexy in her tight jeans and a big white apron, obviously heard him come in. "Perfect timing, the pasta's just about al dente."

"Lottie," he murmured, standing numbly in the doorway. She spun around. "What is it?"

"I think…" He paused, hating to continue. A part of him didn't want to bring the words out into the open, to give them life and make the possibility real.

Dropping a slotted spoon on the counter, she hurried over to him, putting her hand on his chest. "Tell me."

He did. "I think it's possible that my uncle's death wasn't an accident."

At her stricken look, he continued, "As bizarre as it sounds…I think someone who wanted this hotel might actually have murdered him to get it."

IT TOOK A WHILE to make her understand his suspicion. Simon knew it sounded crazy and as he walked back to the shadowy restaurant with her, he told her so.

"I had a feeling. An intuition at first. Seeing the name so many times."

Taking down another chair so she could sit with him at one of the small tables, he began showing her what he'd found. The notes, the planner, the ledger. "One name kept popping up. She came here so often and always stayed in the same room."

Lottie's jaw dropped. "She?"

He nodded. "Yes. The same woman. And apparently she met with Uncle Roger a couple of times during her stays— he had her initials marked in his planner."

"It could have been about something else," she said, though she sounded doubtful.

"It could have. But it wasn't."

He opened a book his uncle had used as a private journal. "Uncle Roger was old-school. The hotel had a computer but it was archaic. He did just about everything by hand, including making notes to himself. Check out the one on May fifteenth."

Lottie looked at the book and read it. "Who's Andrews?"

"The lawyer."

She read the single paragraph to the end, her eyes growing wide. "He scheduled an appointment to talk to his lawyer about L.M. How to convince her he wasn't selling, and to ask if there was a legal way to bar her from staying at the hotel."

"Yes."

"Oh, my God, she was the buyer and she kept coming up here harassing him about it. How bad must it have been if he wanted to try to prohibit her from ever staying at the hotel again?"

"I can't imagine. He was the nicest old guy you'd ever want to meet."

Simon swallowed, wishing he'd done more to stay in touch with his uncle. In May he'd been finishing up the At-

lanta book and preparing for his trip to Charleston. He'd
probably called his only living relative three times that entire
month. "I didn't know this was happening. If I'd realized
someone was bothering him, you can bet I would have done
something about it."

"Of course you would have." She put her hand over his;
reading the next entries in the journal. There weren't many
more—his uncle hadn't written any kind of diary, he'd just
made detailed notes about important things going on in his
life.

One entry the first day of June had mentioned Simon.

S called. Another book in the fall. What a success—his
mother would be so proud.

Simon had had a hard time reading that one. And when
Lottie got to it, she squeezed his fingers hard. The journal
ended three days later. The day before Roger Denton had died.

"Okay," Lottie said, "I think you're right. This potential
buyer wasn't normal. Your uncle was being harassed—stalked
almost by some obnoxious woman. But he doesn't say in here
whether he ever heard from her again. So why…"

He said nothing, merely opening the old-fashioned ledger
book that had once sat on the front desk of the hotel. In keeping with the vintage theme of the place, Roger used to have
his guests sign in the enormous journal, using a big, swooping
feathered pen. They'd always gotten a kick out of it and it had
fit the ambiance of Seaton House perfectly.

"Look at the names of the people who stayed here the first
week of June."

She ran her fingertip over the names—some easy to make
out, some scrawled. She stopped exactly where he had. On a
barely legible signature, scrawled Louisa Mitchell.

All the color left her face so fast, he'd have thought she'd seen a ghost. The ugly possibilities had occurred to her as quickly as they'd occurred to him.

"Do you think she had something to do with your uncle's accident?"

"Lottie, seeing that name and the date…I think it's worse than that. I think she killed him."

HE DREAMED THAT NIGHT. Violent dreams of his uncle not just stumbling over a rock or being startled by a noise. But of a woman's arm coming out of a misty cloud. Pushing against Roger Denton's chest. Then the old man falling away into the nothingness below the cliffs.

Simon woke up several times, and each time Lottie murmured something sweet in her sleep and curled close to him, pressing as tightly to his body as she could get.

He pulled her even tighter. Held her closer.

Tomorrow, he would drive into town and track down this lawyer, Andrews. He'd find out everything he could about the woman he suspected had killed his uncle. Where she'd come from, what she looked like. If the lawyer couldn't help, he'd at least be able to direct Simon toward the former employees of Seaton House. With a guest as regular as that one—especially a pushy one who was bothering the owner—somebody had to remember her.

He had no doubt he'd track down the woman. What would happen when he did so remained to be seen.

At some point during the night, he must have finally fallen into a deep, dreamless sleep, because the next time he opened his eyes, the bedroom was bathed in sunlight. The clock said it was nearly eight.

Beside him, he realized, Lottie was also awake. Lying flat on her back, she stared up at the ceiling. Her lips moved, as if she was talking to herself, and he couldn't help remembering what she'd once said about cursing people she was mad at under her breath. She was obviously very mad at someone because she was frowning as she muttered.

"Hey."

Jerking her head to face him, she murmured. "Good morning."

But she didn't curl back into his arms or offer him a good-morning kiss. Instead, she kept frowning, then slowly looked up toward the ceiling again.

He finally had to laugh, she looked so fierce. "Who are you muttering about?"

"I'm not muttering."

"Ha. There was some definite muttering going on."

Still not looking over, she admitted, "I'm thinking of your uncle. And what's happened to you." Finally rolling onto her side to face him, she continued. "I can't imagine anyone killing someone for a building." She reached up and scraped the tip of her finger against his scar. "But I guess it's no more heinous than someone trying to kill another person for a hundred dollars and a watch."

Yeah. Ugly. He knew exactly how she felt.

"You know," she said, "there's something bothering me. Have you ever had that feeling where you hear something, and you just know it's important—that it has significance—but damned if you can figure out why? It's like a tiny thought running rampantly around my brain, scampering out of reach every time I try to catch it."

"You're good with words."

"I'm going to be a writer."

"Good job," he said, offering her as much of a smile as he could manage.

Lottie wrapped her arms around his neck. "Okay, we have

some more searching to do. And I want to go online and do a little poking around. You think you're okay with cold cereal for breakfast this morning?"

"No eggs Benedict? I'm crushed."

She thunked him on the head. The woman actually *thunked* him on the head!

"Ow! Register those fingers of yours as lethal weapons."

"Mama can leave bruises. But that's not nearly as bad as when she grabs you by the ear."

He immediately lifted a self-protective hand to the side of his head.

She laced her fingers in his and tugged his hand away. "You're safe. For now." Pressing a quick kiss on his lips, she said, "But I need to get moving. I'm going to track down that thought in my head no matter what."

"Lottie," he said, not releasing her, "it can wait a few minutes. I haven't said good morning to you the way I want to yet."

And he drew her back into his arms.

15

Lottie

I LOVE MORNING SEX. I love the laziness of it, when every stroke is accentuated and every touch lingers. At least, that's the kind of morning sex I'd had with Simon.

This morning was no exception. Despite my concerns— and the stress we were both under—the minute I saw that look in his eyes, I knew everything else could wait. This was far more important.

Especially if there were any chance I was still leaving the next day. Because, as of yet, I hadn't figured out a way to get him to ask me to stay.

Lying on Simon's chest, I leaned down and met his mouth in a deep, wet kiss full of promise and hunger. He cupped my face, wrapping his fingers in my hair as he so loved to do. I loved the way he played with my hair—so sensuously, reverently almost.

Ending the kiss, I reached down and shoved the covers away, wanting to see him. Wanting to watch *us*. A sexy, confident smile signaled his approval.

Straddling him, I cupped his sex against mine, not letting him enter me yet, wanting to do much more before we reached that delicious point. In the bright light of day, I looked down at him, studying his handsome face and his stubbled jaw. I stroked his chest, then bent and pressed my lips against his scar, saying nothing. Nothing needed to be said.

I continued kissing my way across his chest, dipping my tongue into the hollow of his throat, then lower so I could swirl it over his flat nipple. He jerked beneath me, thrusting up in reaction. I hissed as he slid a tiny bit into me, loving the feel of him without the separation of a condom. I wanted his hot skin, just him, but I knew we couldn't be so foolish.

He appeared to agree. "You feel amazing. So hot, so wet… but…"

"I got it," I murmured, reaching over to the bedside table and grabbing a condom from the box lying there. My position gave him access and he took advantage of it, sucking my nipple into his mouth and savoring it completely.

Groaning, I stayed still, loving the thorough attention. My body began to move, through no volition of mine, until I was rubbing my wet lips against his erection, dying—just dying— for another forbidden taste.

I like kids. Would he like kids?

I forced the thought away and tore the condom open. He took it out of my hands, which were shaking too much to deal with it. Scooting back, I watched as he covered himself, making a mental promise that someday—hopefully someday soon—I would have him without any barriers. Any separation whatsoever.

"I need you so much, Lottie," he whispered as he shifted me back into position over him.

"I…need you, too." I'd almost said the wrong word. Almost admitted I loved him. But I knew he wasn't ready to hear that yet. Not while living under this cloud.

So I slowly began to move, sliding down onto him, taking him into my body. Imprinting the beautiful sensation into the recesses of my memory.

Just in case the cloud never disappeared. And this was all we had.

SIMON LEFT after breakfast. I know he absolutely hated to go, not wanting to leave me alone here. But since we'd gone through every inch of the place yesterday, I felt pretty safe. "Every door and window is locked and I'll barricade the front door after you," I'd said as I followed him out, practically pushing him out of the house.

Promising to be gone only an hour or two, he left, and I went straight to my laptop. I wished, for a second, that I knew a little more about computers because I'd dearly love to try to track down whoever had been piggybacking on Simon's network. But my knowledge was pretty basic.

I did, however, have a whole lot of experience with that modern marvel, Google. So, not even certain what I was looking for, I went to the familiar site and started typing names into the search bar. I started with the most pressing situation—Simon's ghost.

Louisa Mitchell turned up nothing useful and a million sites that meant absolutely nothing to me. So I moved on, suddenly wanting to know more about Charleston.

Certainly the police in Charleston had searched for Simon's attackers this way, but it was worth a try. So I typed in what I had. And using just the suspects names, Linda and Joseph Harrington, I again got a huge amount of hits.

Most of the first few pages were about the attack in Charleston, but the rest ranged from engagement notices to promotion announcements to articles on economics. Pages of them, and obviously too much to sort through. "This won't work, the names are too common."

I went a step further. Added in the mysterious Uncle Lou and the city of Philadelphia.

Which still went absolutely nowhere.

"Dammit," I muttered, still trying to catch that thought.

I kept playing around with different combinations, using quotations here and there. With no luck.

Finally, realizing my eyes were beginning to get blurry, I thought about the fact that I had never even finished the job I was sent here to do. I'd gotten some good stuff on Josef Zangara for my professor, but I hadn't even sent him all the information I'd collected. So opening my file of notes, I did a quick spell check, intending to zip them right out to him as an attachment.

I barely paid attention as the misspelled words popped up for verification or correction. Most were just formal names the software didn't recognize. I was a pretty good speller. And honestly, I was so anxious to get back to work on Simon's situation that I almost just said to hell with it and sent it without finishing. But there were a couple of typos, so I stuck with it. No sense having my first important, paid job look sloppy.

Then another box came up, with a misspelled word. Also a typo.

"Mrs. Zangara." My eyes focused on what I'd written. Sighing, I said, "Obviously your name was not spelled Loussa unless you were one loose-a woman."

Grabbing my handwritten notes to ascertain what the heck the woman's real name had been, I got it and went right back to the document on my computer scene.

It wasn't until I'd corrected the spelling that the word actually sunk in to my brain. I froze, and at that moment, that elusive, annoying little uncaptured memory burst into my mind like a dazzling ray of sparkling sunshine.

"Oh, my God," I whispered. "*Louisa* Zangara."

Louisa. Like Louisa Mitchell, the woman who'd been

bothering Simon's uncle. Louisa was not exactly an uncommon name but it wasn't run-of-the-mill, either.

That's what had been bugging me since last night. Some part of my brain had obviously remembered seeing the name before, when looking into the Zangara case, but I hadn't been able to pull it into focus.

"Sorry, professor, you need to go back on the back burner."

Immediately flipping back to the search screen, I typed in several new words. Louisa Mitchell. Louisa Zangara. Seaton House.

And immediately found what I had been searching for all along.

"This can't be true," I whispered, staring blankly at the words swimming before my eyes. I had to read it four times before I believed it.

The article was a brief one, from a small town newspaper outside of Philadelphia. It was dated three years ago and was a local interest piece about a woman becoming a centenarian. A Mrs. Louisa Zangara had just celebrated her 100th birthday.

At her side was her loving family, including her son, numerous grandchildren and even some great-grandchildren. Among them, Louisa Mitchell.

That, however, wasn't what had my heart pounding out of control in my chest. No, the absolute stunning part was when I saw the list of names of the other attendees of the big birthday party. And when I saw the group picture accompanying the article.

There were two familiar names in the article. And two familiar faces in the picture. One of those people was alive and sitting in a jail cell in Charleston.

The other had fallen to her death one hot night in June.

The Harringtons were the great-grandchildren of Josef Zangara. And the siblings of Mrs. Louisa Mitchell.

The mysterious Lou had been their sister. The identical twin of the woman Simon had killed.

THOUGH STUNNED by what I'd realized, I somehow managed to keep my head together. I felt certain I had figured out the whole sordid story of what had happened to Simon and to his uncle. I had no idea why, but Josef Zangara's great-grandchildren apparently shared an obsession with Seaton House.

When they couldn't get Roger Denton to sell it to them, they'd killed him. Perhaps they'd assumed Simon would sell right away, not wanting to bother with a broken-down old hotel far away from his busy lifestyle. Or, perhaps the Harringtons hadn't done their homework very well and hadn't realized Roger had an heir. I couldn't imagine how furious they must have been, not only when they made that realization—but also when Simon proved as stubborn about selling as his uncle had been.

Having murdered once, maybe it had been easier to plan it a second time. Louisa had done the dirty work here at Seaton House, but she'd let her twin sister and their younger brother go after Simon in Charleston.

"Oh, God, Simon, where are you?" I asked as I went to the front window, staring outside for probably the twentieth time in an hour. I'd tried his cell phone but either he had it turned off, or else the whole town of Trouble was buried under a cellular curse.

Finally, knowing I'd lose my mind if I didn't keep myself occupied, I decided to go back to the attic, to see if there was anything more I could find out about Zangara and his family. There were still trunks I hadn't gone through.

Careful to take the key Simon had given me, I propped the door open with a chair. Our prankster hadn't taken out any lightbulbs since my attic adventure, and it was broad daylight, so I felt pretty comfortable about being up here alone. My only fear was that I might be too far away to hear if someone tried to sneak into the house. I made a point of going down and checking every ten or fifteen minutes.

Working my way farther back into the attic, I sat in the dusty cavern, going through yet another trunk of old records. The place was utterly silent, not a pipe rattling or a hint of breeze blowing under the eaves. And I began to feel a little more anxious. I was, after all, alone on the top floor of an immense building where a murderer had recently been lurking. And that building stood alone near the top of a mountain.

"Wish I'd told Mark to bring on the cavalry," I whispered, my own voice sounding awkward in the silence.

A few seconds later, however, the silence was broken. I heard a strange sound. Strange, and yet familiar just the same. It sounded electronic, a quiet double ding that was totally out of place in this setting. For a second, I had a mental lapse and thought I'd brought my laptop with me. Because the sound was reminiscent of the one my e-mail system made when I had incoming messages.

My laptop, however, was downstairs, on the first floor. I hadn't brought it up here. There was no way in hell that's what I had heard.

Genuinely curious, I walked toward a shadowy corner of the attic, certain the noise had come from an area behind a huge sheet-draped piece of furniture. Tugging the sheet off, I shrieked a little bit when I caught sight of my own reflection in a warped mirror on the front of an old-fashioned armoire.

Dropping the sheet to the floor, I walked in a circle around the piece. It wasn't until I'd stepped all the way behind it that I realized the floor beneath my feet sounded different here. Less solid. Almost…hollow.

I saw the opening for the trapdoor the moment I looked

down. "Son of a bitch," I whispered, suddenly absolutely certain that there was some kind of secret room down there. A place Simon and I had overlooked when we'd searched before.

The place where his *ghost* had been hiding.

The ballsy girl inside me was reaching for the handle two seconds before my brain screamed *hold it.* Though I'd been sitting here in silence for a very long time, that computer sound had to have come from below this door. And unless I was mistaken, a computer didn't stay on and keep accepting incoming messages for very long without somebody using it.

Somebody's down there.

I slowly backed away, bringing my fist to my mouth to keep myself from shouting. I didn't want to scream in fear— what I really wanted to do was yell, "Come out here, you witch," so I could confront the woman who'd been part of a plot to kill the man I loved.

But I'm not stupid. If it was, indeed, Louisa Harrington Mitchell hiding in that hole, she was most likely armed. I already knew she was dangerous—murderous, in fact.

So still walking backward, never taking my eyes off the trapdoor, I shuffled along the attic floor. Bumping into a piece of furniture, I winced and muttered a curse, then bit my lip, telling myself to stay quiet, not to alert the woman that I'd figured out she was there.

I almost made it. The stairs were a few feet away. But something—my tentative footsteps, perhaps—had given me away. Because, to my horror, I saw the trapdoor slowly begin to rise.

And I ran.

16

Simon

WHEN SIMON PULLED UP in front of Seaton House and saw Lottie running along the cliffs in the backyard, he nearly lost his mind. He'd never felt closer to insanity than he did right then—the sight was something that terrified him more than anything he'd ever experienced.

Nothing during the long drive up here had prepared him for it. He'd been driving quickly, wanting to get back to her, of course, but since the trip into town to see the lawyer hadn't offered any information they hadn't already figured out, he hadn't been feeling particularly anxious.

Then he heard her scream and saw her running.

And saw the woman running behind her.

"Oh, God," he snapped, immediately cutting the steering wheel to the right and driving his car up onto the grass, almost to the front steps. Out of view of the back lawn.

He hadn't been able to make out what the blond woman had been holding in her hand. But if it was a gun, the very last thing he wanted to do was put Lottie in any more danger.

Not even yanking the keys out of the ignition, he leapt out of the car and charged around the side of the house, using the outbuildings and trees to hide his approach.

"Stop running," the woman called. "I want to talk to you."

Lottie, who had taken refuge behind the huge boulder they'd once ducked behind, said nothing. *Smart girl.*

Simon crouched behind a scraggly hedge, mostly devoid of leaves, watching as the blond woman approached the cliffs, looking one way, then the other, trying to figure out where Lottie had gone.

This had to be Louisa Mitchell, the woman his uncle's attorney had confirmed had been harassing Roger Denton incessantly before his death. And now, as he darted from the hedge to the corner of the old storage shed, he saw something glittering in the woman's hand and knew she was holding a gun.

She had to be desperate. She wasn't even going to try to make this look like an accident. Though, Simon was sure, if she could get Lottie close enough to the cliffs, she'd probably try.

Going around to the other side of the small building, he made one more quick dash, until he again caught sight of Lottie. She'd shimmied up the side of the boulder and was trying to get on top of it. In about five seconds, the woman with the gun would round the corner and see her.

Simon wasn't about to risk it. He was preparing to make an all-out run for it, to charge the woman, counting on having the element of surprise. But before he could do it, she spotted Lottie. And his heart stopped.

"Get down or I'll shoot you right now," the woman called, still oblivious to Simon's presence a few yards away.

Lottie, however, wasn't oblivious. She looked past the woman and saw him there. They quickly made eye contact, but she didn't make a single gesture that might tip her attacker off.

Smart? The woman was brilliant. And she had more guts than any man he'd ever met. Because slowly, calmly, she nodded at the woman and slid down the rock, wincing slightly.

Later, when he had her alone, he'd peel off her shirt and

kiss the skin of her stomach, which he knew she'd just scraped. Then he'd kiss every inch of the rest of her body to make sure she was alive and safe and *his*.

"You're Louisa Mitchell, I presume?" Lottie said. Then she raised her voice, and Simon knew she wanted him to hear what she said. "Louisa Harrington Mitchell?"

The woman visibly started. From a few feet behind her, Simon saw the way her whole body went rigid. "How did you figure out who I am?"

"You were sloppy," Lottie snapped. "You left a trail a college student like me could find so you'll certainly never get away with whatever it is you're trying to do here."

Simon immediately stiffened as well, shocked as the implication washed over him. Harrington. He knew that name, it was imprinted in his mind.

This woman was connected to the couple who'd attacked him.

Lousia didn't move and her arm—the one with the gun at the end of it—didn't come down. "And just what is it you think I'm trying to do here?"

Lottie shrugged, still appearing calm, though he knew she had to be terrified. He'd looked down the barrel of a gun. It sure as hell wasn't fun. "You're obviously trying to scare Simon into selling this house. But killing me isn't going to accomplish that—he'll never let you have it."

The woman laughed. That sound was almost worse than the sound of a gunshot because Simon instantly realized she was completely willing to kill again. "If your crazy lover killed you, then threw himself over the cliff in remorse, who do you think will care if someone else comes along and buys this old relic?"

Lottie's face went pale. Simon stepped forward, determined to stop this now, but she narrowed her eyes and gave a tiny shake of her head, telling him to stay back. Maybe she was waiting for a sign—some signal that the woman had let her guard down. She'd tell him when he could make his move, obviously having a better view of what was happening.

It killed him to wait. But if he moved too fast and the woman was able to get a shot off...Lottie could be the one killed. He stayed put.

"No one will believe that."

The woman shrugged. "Maybe. Maybe not. Besides, I don't need to own this place to do what needs to be done."

Lottie looked confused. "But I thought you were trying to reclaim it. For your...family."

He had no idea what she was getting at. But the woman apparently did. "How the hell do you know that?"

"What, that you and your sister and brother in Charleston are descendents of Josef Zangara? That you're trying to get this house back out of some kind of weird, twisted self-righteousness?"

Holy shit, now he was really confused. Lottie had obviously been very busy while he'd been gone. How she'd put all of this together in such a short time was something he really wanted to find out. When this was over.

Soon. Please soon.

"Just because that bastard who killed my sister inherited this house when he isn't *entitled* to it doesn't mean that's what I'm after."

"So what *are* you after?" Lottie asked, her voice low, as if she was trying to calm a vicious animal.

Which she was.

"Money." The woman sounded so matter-of-fact. "My dear old great-grandfather hid a fortune in the walls of that house. A million dollars in cash, at least. And it belongs to me."

Lottie said nothing. She just waited. Simon, though, shook

his head slowly, beginning to understand what had happened. What utter folly the whole ugly scheme had been.

"My brother, sister and I were the only ones who believed it and we cut ourselves off from our whole family because we were determined to find the money. Now it's up to me, and I'm not giving up. So off you go, over the cliff with or without a bullet in your head. It's your choice. Either way, the police will think your boyfriend did it in a jealous rage."

Time was up. Simon knew it by the way the woman shifted on her feet and the muscles of her back tightened. She was going to shoot.

He didn't hesitate. Catching Lottie's eye, he pointed to the rock, then held his hand in the air, three fingers up. He counted down…one step closer. Two. And on three, Lottie did as he'd silently ordered, diving behind the boulder, as Simon charged the woman with the gun.

He didn't think, didn't allow himself to remember what had happened in Charleston, when he'd lunged at a woman and she'd fallen to her death. He didn't question for more than a second that living with the guilt would be worth it to save the woman he loved.

He simply hit the woman around the waist, tackling her to the lawn as she tried to lunge at Lottie. The two of them rolled across the ground, perilously close to the edge of the cliff, the gun flying out of her hand.

She fought. Scratched and kicked, and tried to roll away from him. When Simon saw her body hit the top of the ledge and begin to slide over it, he went from trying to subdue her to trying to catch her.

"Simon!" Lottie called from behind him, obviously realizing, just as he had, that the woman was about to fall.

No. That wasn't going to happen. Now that Lottie was safe, he wasn't going to let this woman die, either, no matter what she'd done. So reaching out, he grabbed her wrist, holding tight as the loose soil, soft after the rain, gave way beneath her and she slid.

Her mouth fell open and terror twisted her features as she realized what was happening. Now, rather than trying to rip herself away from him, she was grabbing Simon's shirt, tearing it as she tried to get a grip.

"I'm not going to let you go," he said, realizing she thought he would let her fall to her death.

Maybe because that's what she would have done.

But he wasn't like her. In spite of what had happened that awful night in Charleston, Simon was no killer.

"I've got you," he added, pulling her, dragging her to solid ground, where she lay panting. Lottie was right there to help him, and when he looked up at her and saw the gun in her hand—which was pointed at Louisa Mitchell—he broke into a wide smile. "I like a woman who thinks on her feet."

She smiled back, but couldn't hide the tears in her eyes. And as he slowly rose to his feet, those tears erupted down her cheeks. Handing him the gun, she melted into his arms and sobbed against his neck until she just couldn't cry anymore.

THE TROUBLE police department might be small, but the chief seemed like a competent guy. He and two of his officers had arrived within twenty minutes of Lottie's call, and they'd spent those twenty minutes watching their *ghost* closely. Simon never took the gun off her.

There had been a lot of questions, but once the woman was in custody, Lottie had led Simon and the chief up to the attic, and had showed them the secret room. It was, as she'd suspected, where the woman had been hiding out.

The room was equipped with a bed, so she'd even slept

here, tucked away in a secret corner, spinning her ugly webs. A laptop computer contained files full of pictures of the crime scene—the ones she'd tormented Simon with. There was a spare skeleton key to all the rooms in the house, which Simon assumed she'd stolen on one of her previous visits, as well as a paint-splattered white blouse, the perfume—everything.

As the police had placed her under arrest, the woman had begun to talk. She'd spat out plenty of choice words toward him, for the death of her sister. But she'd also had a lot to say, confessing to everything despite being told she could wait for an attorney.

Including the murder of Roger Denton.

Somehow, when the police were taking her away, Simon was unable to remain silent about one thing. Following them to the car, he asked the chief for a moment, then faced the woman who looked so much like her dead sister.

"The money," he said, his jaw tight and his head aching from the ugliness of the day. "You said you were after money."

The woman nodded, her eyes still flashing with hatred. "My murderous old great-granddad liked to keep a diary about the sick games he played in this place, and he mentioned having a stash of cash hidden in the house. He was never able to get to it once he was arrested and I guess he didn't trust his loving wifey to get it for him. But if you think I'm going to tell you where he said it was, you can go to hell."

"I've been there," he said evenly. "And you don't have to tell me a thing. I know exactly where the money was hidden."

Beside him, he heard Lottie gasp in surprise. Even the chief looked interested. As for Louisa, she went utterly pale. "You're lying."

He shook his head. "My mother hated this place, you know. She always thought her grandfather had been a crook. So when she was a teenager and there was a fire that destroyed a dozen rooms on the third floor, she wasn't exactly surprised by what they found."

"The third floor…"

"Every room on the west side of the house."

The woman began to shake.

"She and her brother found thousands of tiny bits of burned paper—blackened—like confetti."

"No…"

"Yes," he said, taking satisfaction at showing the woman what an utter fool she'd been. That she'd wasted her life—and had cost other people theirs—for absolutely nothing. Feeling it was almost poetic justice—though, of course, small consolation—he shook his head.

"It was money. And every bit of it was destroyed."

BY THAT NIGHT, Simon began to feel that both he and Lottie were getting back to normal, to recover from the ordeal of not only the day, but *all* the days—weeks, months—preceding it. They had talked for hours, and when she'd told him how she'd put everything together, he'd been very impressed.

He *hadn't* liked hearing about how a psycho had risen out of the floorboards of the attic and chased the woman he loved down the stairs and out of the house. But she was safe. She was in his arms, in his bed.

Preparing to go away.

"So, your family's expecting you back tomorrow night?" he asked, trying to sound nonchalant when a voice inside his brain was screaming at him to demand that she stay with him instead.

Her head was resting on his shoulder, her faced tucked against his neck, but she nodded. "Yes. I have to leave in the morning."

"As long as your car starts," he said, only half joking.

She didn't even try to force a laugh. "I got an e-mail from

my professor asking for my notes a couple of hours ago. I sent them…and told him I'd finalize everything and see him in person on Wednesday."

Nothing in her voice indicated that the idea bothered her. She sounded ready to go, to move on with her life.

Well, why wouldn't she be? Since being in his house, she'd been stalked, attacked and nearly killed. Who wouldn't want to get away from here—away from him, the man who'd caused it all?

"Will you be all right, Simon?" she asked. "I mean, if you need more help…"

She didn't continue, letting the words hang there unsaid. He knew if he asked her to extend her trip, she'd do it. If he told her he needed her, nothing would make her leave. After all, her loyalty and kindness were two of the things he loved most about her.

But he couldn't ask. Having her stay here because she thought she needed to take care of him was almost as bad as letting her go. Almost.

He thought about just telling her the truth—that he wanted her to stay because he loved her. Or that he'd go with her anywhere she wanted to be…again, because he loved her.

He didn't do it. Laying the "L" word on her would make her feel obligated to use it back. That or make her pity him more.

So he kept silent. He asked for nothing, he told her nothing, he promised her nothing.

He simply made love to her all through the night, asking her, telling her and promising her *everything*. Without saying a single word at all.

And by noon on Halloween, she was gone.

17

Lottie.

Four weeks later

I LOVE THE HOLIDAY SEASON. Right after Halloween rolls around, I start jonesing for turkey and pumpkin pie. I pull out my favorite winter clothes and love walking outside, feeling ice-cold air kiss my cheeks and seeing my breath dissipate in a mist just past my lips.

Thanksgiving with the Santori family is a huge affair. On every other Sunday, and every other holiday, the immediate family gathers at my parents' house, the same one where I'd grown up. But on Thanksgiving, Mama and Pop invite all the relatives, not just the close ones. So they have the celebration at the restaurant, which is closed to the public that day.

Getting the meal ready falls, as usual, to the females, but at least Pop and Tony, who runs the restaurant now that our father is somewhat retired, are responsible for the turkey.

It smelled good, the odor permeating through the restaurant like a cloud of positive feelings and joy.

Only, I wasn't feeling any of it. Sure, I was smelling it. But positive feelings and joy weren't part of my repertoire. They hadn't been since Halloween.

Driving off that mountain, watching Simon get smaller and smaller in my rearview mirror, had been the most difficult thing I'd ever done. More difficult by far than outrunning a psycho bitch with a gun.

Uh, the family still doesn't know that part of the story. And I don't plan on telling them.

They know I'm miserable, of course. That I've lost weight, that there are tire-size bags under my eyes with treads deeper than a Michelin. That I don't laugh and seldom smile.

Every woman in the family knows I'm in love, and so does my brother Mark. He's also the only one who knows who I'm in love with, and I'm inclined to keep it that way.

I just couldn't believe Simon hadn't gotten in touch with me. "You jerk," I whispered under my breath as I sat in a booth in the back corner of the room, watching as the door opened again to let in another bunch of loud, laughing Santoris bearing food.

I knew we'd said goodbye. But when I made the choice to leave, rather than forcing Simon to admit what he felt about me—I felt sure it was only for a short time.

Simon had been through hell. If there was ever a man who needed to get his shit together and his head on straight, it was him. Having discovered that his uncle had been murdered—and that he himself had been targeted by the same group of killers—wouldn't be easy to get over.

I'd needed to *let* him get over it. On his own terms. In his own time. "But I didn't count on it taking so long," I muttered as I reached for the big glass of wine I'd snagged from my father's secret stash in the kitchen of the restaurant.

"Taking so long for what, honey?" someone said in a soft southern drawl.

Looking across the table, I saw my sister-in-law Rachel, who'd plopped down across from me. Her bright, blond hair was out of place in this sea of dark-haired Italians, but with her smile and her enormous heart, she fit right in. "I was talking to myself."

"No kidding," someone else said. "You been doin' nothin' else but mopin' since you got home last month. When you going to get off your keister and do something about this guy who has you tied up in knots?"

No mistaking that voice, either. Gloria, Tony's wife, had been a member of my family since I was a teenager. She was an inner-city girl, raised just as we had been by another big Italian crew a few blocks away from us. She was brash and bossy, confident and sexy. And she kept Tony on a tight leash, though she let him pretend he was in charge of their household.

My other brothers used to call Tony whipped. Until they got married. Now I'd say they're all pretty much whipped. *Ha*.

I couldn't even imagine the kind of woman it would take to calm wild-man Nick down though. Neither could anyone else, which was another reason everyone was anxious for him to finish his tour of duty and get home, safe and sound.

"So what are you going to do?" Gloria prodded, not taking my silence as a hint that I didn't want to talk.

Nobody in my family takes hints very well.

"There's nothing I *can* do. The ball's in his court."

"Sounds to me like you need to pick the damn thing up and run it back into your end zone, then," Gloria said, snapping her gum. Her eyes scanned the crowd, watching, as always, for her two sons, both under the age of five. We affectionately called them "the heathens."

"Leave her be," Rachel said, reaching over and taking my cold hand. "Sugar, you look like your heart's near to breaking. Now I know you haven't wanted to talk but you know we're all here for you."

Behind her, two more female heads suddenly popped up from the bench behind this one. Meg and Noelle had obviously been sitting there, waiting for their chance to jump into this conversation. They wore similar, mischievous smiles.

"Jeez, is Mama going to come crawling out from under the table next?" I muttered.

"She knows you won't open up about *everything* that happened if she's here," Meg admitted, a pink flush rising in her soft cheeks. That gentle, darling face was quite a contrast with the woman's knockout figure. "I mean, we can all tell you've…changed. But I don't think she wants to know the details."

Mama would have a heart attack if she knew the details.

Before I could answer, I heard Noelle, my newest sister-in-law, let out a low wolf whistle. "Whoa, Nellie, who's the hunk who just walked in the door behind Aunt Carmela?"

I couldn't even muster enough interest to look up.

Then Gloria let out a loud sigh. "Somebody tell me if you hear my knees knockin' together. Talk about tall, dark and dangerous."

I immediately went still. A sudden flow of electric tension washed over me, and I knew I was being watched. I also knew by who.

I slowly looked up, toward the door, and saw him standing there. Aunt Carmela, who probably stood only as high as Simon's throat, was chattering up at him and one of my cousins had walked over to greet him. But he paid no attention.

Every bit of his attention was focused on me.

Feeling the cold, hard knot that had been in my stomach for a month begin to unfurl, I put my hands flat on the table. Knowing I was going to be all right, I murmured, "Ladies, if you'll excuse me, I think I have a ball to go pick up."

It took maybe five seconds for my meaning to sink in. Then one of them gasped. Or they all did. I barely noticed.

Slipping out of the seat, I walked slowly across the room. He came forward to meet me, his dark, blazing eyes never shifting left or right. They were locked on me, burning with emotion.

From a few feet away, I noted the changes. His face had more color, the hollows beneath his eyes were gone. And though he wore a heavy overcoat, I could see his muscular body had filled out a little bit, erasing any sign of illness.

He looked, in fact, delicious.

"Hi," I murmured when I got to within a foot of him. "Happy Thanksgiving."

He stepped in close, sliding a hand around my waist and tugging me against his body. "And Merry Christmas," he growled before lowering his mouth and catching mine in a hungry, desperate kiss.

Elsewhere in the room, I'm sure, we had a wide-eyed audience. But frankly I just didn't care. His arms held me tight, and I slid mine around his neck. Our deep, intimate kiss continued silently, but with our bodies, we cemented one certainty—neither of us was letting go. Ever.

Finally, apparently realizing everyone around us had stopped talking and was watching in shock, Simon ended the kiss and looked into my eyes. "I love you."

"I love you, too."

"Yeah. I know. I'm ready to let you now."

He didn't have to explain. I understood.

"I'm fine, Lottie. I'm *whole*."

I nodded. I could see that. The shadows were gone, the pain and guilt had finally disappeared from his beautiful, scarred face. This was the Simon I'd seen more and more of at Seaton House. The other one—the dark, angry one—had disappeared.

"I'm really fine," he added. He lifted a hand and brushed my hair back, frowning as he ran the pad of his thumb under my eye, as if rubbing away the tired circles there. "Are you?"

Catching his hand, I brought it to my lips for a kiss. "I'm fine now, too. I was just getting a little tired of waiting."

"Thank you. Thank you for waiting."

"You're worth it. How did you find me here?"

He shrugged. "You said whenever you weren't home, you were here. This place wasn't hard to find. I scout out great restaurants for a living, remember?"

"It's the best in town."

All around us, conversations began to buzz again, and out of the corner of my eye, I saw one of the little ones come racing out of the kitchen, my father and oldest brother hot on his heels. I could just imagine the story they'd heard about Aunt Lottie kissing some stranger in the middle of the room.

"You really sure you're ready for this?" Gesturing my head toward my family, I added, "They're a bit...overwhelming."

He finally let go of my waist and stepped back. "Well, I think they should meet me on the right terms." He pulled a small black velvet box out of his pocket. "Which one's your father?"

"Oh, my Gawd, he's got a ring. Lottie's getting married!"

Gloria. The queen of tact strikes again. "Welcome to the family," I whispered with a sigh.

"Does that mean your answer's yes?"

"If you ever get around to asking the question," I said, "it'll be yes." Throwing my arms back around his neck and pressing a kiss on his lips, I whispered, "Oh, *yes*."

Then we were surrounded. My brothers formed a half circle around Simon. I stalked over to them and glared. "Any one of you steps out of line with my future husband and I swear I'll make you sorry I was ever born into this family."

"Oh, you mean like we were every day of our childhoods?" Lucas asked, completely deadpan.

Knowing my parents were behind me and couldn't see, I flipped him the bird.

"Husband?" Tony said, obviously not having heard his loudmouthed wife. "He's marrying her? Well, what's the problem then?" He walked over to their father. "False alarm, Pop. Lottie's gettin' a ring on her finger." He glanced back at his brothers, adding, "We don't have to get the shotguns."

I groaned, closing my eyes and shaking my head as I imagined Simon's expression. But suddenly Tony burst into laughter, with my other brothers joining in.

Then Tony walked over and picked me up in his arms, crushing me against his beefy chest. "You should've seen your face, Lottie. You really thought we were going to do somethin' to the guy you've been moping over for a month?" He looked at Simon. "Please, please, take her…my sister's whining is worse than her yelling. I don't think any of us can stand another minute of it."

"Hear! Hear!" one of the others said.

My brothers. Have I told you how much I love the big jerks?

"You're Simon?" Mark said, stepping out to extend his hand.

Simon took it, but his eyes were on all the guys, not just Mark. "Yes. And no shotgun necessary. Your sister's stuck with me. I'm not going anywhere."

Mark nodded once. "Good."

"Now," Mama said, her arms thrown up in the air as she walked over to meet the newest member of the family, giving him a kiss on each cheek, "come, *mangia, mangia.* You are skin and bones." Then she stepped back and gave him a thorough once-over. "But on you, this looks not so bad. Not so bad *at all.*"

I groaned. He didn't even bat an eye.

"Thank you, ma'am, but I would like to speak to your husband first."

My sisters-in-law surrounded me as the family drew Pop over to Simon. I heard lots of "Oh, my God, what a hunk," and "Those eyes, that body," kind of comments, but I paid no attention. I didn't realize I was holding my breath until my father and Simon shook hands, and Pop clapped him on the shoulder in that odd gesture of male acceptance. *Whew.*

Then they both walked over to me, Simon hanging back a little. Pop put both hands on my face. "My leetle girl. You'll be a beautiful bride." His eyes brightened. "You know I'm not going to be a-giving you away. Just letting him borrow you some of the time? Okay?"

Crying myself, I nodded, then kissed my father and hugged him tight. After a long moment, he let me go, calling to Tony, "Come on, for this kind of celebration, we need more food!" and the pair of them headed for the kitchen, my mother almost tripping in her hurry to supervise.

Simon still watched me from a few feet away. The women scattered, disappearing but, I would bet, staying within earshot. "Thank you for doing that. My family can be a little old-fashioned."

"I'd expect nothing less. And I'll demand the same thing someday."

We hadn't talked about children. Even the brief mention made me get all teary-eyed again.

"Can I at least give you the ring in private?" he asked, coming close and kissing my temple.

I sighed, lowering my lashes to hide my disappointment. I'm not the most patient sort. But when I heard Simon burst into laughter, I knew he'd been teasing me.

Which was why, without a moment's remorse, I said, "Isn't it customary to be in a certain position?"

His eyebrows waggling suggestively, he murmured, "I can think of lots of them."

Oh, boy, good thing my parents weren't around for that remark. Bad enough that Noelle and Meg had heard and both started snickering.

Then Simon dropped to one knee in front of me. Again all conversation ceased, as if he'd turned off a giant volume switch in the room. Taking my hand, he looked up at me, every bit of emotion a human was capable of feeling shining in his eyes.

"Lottie, you brought me back to life. Please tell me you'll let me live what's left of it by your side."

Sniffling a little and biting my lip, I nodded as he slid a beautiful ring on my finger. "We're going to be very happy, Simon."

He rose. "I know."

He had just enough time to give me a sweet kiss on the lips, then we were once again swept up in the madness that lasted throughout the entire celebratory evening.

I watched him meet my whole family. I heard him repeat their names throughout the night, never forgetting one. I saw them fall under his spell. I fell in love with him even more.

When it was all over, I took him home and slept in his arms, knowing one thing more. I hadn't brought him back to life, we'd created a new one together.

And I could hardly wait to start living it.

* * * * *

*Wait, there's still plenty of fun—and the occasional
dead body—to be found in Trouble!
So be sure to come back for the next story of
Mortimer Potts and his super-hot grandsons.
When Michael Taylor comes to town, he meets
the murderous Feeney sisters' grandniece,
it's...*
TROUBLE OR NOTHING
Coming from Harlequin Books in July 2007

*Did you miss the first Trouble story?
Mortimer's playboy grandson Max Taylor
met his match in sultry Sabrina Cavanaugh.
Their story,* HERE COMES TROUBLE,
*was released in August 2006 from Harlequin Books.
And are you dying for the last Santori brothers' story?
Ex-Marine Nick Santori is going to tangle
with the wrong kind of woman...an absolute
bad girl...in the summer of 2007.
Watch for his story in the Harlequin Blaze*
BAD GIRLS CLUB *miniseries.*

RUN, ALLY! Don't be fooled by him. He's evil. Don't let him touch you!

But as the forbidding figure came through the mists toward her, Ally knew she couldn't run. His features burned with dark malevolence, and his physical domination of everything around him seemed to hold her like a net.

She'd heard the tales. She knew all about the Wolverton legend and the ghost that haunted The Willows, an elegant old mansion lost by Micha Wolverton nearly a hundred years ago. According to folklore, the estate was stolen from the Wolvertons, and Micha was killed, trying to reclaim it. His dying vow was to be reunited with the spirit of his beloved wife, who'd taken her life for reasons no one would speak of, except in whispers. But Ally had never put much stock in the fantasy. She didn't believe in ghosts.

Until now—

She still didn't understand what was happening. The figure had materialized out of the mist that lay thick on the damp cemetery soil. A cool breeze and silvery moonlight had played against the ancient stone of the crypts surrounding her, until they joined the mist, causing his body to thicken and solidify right before her eyes. That was when she realized she'd seen this man before. Or thought she had, at least.

His face was familiar. . . so familiar, yet she couldn't put

it together. Not with him looming so near. She stepped back
as he approached.

"Don't be afraid," he said. His voice wasn't what she expected. It didn't sound as if it were coming from beyond the
grave. It was deep and sensual. Commanding.

"Who are you?" she managed.

"You should know. You summoned me."

"No, I didn't." She had no idea what he was talking about.
Two minutes ago, she'd been crouching behind a moss-
covered crypt, spying on the mansion that had once been The
Willows, but was now Club Casablanca. And then this—

If he was Micha, he might be angry that she was trespass-
ing on his property. "I'll go," she said. "I won't come back.
I promise."

"You're not going anywhere."

Words snagged in her throat. "Wh-why not? What do
you want?"

"If I wanted something, Ally, I'd take it. This is about
need."

His words resonated as he moved within inches of her. She
tried to back away, but her feet were useless. "And you need
something from me?"

"Good guess." His tone burned with irony. "I need lips, soft
and surrendered, a body limp with desire."

"My lips, my bod—?"

"Only yours."

"Why? Why me?" This couldn't be Micha. He didn't want
any woman but Rose. He'd died trying to get back to her.

"Because you want that, too," he said.

Wanted what? A ghost of her own? She'd always found the
legend impossibly romantic, but how could he have known
that? How could he know anything about her? Besides, she'd
sworn off inappropriate men, and what could be more inap-

propriate than a ghost? She shook her head again, still not willing to admit the truth. But her heart wouldn't play along. It clattered inside her chest. The mere thought of his kiss, his touch, terrified her. This wildness, it was fear, wasn't it?

When his fingertips touched her cheek, she flinched, expecting his flesh to be cold, lifeless. It was anything but that. His skin was smooth and hot, gentle, yet demanding. And while his dark brown eyes were filled with mystery and wonder, there was a sensitivity about them that threatened to disarm her if she looked too deeply.

"These lips are mine," he said, as if stating a universal fact that she was helpless to avoid. In truth, it was just that. She couldn't stop him.

And she didn't want to.

* * * * *

Find out how the story unfolds in...
DECADENT
by
New York Times *bestselling author*
Suzanne Forster.
On sale November 2006.

Harlequin Blaze—Your ultimate destination for red-hot reads.
With six titles every month, you'll never guess what you'll discover under the covers...

Silhouette®

nocturne™

HER BLOOD WAS POISON TO HIM...

MICHELE HAUF

FROM THE DARK

Michael is a man with a secret. He's a vampire
struggling to fight the darkness of his nature.
It looks like a losing battle—until he meets
Jane, the only woman who can understand his
conflicted nature. And the only woman who can
destroy him—through love.

On sale November 2006.

nocturne™

Save $1.⁰⁰ off

your purchase of any
Silhouette® Nocturne™ novel.

Receive $1.00 off

any Silhouette® Nocturne™ novel.

**Available wherever books are sold, including most
bookstores, supermarkets, drugstores and discount stores.**

Coupon expires December 1, 2006. Redeemable at participating
retail outlets in the U.S. only. Limit one coupon per customer.

5 65373 00076 2 (8100) 0 11265

SNCOUPUS

nocturne™

Save $1.00 off

your purchase of any
Silhouette® Nocturne™ novel.

Receive $1.00 off
any Silhouette® Nocturne™ novel.

Available wherever books are sold, including most bookstores, supermarkets, drugstores and discount stores.

Coupon expires December 1, 2006. Redeemable at participating retail outlets in Canada only. Limit one coupon per customer.

52607136

SNCOUPCDN

REQUEST YOUR FREE BOOKS!

2 FREE NOVELS PLUS 2 FREE GIFTS!

HARLEQUIN®

Blaze®

Red-hot reads!

COMING NEXT MONTH

#285 THE MIGHTY QUINNS: IAN Kate Hoffmann
The Mighty Quinns, Bk. 2
Police chief Ian Quinn should be used to the unexpected. But when free-spirited
Marisol Arantes arrives in town, scandalizing the neighborhood with her blatant artwork,
he doesn't know what to do with her—that is, until she shows him the joy of
body paints....

#286 TELL ME YOUR SECRETS... Cara Summers
It Was a Dark and Sexy Night..., Bk. 3
Writer Brooke Ashby has been living vicariously through her characters...until the
day she learns she was adopted, and that her identical twin sister has mysteriously
disappeared. What else can she do but uncover what happened by taking her sister's
place—and falling for her fiancé...?

#287 INFATUATION Alison Kent
For a Good Time, Call..., Bk. 3
Three dates! That's all Milla Page needed to write a sexy, juicy story on San Francisco's
hot spots for her online column. But was calling her ex—bad boy Rennie Bergin—
to go with her the best idea? Especially since she was still hot for him six years later...

#288 DECADENT Suzanne Forster
Club Casablanca—an exclusive gentlemen's club where *anything* is possible, as
Ally Danner knows all too well. Still, she has to get in, to rescue her sister from the
club's obsessive owner. But when she catches sexy FBI agent Sam Sinclair breaking
in, too, she has to decide just how far she's willing to go....

#289 RELENTLESS Jo Leigh
In Too Deep..., Bk. 1
Kate Rydell is living under the radar. When she witnesses a murder, the last people who
can help her are the police, especially red-hot detective Vince Yarrow. But he's determined
to protect Kate, even if he has to handcuff the sexy brunette to his bed....

#290 A SCENT OF SEDUCTION Colleen Collins
Lust Potion #9, Bk. 2
The competition for reader votes is heating up between journalists Coyote Sullivan and
Kathryn Walters, and they're both determined to win. So what's going to give her the
edge? A little dab of so-called lust potion and she'll seduce him out of the running!

www.eHarlequin.com

HBCNM1006